THE SOUND OF GRAVITY

Joe Simpson

WINDSOR
PARAGON

First published 2011
by Jonathan Cape
This Large Print edition published 2012
by AudioGO Ltd
by arrangement with
The Random House Group Ltd

Hardcover   ISBN: 978 1 445 88643 5
Softcover   ISBN: 978 1 445 88644 2

British Library Cataloguing in Publication Data available

Printed and bound in Great Britain by
MPG Books Group Limited

Please return / renew by date shown.
You can renew it at:
norlink.norfolk.gov.uk
or by telephone: 0344 800 8006
Please have your library card & PIN ready

DS 3/15

14 APR 2015

THE SOUND OF GRAVITY

This novel is dedicated to Tony Colwell and Val Randall.

Friends and mentors who have shaped my writing life.

PART ONE

In the depths of your hopes and desires lies your secret knowledge of the beyond. And like seeds dreaming beneath the snow, your heart dreams of spring. Trust the dreams, for in them is hidden the gate to eternity.

'The Prophet' by Kahlil Gibran

1

He held his breath as she died. She vanished with a swiftness that unbalanced him. It snared him from a weary sleep, waking him with icy immediacy. She simply fell away and out of life, dropping noiselessly down into the cold air, falling into the dark. He was motionless, trapped in the bitter tranquillity of her leaving.

There had been a heavy thump as her hip slid past her sleeping bag—lying, still warm, on the ledge. Her thrown arm hit hard against his chest and he held tight as the yellow nylon slipped through his fingers. Her grasping fingers stopped abruptly at his wrist. He held her weight but was pulled towards the side of the ledge. As he slid across the ice he reached back to grab for the orange sling hanging behind him. He heard the rustle of her legs as they swung across the ice and a shocked word squeezed out from her in a regretful, plaintive voice, quiet, almost embarrassed.

'Both hands,' he said and the strain cracked his voice. 'I need both hands . . . I've got you, hold—'

She was gone with blinding speed and he watched her fall, becoming smaller and smaller, watched her die. It was endless. Then she vanished.

Part of his brain registered her appalling acceleration away from him and yet his eyes and his memory seemed to be telling him that it was happening slowly. She fell away in a staccato rush of monochrome images flashing across his eyes,

3

burnt into his memory. They swam like film rushes across his mind the moment she vanished. He looked away, shook his head, eyes tight shut, but the picture remained. He had held his breath with ease for the entire fall and quite long after.

The images would not leave him.

He had felt the pressure of her hand on his wrist, felt the warm touch of her skin, and now he stared at his empty, outstretched palm. *He had held her.* He had held her hard and tight. The pain where the metal bracelet of his watch had cut into his skin was fading but showed how hard she had held to him. He turned his hand over. *How had he let her go?* He saw a livid weal where the skin had peeled from his wrist bone and three thin lines scratched by her nails.

He had let her go.

He turned and stared numbly into the wintry gloom.

An eerie stillness deafened him. Then he heard the lonely sounds: blood pulsing loudly at his temple, the wind brushing his ear, the cloudy plume of a long, soft exhalation—all the quiet, living sounds that went with her death. He remembered the rush of expelled air as she hit the ledge, the hiss of nylon on ice—not the sounds of terror. There was no pain or violence until the very end and then came a high, keening wail reaching up to him from the depths.

Their eyes had met, held in a desperate silence, before she fell away and down. She must have twisted as she fell, spun around as her smooth-soled inner boots slipped on the exposed ice at the side of her sleeping mat. Whatever happened, and he would never be sure, rising as he had through a fog of sleep, she suddenly bounced hard down against him, face upturned and eyes locked on his. For a fragment of time her face almost touched his as she thumped into his chest. He grabbed her wrist. Her arm flapped up and outwards. He felt his shoulder muscles clench but she was falling before his arm could move to her. His grip had failed.

He thought he might reach swiftly out and draw her back. For a moment he thought he would hug her and laugh. Instead he watched her fall. Then guilt consumed him. *Why had he not held her?* It had seemed so easy; such a simple, natural thing.

He knew with the logic that never helps survivors that it would have been a miracle if he had caught her, held her fall. He had shuffled in his sleep when she had stirred to stand and relieve herself. Drowsily aware of movement by his side, he had released the tightly cinched draw cord on his sleeping-bag hood, then slumped back as lethargy dragged him down again. She was silent but the fall was not. A hissing, rushing sound rose up as she dropped—clothing against the ice, the distinctive harsh friction noises a body makes when it falls; the sound of gravity.

He had leaned out to follow her fall. Her arm remained outstretched, fingers splayed towards him. The hood of her vivid yellow down jacket was blown up by the wind of her fall, framing her face. It seemed to stay there for a long time—the bright yellow and her face set in the middle, eyes wide and surprised. Her mouth was set in a rictus gape of a petrified, voiceless scream and he heard only the falling noises. They faded swiftly to silence as she plummeted into the lifeless void beneath the ledge. He felt the warmth and the tingle in his lap where her shoulder had struck him. It was as if she was still with him.

And then out of the silence the scream came up on the wind—an eerie, feral noise. At first he did not think it was her. She would not make such a cry, he thought, as he watched her dwindle to nothing. He shuddered at the thought. It was her last voice. This was her leaving, dropping into cold oblivion with a high-pitched, brutish shriek. She was in a place he could not imagine and all that he had ever loved went down with that last maddened, agonised terror—the pitiless sound of fear.

Then she seemed to stop, to freeze her headlong plunge. It made no sense, since she was hurtling down a thousand feet of ribbed water ice. Constant powder-snow slides in the fierce winter storms had hard-polished the ice until it had darkened in the bitter cold. There were no ledges to halt her fall. Yet for a moment she seemed to come to a sudden, softened stall. He scarcely registered the tiny dark shape whip away beneath her hovering yellow down jacket. It hung in the frozen evening air, supplicant arms outstretched. Then a gust of wind caught it in a rising eddy of turbulence and as it floated out from the ice field he saw her speed-smudged form racing away below. He sensed a faint, distant noise, a sound on the very edge of his hearing like a dog whistle set high and thin and piercing. It stopped abruptly. He told himself it was the wind.

He struggled to sit up in his sleeping bag and the cold cut into his bare hands. Turning towards the mess of slings and hardware hanging from the

6

pitons in the rock wall, he looked at the orange sling that he had reached for when she had fallen against his body. It hung slackly across the ledge. He stared mutely at the sling lying limp in his hand. Her karabiner was missing. He rested his right hand absently on her sleeping bag. The soft down was warm from her body. He looked down at the bag, feeling the cold air eating away the last residue of her life. He leaned over and pressed his face against it.

He felt the warmth of her on his face, inhaled the musk of her scent, and cried until the cold came into his shoulders and he sat up and pulled his bag around him. Night was coming on. There were storm clouds on the lowering horizon.

*   *   *

They had climbed hard all day, starting at first light in that dreary time when the mountain face looming above them seemed at its most inhospitable and menacing. It was that early-morning hour favoured by policemen making their arrests; the time when victims are most feeble and compliant. She thought to ask him to turn back and retreat to the shelter of the wooden hut still snug from the morning's cooking, but he had a determined look and a distant gaze as if he were already far up on the wintered north face. As she turned to him, half-tempted to ask, he looked sharply at her as if sensing her scrutiny, and smiled his wide smile, his eyes glittering with excitement.

'Shall we do it, then?' he asked in a rush, sensing her retreat. He leaned towards her to hold her arms urgently. There was joy in his face as if he

7

had been released from the toils of mundane exertions. He grinned broadly. 'It'll be fine.'

'You always say that.' She smiled, despite her nerves.

'But it will. We'll be okay. Think of it, just the two of us . . . taking as long as we like.'

'What about the weather?' she said and glanced at the leaden blue-black sky on the horizon with the thin streaks of cloud heaped darkly on the retreating edge of dawn. 'Looks like a front moving in.'

'Only a small one.' He grinned. 'Come on, it's going to be fine. The pressure's steady. We can always back off if it turns bad. We've got plenty of food. We'll take it easy, go slow and careful. If we don't like it we can traverse to the ridge.'

'Difficult in a storm,' she said with a enquiring lift of her eyebrows but she was unable to hide the amusement in her eyes.

'We'll sit it out then.' He reached his arms around her and hugged her, then pulled away, rubbing his hands up and down the bright yellow sleeves of her down jacket. 'It'll be an adventure,' he added, sensing her compliance. He looked at her quizzically, noting her hesitancy. 'What's up? Got a bad feeling about it, touch of cold feet?'

'Yes, I have,' she said, stamping her boots in the snow. 'Cold feet, that is. I don't get bad feelings.'

'Never?'

'No, don't believe in them. Oh, and no, I'm not scared—well, only a little, but that's good.'

'Me too.'

'I'm just being wet.' She tilted her chin and looked up at him. 'You know I'm never good in the morning.'

'It's not what I've found.' He laughed as he ducked away from her swinging arm.

She looked at her ice-crusted boots, then continued stamping up and down in the snow.

'Go on then,' she said at last. 'You first. I hate crossing bergschrunds.'

She watched as he tentatively stretched his foot out over the dark maw of the bergschrund. There was the sound of breaking glass as the front points of his crampons bit into the ice, knocking splintered shards from the wall. The tinkling chandelier sounds faded deep below her in the guts of the glacier. She shuddered and stepped nervously away from the fragile, gaping edge.

It had been a long, slow day on the ice field. They had hoped to make fast progress but the ice was brittle and hard; black in some places, polished by winter avalanches to a glassy, steel-hard sheen. They had struggled to make their picks and crampon points stick and the shattered leaves of ice breaking from their axe blows almost knocked their footings loose. Ice screws blunted quickly, the ice screeching and fracturing when they drove them in, not trusting them to hold a fall. They climbed cautiously.

Speed was not important because they knew that they would not start on the forbidding rocks of the mixed ground until the following day. They planned to make an early bivouac at the top edge of the ice field where the rock band reared up. Their sacks were heavy with fuel and food. They wanted it to be a long climb; long enough for it to become their entire world. This was what they had talked about when they had huddled in the small wooden hut perched on the ridge above the

9

glacier. If it was too hard they would come down. If fear began to swamp their courage they would retreat leftwards to the ridge and hurry down in long abseils to the comfort of the hut. They climbed for their time together—not for the difficulty of the ascent or the seriousness of the experience. They were confident mountaineers, happy, that is, with their sense of what they were doing. It was winter and there was no one around. It would be a true test, they told each other, since as far as they knew their route had never been climbed in winter.

It was January and winter was well set in. Not even the guides came at this time of year. They had battled through the drifts of powder snow that guarded access to the ridge upon which the hut had been carefully sited. It had been closed at the end of the summer, five months earlier.

The warden had lodged the door shut with heavy rocks. Firewood had been stacked by the side of the door and a few unopened cans of vegetables, some rice in a glass jar, a packet of cigarettes with one missing, a half-empty bottle of cheap brandy and a withered salami had been left on a shelf above the single-ring gas cooker. A large gas cylinder for the stove had been disconnected but was almost full. It had taken them five round trips to carry up all their supplies—the climbing gear and the food, books to read and extra firewood for comfort, wine and candles, cured meats, bread that swiftly staled, cheese, biscuits and tea.

They had spent hours reading on the rocky ledges outside when the sun eventually came round and warmed the hut walls. Evenings were spent huddled over a chessboard on the damp and musty mattresses which covered the cramped wooden bunks. One bright day they crossed the glacier, roped together, stood beneath the ice field and tried to follow the line they would take from the top of the ice and on through the black rocks. The mountain towered over them and everything became distorted—foreshortened and confusing. A single stone flew out into the icy sky, ejected from the mixed ground a thousand feet above them. Its high-pitched whistle had them searching the sky in momentary panic, until they spotted the speeding black shape and laughed as the tension eased and they felt foolish to have taken fright. The stone hit the soft snow of the glacier with a muffled thud several hundred yards to their left.

The following day they climbed far up the ridge that bounded up above the hut in a series of knife-edged towers of rock. Stopping to gaze across the acres of hard ice a thousand feet above the roof of the hut, they spotted a bivouac site. A short shadowed wall at the lowest point of the rocks overhung the ice to form a protective angled roof. It would be a good place to sleep, they agreed. He leaned out over the crest of the ridge and she let the rope slide slightly under pressure so that he could look straight down. A steep ice gully led up to a short overhanging rock wall beneath where they stood. She could see the meandering trail of yesterday's footprints on the glacier a thousand feet below. It was a long way down, she thought idly, then glanced up to the summit ridge—they were only a third of the way up.

He said the ice gully might be a good escape line off the face and onto the ridge if things turned bad. She muttered disapproval when she leaned

11

over to examine it. The ice looked thin and fragile and the rock walls were smooth and fiercely steep. She looked across the ice field and tried to imagine how hard an escape it would be. The entire mountain face would be moving, a continuous surge of powder-snow avalanches streaming down from above, heavy enough to rip them from the face. She glanced at his eager expression. He wasn't thinking of escape, she thought. He raised an arm and pointed at the climbing line. She smiled, charmed by his enthusiasm.

Then they climbed higher up the ridge in the hope that they might see better across the rocky buttresses of the upper face, but it was no help. The air was glacial despite the weak winter sun shining on the east ridge. Their hands soon froze numb in contact with the rock and they blew their warm breath into cupped palms and slapped life back into whitened fingers.

Looking sideways across the north face they saw a series of sombre walls looming above the ice field. Imposing rock buttresses seamed with snow-choked cracks reared up towards the summit. Here and there they marked powder-snow-covered ledges, sanctuary to aim for amidst the vastness of ice-marbled rock. They tried and failed to trace the ice line, a weakness leading up through the rocks that they had spotted from the balcony of the hut. Nor could they see the telltale white lines of snow and connecting grey tails of ice that revealed the shallow slanting gully leading to the summit ice fields.

They watched the wind blowing snow in a spreading veil out from the ridge high above them.

12

There was no easy escape line from the upper slopes. If the powder was bad it would make a retreat down the face impossible. She watched as he studied the mountain wall with keen anticipation, then turned to look down far beyond the glacial foot of the mountain where early evening's long light was shadowing the western slopes of the valleys. Clouds clung like drifted smoke to the cliffs and the steeply forested hillsides. As the overlapping ridge lines stepped down towards the valley depths, each was defined by skeins of thinning mist, interlocking smoke-grey layers in fading shades—the iron-hard frozen land blackened by winter shadows, its streams silent, gripped by frost.

The long western horizon glowed with a pale, cold shimmer. The exposed craggy precipices and wind-blown, snow-freed trees now seemed starkly black and skeletal against the bleak winter land. It was strange to sit in the fragile warmth of the failing sun high on the jutting ridge of the mountain and look down into an inert world, still, abandoned, empty and left to drift between the seasons.

She felt a sense of freedom on the sun-bathed mountain rocks, a bright lightness of spirit—yet as she peered into the shadows of the distant valleys it seemed as if that strangely disconnected world had about it the gelid stillness of pooled black water on the point of freezing. She shivered at her gloomy thoughts, feeling a tingle run up the hairs of her back.

'Let's go,' she said. 'We'll lose the light.' He turned to her with smiling fervent eyes until they stilled at her expression.

'You okay?' he asked and touched her shoulder. 'Something wrong?'

'Getting cold,' she said and looked into the deepening valleys. 'It looks grim down there.'

They had thrown their ropes down the ridge line and swung down towards the far-off, sunlit roof of the hut. Their calls echoed in the still evening air as they slid fast and smoothly on the ropes and watched the night shadows surging up towards the mountain foot, spreading out like spilt ink. They laughed as they pushed open the wooden door. Their breath pooled in the windless evening air as they pulled it shut behind them. The weather was calm, the sky was clear, but the mountain was gripped in a snow-bright cold. The black of night chased the fading sun westward until it was brilliant with a wash of strewn stars.

Now, as they climbed the ice field, the face was silent; the surrounding peaks watchful. The blows of their axes seemed to echo in the amphitheatre of the wintry north face. Their voices hung in the air when they shouted instructions to each other, breaking the tranquillity of the day. Splintered ice tinkled from beneath their boots and they glanced with increasing anxiety at the mountain wall looming over them. The silence, at first enjoyable, became oppressive. Conversation became clipped, muted by an ominous expectancy. The winter-hardened ice demanded delicate and precise power. It repeatedly shattered, brittle leaves of glass exploding under their hammering picks, increasing their sense of insecurity. They tiptoed gingerly up a wall of splintered mirrors, wincing at the sudden sounds of cracks unzipping all around them. Crampon points sheared away with sudden

14

and shuddering frequency; gasps and muttered oaths broke the vigilant quiet.

The cold stung their faces until their skin tingled with a crisp sensation as if they and the day had been washed clean and left suspended to dry in the frigid air. They exchanged glances as they rested on belay ledges hacked from the ice. The menace was electric. They climbed with wary calm, only their eyes betraying the uneasy conflict of apprehension and excitement. Nothing was said, but an air of grim resolve had replaced the nervous humour at the start of the day. Affectionate companionship became competent determination. There was no need for words.

As the sun rose behind the mountain the light became vibrant with sharp detailed colours. The winter sky had a keen polished clarity and the clinking of metal-ware on their harnesses and the hammer blows of their ice axes hung in the still air. Menace surrounded them. There was an edgy resonance to the day. Mostly they looked upwards for the easiest line, seeking the danger. It would come with a fast and brutal unexpectedness.

The calm was uncanny; quiescent and watchful, disconcertingly hushed. She kept glancing down to the valley's floor as if searching for some threat. He noticed her distraction and followed her gaze, checking the weather signs above the dawn-darkened valleys. Later, he would wonder about that sinister stillness and the violence it ushered in.

He grinned with pleasure as he watched her delicately threading her way above him, teetering carefully on millimetres of steel biting into the frail ice. He admired the dancer's grace of her fluid movements which made him feel crudely clumsy, hammering hard with his axes and kicking brutally at the unyielding ice.

The day was so distinctly quiet that they came to accept it as theirs—a perfect day; a day to remember. Yet he would never forget that sense of patient watchfulness as they climbed, a tense, expectant atmosphere; the feeling of being preyed upon. He shook the thought from his mind, admonishing himself, knowing it was simply natural nervous anxiety. The quiet, hovering threat unnerved him. It was as if he were just failing to catch sight of something. Fleetingly, at the edge of his vision, he seemed to glimpse a shadow of danger, a sense of being hunted, a formless threat. They were tense, but then it was a serious climb. They could expect the unexpected. They had planned carefully and well but they had not counted on the silence.

A rime of fine, hoary frost fringed and whitened the curls of auburn escaping from beneath her helmet. Her breath hung like vented steam as she recovered at the stance. Only the constant cracking of ice particles from beneath their feet suggested movement—that, and the alertness of the ice, the way it creaked as if its vast, flat body had just flexed in a great, slow, elastic shudder. They heard no movement but felt the strange dissonance ripple through the ice.

Then a rifle-shot detonation startled her as she fed the ropes through her belay device and she jerked her head up, searching for the threat with urgent fear. He stopped, axe poised in mid-swing, one hundred feet below her and glanced upwards, fearful of the sudden exploding impact of a stone. A flurry of rocks like wheeling starlings flew out,

16

spinning clear of the face, hurtling down with a chilling whirr and thrum. Then they bounced down the ice in a clatter of sharp-angled ricochets. The abrupt cracks of the impacts echoed around the concave face. He hurriedly clipped a sling to an ice screw and leaned back to watch the fusillade of stones. The slings creaked stiffly in the cold and the screws contracted in the brittle ice. They grinned uneasily. Quietness seeped back.

They reached the upper rim of the ice field where a short rock wall reared out from the ice. It formed an angled protective roof, a safe bivouac. It was the work of an hour to excavate a ledge at the foot of the wall. Digging quickly into the soft snow, they soon reached unyielding winter ice. The heavy axe work kept them warm as they hacked, cutting the sleeping platform so that it sloped into the rock wall. A long, orange sling was tied to well-seated rock pitons and they clipped extension slings to the rope and to their harnesses so that they could move freely as they worked.

They kicked their spiked boots high up and backwards like territorial dogs and the accumulated ice shards slithered down the ice field. They coiled the loose ropes in layers across the ledge on top of which they laid their thin foam mats. Then they knelt on the mats to lay out their down sleeping bags and bivouac sacks. He fixed the hanging stove by its chain to a piton hammered into a crack in the wall. He filled the pan with ice chips and sparked the propane-butane gas mixture into hissing blue life.

She removed the plastic shells of her outer boots and carefully hung them on the handrail rope. Then, shuffling her legs into the mouth of the bivouac sack, she reached in with her arms to feel for the neck of her sleeping bag. She pulled it up her thighs, shuffled her buttocks on the mat and twisted and pushed with her legs, wriggling them into the bag. An orange sling crept out from the edge of the bag and stretched tightly up to where it was clipped to the handrail rope. Her harness with its stiff, knotty stitching might dig into her flesh, but she was safe. Before clipping the orange sling to her harness she tested the belay system to check if there was enough slack to lie back in comfort. If she fell she would only swing a few feet off the ledge.

He passed her a steaming mug of tea. Reaching for the mug, she let go of the sling. It hung slackly from the handrail rope. The karabiner at the belay loop on her harness hung empty and unclipped. She leaned on her elbow to sip her tea and peered down the sucking fall of the ice field.

They drank thirstily and took turns at preparing food and more hot drinks. He rolled a thin cigarette between cold fingers and smoked it slowly as he looked at the clouds building on the horizon. He liked the strong, bitter taste and the dizziness induced by the heady nicotine rush. He smiled as he sensed her disapproval.

They lay curled together on the ledge, their murmured conversation eventually petering out as the rigours of the day overcame them and the heat of their bodies lulled them into drowsiness. He fell quickly into deep sleep but she hovered on the edge of it, conscious of the rutted, sloping ledge and the hard discomfort of her harness, sore where it cut in at the sides of her hips and plagued by a faint unease, something she had to remember but could not reach. She thought of the bleak stillness of the valleys and how it had unsettled her. She would have slept but for this nagging uneasiness. After an hour's fractured rest she lifted her head and reached for the draw cords of her sleeping bag. She had drunk too much tea.

She could feel the warmth from his back pressing comfortably against her. She had managed to sneak herself onto the inside slope of the ledge while he had been working the stove. Although sometimes she was crushed, she felt safer when he relaxed in his sleep and slid down the incline, pressing her firmly against the rock wall. Sheltered by his warmth, she also had the comfort of knowing that she would not slip from the ledge during the night.

She carefully opened the neck of the bivouac sack, letting the cold air rush into their warm cocoon. He murmured a protest in his sleep but she ignored him, preoccupied as she was with the problem of safely relieving herself from the edge of the ledge. She had roused herself from a fitful slumber, wakened by the insistent pressure in her bladder. She stood up and looked down at him sleeping on his left side. She felt stiff from the climbing and her knees protested. It would be dark soon and she preferred to do this in the light. She saw the stove hanging by its chain clipped to the piton. It stirred a warning memory.

As she turned towards the mountain she noticed the orange sling hanging empty against the rock wall. The remembrance of what she had to do came the instant she saw the empty sling and her hand felt the snaplink hanging loose on the belay loop of her harness. She wondered how it had become detached. It made no sense.

As she leaned towards the handrail rope, reaching for the empty sling, the sleeping mat shifted under her foot. She had a fleeting glimpse of ice as the yellow foam of the mat slid up, exposing the ledge near her inner boot. Then her foot slipped, snapping sideways, and spat from the ledge with stunning swiftness.

She went down sideways, falling across his chest, her fingers flailing at the handrail rope as she fell, her mind screaming at her that she was not clipped in. As she hit him she felt events were happening in an odd, slow way: there was guilt at hitting him so hard and waking him and then there was his face close to hers, eyes wide and staring. Her arm was whipped away from the handrail by the impact and she felt her legs and hips swiftly pulled down below the ledge as she tried to grip onto something solid.

Her fingers raked across the bivouac sack, hooked around the crook of his elbow and clamped down in a fierce grip. She felt the material of his sleeve rasp as her palm slid down his forearm, then the rigid edge of his watch cut against the ball of her thumb as she swung, full-bodied, off the ledge. Her legs skated across the ice, the cold pressed against them and a hot wetness flooded down her thighs.

It happened in a series of jolting, staccato snapshots: the slip, the impact, her thrown-out hand, and then she was no longer on the ledge but looking up her stretched and jolted arm as her fingers seized onto the bracelet of his watch, looking up at his ashen face, wide eyed staring, shocked. His torso was dragged forward and out

20

from the ledge.

Her cry of alarm stilled in her throat as she came to a stop and saw the empty sling. It was their anchor, their link to safety. She had unclipped them both. He had instinctively reached back for it with his free hand as her weight tugged him outwards. She stared at his hand reaching for the sling for support. She saw the strain show in his face as he strove to twist his fingers around her wrist, but she had caught the back of his forearm and couldn't twist round enough to match the grip.

'Both hands,' he said. 'I need both hands . . . I've got you, hold—' She knew at once that he meant to let go of his hold on the sling. She had detached them both and he didn't know. The moment he let go of the sling and leaned down to reach for her with both hands, he expected to be held hard and safe by the anchor. She stared at his hand gripping the sling. They would both fall. No time to shout. His body shifted forward and her legs dropped down the ice.

She must let go or they would both die. 'Let go!' She wanted to say it but fear made her dumb. She released her fingers from around the watch band. His arm whipped upwards and she fell.

As she dropped away from him she felt, rather than saw, the fall. She registered the rushing wind that suddenly battered her jacket up around her shoulders and the corrugated surface of the ice rattling her elbows and knees as her brain told her that she was gone and she refused to believe it.

She kept thinking she would stop, hit the end of the rope, jerk to a halt safe in her harness, stop, just stop, but she swooped down faster, pitched forever down, faster again, accelerating without

21

friction, without end. It seemed as if she was hurtling into a narrowing cone of speed and flashing light and gathering menace.

The juddering of the ice spreading through her body melded into a continuous, droning vibration. Her vision blurred. His face shrank abruptly from her; his heart-torn eyes vanished. The hunched, still form staring from the ledge blurred through wind-stripped tears. Then he was gone and part of her howled inside.

She tried to dig her fingers into the ice. Her fingernails ripped off, leaving bloody smears. She recoiled from the pain and eased the pressure until something told her that it was all she could ever do. She forced her fingers back down hard into the unyielding ice as their tips shredded, nails split to the roots and torn back, and she pressed all her weight over her hands, pushing her head down towards the flashing ice until her chin battered against a rib, lashing her head back and stunning her momentarily.

There was a whoomping sound and a sudden ripping tug as the duvet jacket ripped over her head and whipped off over her arms, pulling her bloodied hands from the ice. She felt the cold wind knifing through her thin thermal shirt. The surging pull had flipped her up and over and spun her around on the ice and she glimpsed the bright yellow jacket hover above her, suspended like a yellow cross. Then she was falling sideways, twisting around on the ice, spinning as she fell away until she was facing head-down on her back. She glimpsed the rocky ridge passing by on her right, then the glacier came into view and the ominous shadow of the crevasse and she saw it was close. An alien sound started deep in her chest. She heard it come out and shut her eyes and let it go.

It came up rising from deep inside, a wild maddened cry; it was denial. A part of her wanted to be calm, to think of him, to be accepting and resigned and quiet, but this animal scream ripped out from her and she seemed to be hearing it from a distant place.

As she rushed over the edge of the crevasse she burst out high into the air, launching off the ramped lip and, for a moment, with her eyes closed tight shut, she felt weightless, free-moving and released and she was glad to stop the piercing noises emanating from deep within her chest. There was a comfortingly familiar sensation to this new falling through the sharp whistling air with her eyes closed. It reminded her of childhood, eyes shut on swings, going so much faster in the darkness, feeling scared and happy all at once, watching the blood spots on her eyelids against the sun and smiling at the feel of the cool summer air. It was the same feeling and she was glad.

She hit the glacier with brutal force. The impact drove her deep into the surface layer of snow until she exploded through the thick ice roof that covered the tight throat of the crevasse. Her spine sheared low down and she felt nothing, unaware of her slowing fall into the chamber below. She didn't feel the fracture rupturing her thigh as the femur punched through the fabric of her trousers and the greasy, splintered bone-end ripped against the ice of the crevasse. As she was punched into stillness her neck snapped cleanly near the base of her skull.

She was not even aware of having stopped. The impact did not render her unconscious but her injuries had mercifully ended the pain and fear.

Memories flashed through her dying mind, disconnected sequences of images released from her brain. The crazed signals flickered like a misfiring film projector across her eyes as the electrical impulses of dying neurological codes sparked and shorted through her brain. Blood flow failed, oxygen finished.

She was not breathing. She lay on her side, her shattered leg twisted cruelly out of sight beneath her. Powder-snow flurries eddied down into the still air in the chamber. A faint light glimmered from the entry hole in the ice roof twenty feet above her body.

She felt something rolling inside her, something empty and hollow and cold. She tried to speak but had no commands to make it happen. A tear welled, spilling glutinous and slow on her cheek. She sensed herself sinking into darkness, a chill seeping through her body, as a weak white light flickered across her eyes. She tried to resist the going down but the dragging heaviness was insistent. She heard the fading pulse of blood at her temple—then silence. Her fingers fluttered in spasms against her cheek. She thought of him, almost formed a ghostly flickering memory of his face, a fading inarticulate impulse as a long, slow exhalation drifted from her lips. Shorting, disconnected signals fizzed through the dying synapses in her brain and the sight of him flickered into black and she was gone.

2

The storm swept over his bivouac just as night approached and darkness seemed to increase its fury. He crouched inside the billowing two-man bivi-bag, making no effort to contain the flapping fabric or secure his position on the ledge. He could hear the aluminium gas stove swinging on its chains and rattling against the rock wall. He knew he should bring it inside but he did not move. Snow slashed across the nylon with the harsh rasp of blasted sand. The bivi-bag cracked back on itself, a stinging whip lashing his face.

He squatted on his haunches, pressing his back against the contours of the rock wall. His head was uncovered and his sleeping bag open to his waist. Cold seeped into his spine and he shivered convulsively. The air temperature had dropped close to minus twenty and, with the gathering storm-force winds, the wind-chill factor was already fast approaching minus fifty. From far above the ledge came the steadily increasing howl of the wind blasting across the summit ridge. He bowed his head, letting the cold seep through him. It was a precise, sinister invasion, easily monitored, yet he impassively ignored the frantic defence signals that his body was sending out. He felt the stiffening current flowing through his veins with glacial resolve: it made him drowsy.

When the first winds had tugged at the bivi-bag he paid no attention. He had sat numbly, aware of her body heat draining from her empty sleeping bag. He had no sense of time passing, only an

25

awareness of darkness gliding across his face and the cold sliding into his chest. His legs felt dead, his fingers white and wooden. He stared fixedly at the hands that lay bare on his lap. They looked very pale, almost lifeless, in the dour light. He flexed his right fist repeatedly in a catching motion. The fingers seemed to move stiffly and with slow disconnected co-ordination as if each digit was responding to separate commands. He made a fist and squeezed hard but the hand felt soft, sleep-weakened as on waking.

Was that what had happened? He had let her go because sleep had weakened him? He stared at the hand. It had always been strong. Not pretty perhaps, rough and scarred from the rock, but always powerful. These hands were his tools; they had never let him down and yet he had dropped her.

He bowed his head and tried to remember how their hands had felt. It had been so swift: the sudden clench onto his wrist, the sense of her weight pulling him out, the heavy solidity as he resisted and held her for the briefest moment and then the shocking recoil and lightness and flying backwards as she fell away. He opened his palm, peering helplessly into the gloom, searching for an answer. He closed his eyes and cried.

Then he was struck hard from the side and shaken violently from his reverie. When the main storm winds came he was instantly scared. It was a fierce physical shock as if some great hand had suddenly pressed hard against his shoulder. He was being attacked. The wind threw him sideways across the rock wall and kept pushing him so that he had to thrust out his right arm to steady

26

himself. It was no abrupt gust but a firm, insistent, pulsing force. With the pressure came the sudden rising roar of the wind. He began to shake. He had never experienced a wind like this, never lived through such elemental brutality.

He had thought to quietly drift down with the cold, slipping into a warm befuddled sleep and, but for the storm, he would have done so with ease. Yet the urgent force that threatened to rip him from the ledge and hurl him out into the darkness drove away all thoughts of sleep. He instantly forgot his misery and, without thinking, began to fight for his life. No one could have heard that wind and not been frightened. It was darkly overwhelming. No state of guilt and despair could have sustained itself against such a brutal assault. It attacked his senses rather than his mind. Instinct made him fight back. He knew that if he let the fear in he was finished. Fear was an infection. It would crawl inside, deep into the heart of anyone who engaged with it. It must never be acknowledged. He must strike it from his heart. *Do something!*

Unbalanced by his sudden sideways movement, he was immediately confused by the frenzied thrashing of the loose folds of fabric whipping around his face and shoulders. Blinded by the slapping, claustrophobic material, he fumbled with his left hand, searching for the sling that he hoped was still attached to his harness. A ghastly dread seized hold of him as the unrelenting wind slid him inch by inch across the ledge. His fingers scrabbled fretfully at his waist, anxious to feel the comfort of the cold steel link clipped securely to its sling. He grasped the woven tape leading up and out from

27

the dark warmth of his sleeping bag. Clutching the sling, he crouched on his knees and walked his trembling, numb fingers along the inch-wide strip of fabric until they rapped against the abrupt coldness of the karabiner. Its gate was locked, clipped tight to his lifeline—the sling.

He let out a tremulous sigh, unaware that he had been holding his breath as he had made the search. He felt the surge of fear rising tight in his throat, threatening to overwhelm him. He clenched his jaws until the muscles ached, as if pain alone could push the fear away. When he jerked on the sling he felt the reassuringly firm tug of the handrail rope. Above the clamour of the gale he faintly heard the metallic jangle of hardware and the rattle of the stove hanging from the rope. He was safe.

The wind intensified. He had hoped that after the initial fierce bursts it would settle itself into steady storm-force gale, but it seemed to be surging to higher and higher speeds. He could hear a distant booming roar; a deep and constant thrumming noise that he could not comprehend. Close by, the wind seemed to be tearing the air apart. Snow and ice particles hurtled across the mountain face, strafing his exposed ledge with a high-pitched slashing sound, adding to the demented cacophony.

He remained curled over on his knees, this foetal cringe felt safe. He could hold out against the force of the wind. For a long time he simply braced himself and dug his knees and hands into the ledge, sensing the mats sliding beneath the sleeping bags and the bivouac sack. He could feel the wind slipping under the mats and he sensed a lifting, buffeting sensation and the slight creep

28

over the ice as he hovered along the ledge. Raw panic gripped his stomach and he hurled himself sideways towards the rock wall, feeling the solidity of the wind. *Fight it, fight it. Don't let it win!*

The thought shocked him as he felt himself lifted, suspended on the edge of friction. He remembered the slings and the handrail rope and the well-seated pitons driven tight into the cracks in the rock wall and he told himself he would not go far. The suddenness of the wind and its abrupt intensity had deadened his mind. He felt that there was nothing to be done—no way to resist. He would not fall. He repeated it like a mantra, murmured desperately against the storm.

He twisted inside the bivi-bag and tried to gather in the folds of bucking material, bunch them together and trap the fabric under his thighs. The warmth advantage of the large two-person sack had disappeared and it was now threatening to become a great billowing sail catching the full weight of the wind and dragging him from the mountain. Once he had gathered it tight around him he could feel the cold pressure of the wind steady on his back and thighs. Perhaps what he had gained was a small victory, but he had prevailed. It was enough.

The power of the gale seemed to lessen and he realised that it had been the sack that had been causing the trouble, sucking him inexorably across the ledge. The maddened slapping of the fabric had made him think the wind was a living thing, a harrying, malevolent force. It was better now. There was still a booming roar from high above and the seething rush of ice particles shredding over him, but the strength of the wind had lessened. A swell of courage began to rise and with it a determined anger.

He pulled open the sack, struggling with deadened fingers to release the toggle on the draw cord. Poking his bare head through the gap, he flinched at the raw frenzy of the storm. The cold tore at his face, stinging his slitted eyes and burning his exposed ears as the ice particles lashed him. His skin hardened in the piercing bite of the wind and he could scarcely keep his eyes open against the onslaught. Groping his hand through the entrance, he pushed his arm out, reaching down to the side where he found the sling. It hung slackly against the rock. He knew that he needed to stand or half-crouch and use both hands to tighten the anchor system. He could feel the pull of the abyss in the darkness beneath the ledge.

When he had cinched the draw cord of the sack tight around his waist he was chilled to his core and shivering spasmodically. He wished that he had put on his down jacket, for the wind stripped the body heat from his thin thermal shirt. He braced himself against it and feverishly began to fix the anchors, binding new lengths of ropes directly to individual pitons.

Despite the shivering he carefully adjusted the knots so that each rope came tight against his harness, sharing the load equally. Then, shaking, he crept into the dark shelter of the sack. The ropes now pinned him in place on the ledge, preventing him from moving from side to side. They pulled him against the rock wall, holding him tautly secure at the back of the ledge. He pushed himself from side to side to test the tension in his cat's cradle of ropes and slings. Only an avalanche could threaten him now and he forced himself not to think of the dangers lurking above him. He was safe, he told himself, and the wall would protect him.

Shrugging himself deep into his sleeping bag he scrunched up the ropes and mats into a thick layer and partly pushed them up the wall at his back. By twisting his body in the sack and squirming in his sleeping bag he managed to squeeze himself behind the cradle of ropes stretched down to the ledge so that they held him tight against the wall. When he was satisfied with his half-sitting position he relaxed, dropping his shoulders and letting the curve of his back press against the rock wall.

He clenched and unclenched his fingers, fighting to regain circulation. He would need his hands. He searched in the loose areas of the sack until he found her sleeping bag. He pulled his legs into the open neck, easing the half-zip to allow him to shuffle deeper inside. It would not close over the bulk of his own bag but it provided welcome extra insulation from the pummelling wind. He ducked his head away from the wind, down into the lofted folds of nylon. He smelt her soft, lingering odour and squeezed his eyes tight shut, flexing his fingers and crying with the pain of the returning blood and the unexpected swell of memory.

The hours passed interminably as the storm intensified. He was warm enough to survive, but gradually the cold began to eat into his bones and forced away any hope of sleep. He slumped forward mutely, listening to the howl of the wind. It steadily rose in volume and tone as the night darkened. The weight of snow pressing against him increased. Down in the valleys the snow was

31

settling heavily. High on the exposed flank of the north face it was ripping across the face of the mountain, flooding around his rocky eyrie. He had the uncomfortable sensation of being slowly smothered.

He wondered whether the wind might weaken the summit cornices until they wrenched free and tons of ice and snow plunged down the face. They would come thundering down onto his fragile shelter and hurl him into blackness. He thought of the pitons ripping out and tried not to think about the cornices, but with every swelling storm gust he could hear the bellow of the wind scouring the summit ridge.

He had never heard a wind like it. It seemed alive. It ripped across the surface of the ice field like tearing steel. With each new sudden sound he seemed to become smaller, burrowing deeper into the taut mesh of ropes and slings. He could feel the wind worrying at the edges of his body even as he pressed harder against the base of the overhanging rock wall. It prised at him, sliding long, powerful fingers beneath his back, probing for weakness. He felt himself shift. The ropes stretched and held.

As the hours battered past him he drifted through a daze of thoughts, memories of what had been, of what had so suddenly been lost. He pictured her sleeping, curled as she always slept, lying on her side, turned away from him, in a neat bundle, easy to enfold. He rocked on his knees to the rhythm of the wind, inhaling her fading scent on the sleeping bag, holding hard to the memory of her. She was drifting away from him in this fierce world. He knew that he must hold on to her through the night or there would be no dawn for him.

He loved to watch her sleep. She slipped into it with fast, sure ease, her breath calming to faint murmurs. He would lie awake, head supported by an elbowed hand, gazing at her shadow-lined face as pale street light leaked through a gap in the curtains. He wondered where her dreams were taking her. There were different currents running through her unconsciousness that he could never fathom. From the hushed swell of her breathing he could draw the form of her body and in the stillness of her sleep he sensed a tranquil contentment. She sank into sleep as if taken by the ebb of a warm tide, confident of safety till morning, and when he was sure she had slipped into her quiet, stolen place he would bend to kiss her neck.

He knew then that she loved him. That silent unconscious movement touched a secret wellspring of his feelings for her. Sometimes he kept the moment as a tiny secret pleasure of the night, all his own, and at other times he had to wake her and remind her of his love and she would turn her face to him and he could see it in her eyes. The truth of it shone through.

He tipped back and forward on aching knees, felt tears on his cheeks and raised his head, confused. How long had he slept? Had he dreamt or was she with him? He pushed out a forlorn, seeking hand, then stopped as he felt the sickening dread of remembrance flooding back. For a moment he was overcome, drenched deep in sadness like a hunger he could never satisfy. He had lost her. He balled his hand into a fist and remembered the sudden emptiness around his wrist. Why had he let her go?

The stove jangled on the ropes, clattering across the rock. He thought to stir himself and reach out for it before it was lost in the storm. It was his only source of water and warmth and hot food. He must not lose it. He roused himself reluctantly, wary of the cold and the wind and the night outside. *The stove is metal,* he told himself, *it is tied to the anchor ropes and pitons and it can't be detached.* He settled back against the comforting pressure of the slings and thought about her and where she was now.

He imagined a cold and soundless place—not some suspended sleep from which she might wake but a chilling emptiness. There would be no safety till morning, no quiet exposure of love. She was there now as the storm raged outside his nylon shelter. She lay alone in darkness, preserved by winter's grip. He had to find where she had gone to and tell her what he had done. She was absolution.

Earlier he had thought of joining her, slipping soundlessly off the ledge down her fall line. As the storm raged to a furious intensity the shriek of the wind made him strain into himself and cringe with fear. It would rail at his vulnerable bivouac until he had the nerve to slip down after her. The wind would then die with him, the storm quieten to silence as a debt was paid.

He knew this was the cold talking. It was the way of storms. He thought of it as an enemy probing for weakness, creeping inside to kill from within, sliding knife-like into his core, edging him inexorably towards the abyss.

All he had to do was endure. The storm had to end. They always ended. Then he could shake himself, dog-like, free of the snow, dig out his frozen ropes and begin to descend the face. He would go straight down the fall line and find her. He had only to endure.

3

The worst storm in living memory buried villages in silent drifts, cut off roads and froze unwary travellers. High on the shoulders of the surrounding mountains, snow settled heavily on over-burdened slopes until they broke free, spewing thousands of tons of snow into the valleys below. In small hamlets people struggled to move against the wind as they secured shutters and chained fences. Some were forced to their knees to wait for lulls between gusts, many fled for safety. Strange things happened. Barely perceptible electromagnetic pulses were generated by the violent winds. Birds fled. Men were driven to madness. Far above could be heard a low, intermittent roar tearing across the highest ridges. The chaos of the *Föhn* had begun.

A sleek-feathered Alpine chough hung on a flurry of rising air, then looped acrobatically, darted to one side and took a small insect on the wing. The atmosphere was charged, crackling with energy. Disturbed, it dived away from the summit rocks, swooping down towards a large flock of birds that was rapidly losing height in a swift spiralling descent. Fleeing the dipping air pressure, the birds sped for the safety of the valley. A sudden breeze swept powder snow from the length of the summit ridge. A white plume arced back into the late afternoon sky. The storm was approaching.

The birds had long since gone. Far below the summit cornices came the tiny metallic sounds of climbers at work, their thin cries rising in the wintry air. At the top of the lower ice field two ant-like figures cut at the ice with their axes. Laughter mixed with the chinking sounds of axe blows. Clouds streamed across the summit, pushed by relentlessly hurrying winds. Hours later, as the advancing cloud wall swallowed the last of the neighbouring peaks, a high keening scream rose on a strengthening wind as a dark speck plunged down the ice field.

High in the upper atmosphere, above the spreading sea of cloud, a mass of dense, cold air was punching down towards the Alps. A bleak cloud wall marked the distant edges of the horizon. As night came on, the mountain stood within a diminishing patch of clear sky. A long melancholic lens of cloud streamed from its stony crest. Adjacent peaks thrust above the clouds that lapped at their summit rocks. The bitter wind, gathering in strength, pushed ahead of the advancing storm front. Flurries of snow scurried across the rocky summit, catching in crevices, forming white lines like seams of quartz. The mountains began to disappear.

Massive cornices draping the steep upper ridges threatened the darkened bowl of the north face. This immense frozen surf hung far out from the ridges, suspended precariously above the abyss. On the southern side a long fissure began to cleave the snow open. The vast weight of compacted snow-ice was losing its battle with gravity. Blue ice glinted deep within the cleft. The cornice shifted, then settled with an ominous groan. Again the fracture widened, snow slithered into the depths and ice like crushed glass splintered apart. The cornice shuddered and the widening crack raced along the ridge line. The storm hushed the catastrophe.

As night wrapped around him the noise of the wind seemed to heighten. The darkness unnerved him. It was as if the storm were a living entity intent on his destruction. His senses were battered, punch-drunk and disorientated by the cacophony. He rocked on his knees, hands at the sides of his head, clutching the down bag hard against his ears as if he could silence the din. He lost the sense of time passing as his world shrank into a helpless acceptance of blows raining out of the night, shredding his sanity. He felt consciousness recede dimly.

Later, despite the ferocious maelstrom, he noted the urgent pressure in his bladder and the shuddering spasms of his shivering forced him into a dulled wakefulness. He searched for the hard, cold shape of his water bottle, finding it under his knee. He let go a hand and groped for it in the darkness. Fumbling with his head torch, he squinted as a sodium-yellow blaze filled the billowing shelter and he saw a blue metal bottle. He struggled to understand what he was seeing. His water bottle was red.

He shook the bottle, feeling a light sloshing within. Almost empty. He unscrewed the top and sucked down the few mouthfuls of orange-flavoured liquid. Her bottle. He saw her slipping from the ledge, saw her fall and stared blankly at the blue metal bottle. The wind veered suddenly, catching him from an unexpected angle and he slipped hard against the rock wall, tight onto the slings and ropes. Crouched on his side, he tugged clumsily at the zipper on his trousers, pulling the harness belt as high as he could and shuffling his pelvis forward. He clenched his stomach and groaned as he felt the metal bottle heat in his hand with the urgent rush spattering the inner surfaces. As he finished, the wind caught him again, slopping the sour, warm stench foaming across the soft down of his sleeping bag. Clutching the bottle upright, he searched for the screw top that he had dropped as he had instinctively put a hand out to steady himself. It was nowhere to be found.

As he pulled open the neck of the bivouac bag the fury of the gale numbed him. Ice crystals needled his face and he gasped. He pushed the warm bottle out into the storm, shaking the dregs into the wind as his hand was wetted by rapidly freezing urine. Crouching once more on his knees, he clenched his hands together, rubbing warmth back into his fingers. The cold was seeping deeper into his body. He rocked back on his heels, moaning, and tried to understand what was happening. His mind felt sluggish, distracted. He slapped his cold, sour-smelling hands against cheeks still numb from the unforgiving wind. The air had seared his lungs.

He shook his head and tried to marshal his thoughts. He had knelt unmoving in the dark for too long. As he flexed his fingers, feeling their deadened stiffness, he remembered how difficult it had been to open the zipper and close the draw cord. Motor co-ordination was deteriorating.

If you stay like this you will die. How long have you been shivering? He couldn't remember. *Was it continuous or coming in convulsive waves?*

Shivering meant his core temperature was plummeting. The chemical reactions created by the rapid muscular activity would generate heat, but only while the glucose in his muscles lasted. He wanted to piss again. He knew it was a symptom of the cold eating into his bloodstream. His blood vessels were contracting by the minute. He felt the tightened, deadened feeling in his limbs. His diving core temperature and his blood-pressure receptors were conspiring against him, telling his brain that there was an increase in the volume of his bodily fluid. It stimulated the urge to pee. He rocked forward, feeling his muscles vibrating under his hands. The cold was seducing him.

Rolling into an upright sitting position, he stamped his feet against the ledge and windmilled his arms. He beat his fists into his chest with heavy punches, rolling his shoulders and rocking back to hit hard against the rock wall. His breathing increased in the airless bivouac bag and he threw his head back and began to shout—screaming meaningless, angry sounds into his sleeping bag. After fifteen minutes he stopped and relaxed back on the support of the slings and monitored his body. The shivering had stopped. He felt a little livelier. He no longer need to pee. *Food. You need food, sugar, energy.*

Leaning over his knees, he pushed his hands deep into his rucksack. His fingers clasped a hard edge and he pulled. A leather boot appeared in the beam of his torch. He placed it by his hip, then

39

reached deeper—another boot, blue leather, smaller. He stared at it in the torchlight, then pressed it carefully into his lap. When he had found all the boots and wrenched the food bag from his rucksack he sat back and stared at the blue boots in his lap. She had no need of them now. He pulled open the draw cord and pushed each one out into the storm, feeling them bounce against his legs before they spun off into the night.

Rummaging in the bag, he found dried fruit and chocolate bars. The thought of hot noodle soup was briefly tempting until he heard the stove jangle against the rock. It would be impossible to light. He ripped open the ring pull on a tin of sardines. He scooped the contents into his mouth, sucking the sauce from his fingers and feeling the frozen fish crunch between his teeth and the fine bones scratch against his palate. He crammed his mouth with frost-hardened apricots and blackened dried banana, chewing long and methodically. He felt his cramped cheek muscles thaw and relax. Chunks of chocolate followed, held unsucked on his tongue, melting slowly in the warmth of his mouth. He sucked the viscous sweetness through his teeth, rolling it over his tongue, luxuriating in the instant sugar high.

Placing his boots side by side on the ledge inside the bivi-bag, he covered them with his rucksacks and placed a folded layer of insulating mat on top. Sitting in two sleeping bags on his new seat, he felt cramped and unbalanced as the wind pushed hard against his side, but he was warm. He could stretch his legs, kicking life into them when they cooled and stiffened with inactivity.

The food revived him. He listened to the sound

of the storm and watched the sack thrashing in the beam of his torch. Reluctantly, he turned the light off. The storm seemed louder. Resting his chin on his knees, he made a mental list of the food and batteries, gas and hardware he had with him. Riffling through her rucksack, he found the spare head-torch batteries he was seeking and placed them in the food sack. In the top pocket he found chocolate bars and dried fruit. While the wind remained strong he would be unable to make drinks or hot food. He had to conserve his supply of snacks and fruit. When the wind calmed he knew that the snow fall would come, heavy and claustrophobic. The rock wall would provide some protection but it would build up behind him, steadily pushing him from the ledge. Powder avalanches would make cooking difficult and infiltrate any gaps in the bivi-bag, melting in the warmth. His down sleeping bags would quickly lose their insulation. He must be careful. He rummaged in the rucksack once more until he found her woollen balaclava. It would make a brush of sorts to keep the powder snow off the bags.

The red water bottle was three-quarters full. He rationed the liquid, sipping infrequently until the wind died. At the first opportunity he would light the stove, refill the bottle and prepare a meal of soup, noodles and hot sardines. Then he would wait. He would wait for the snow to stop falling and wait longer for the avalanches to shake themselves free and the face to consolidate itself. Only then would it would be time to move.

Rocking gently on his seat, he considered moving. *Move where? Down or up?* There was more than two thousand feet of hard mixed climbing above him. Below lay a sheet of polished ice, dropping a thousand feet to the glacier. He had eight ice screws, enough to be able to abseil the entire length of the ice field, so long as they remained sharp. He remembered the ice work of the morning and knew that some of the screws would be unusable. Descent was still his fastest and safest option. He doubted his ability to climb alone to the summit. The thought scared him: down it would be.

The food and exercise had given him energy and confidence but it soon seeped away as the hours drifted past. He listened to the hypnotic cadence of the wind, hoping to detect some sign of it weakening. Occasionally, he opened the sack and pushed his head into the night, feeling the wind on his face, gauging its strength more accurately than from the distorted hubbub inside his shelter. Above the sound of gritty snow rushing against the nylon he listened to an ominous growl rising and falling from far above. The wind was building remorselessly.

Turning off his head torch, he stared hard into the blizzard, trying to detect a glimmer of light softening the night. He saw only the dark mass of the storm surging around him. When he turned on the torch he was dismayed at the way the storm devoured the light. The snow had come. He pulled the draw cord tight and began swaying on his haunches. An uneasy tremor rippled down his spine. He felt the first low resonance of fear grip his stomach as a cold wash of adrenaline flooded his system.

The white noise of snow rustling against him

began to unravel his mind. He felt trapped. A vast, demonic generator seemed to be humming and fizzing around him. The incessant pandemonium battered at his brain, ripping him from a delirious slumber to an abrupt, demented wakefulness until exhaustion took hold and he slipped into fitful sleep again. The storm raged fiercely, yet he seemed no part of it. As the wind eroded his senses he felt cowed and defeated.

Far above him, a gibbous moon lit a raging mercury-silvered sea where hunting clouds scoured high into the heavens and an unnatural darkness lay below. Hurrying banks of mist, torn through by wind-rent snow, whipped past him as the gale swept the face of the mountain. The desolate tide of night flooded slowly by as he struggled with his unhinging mind, feeling as if he were drifting, self-absorbed, in a bleak and lonely place surrounded by noise and catastrophe. He endured.

As the darkness stretched towards a feeble dawn, an exhausted light leached into the sky. He stayed within the darkened shelter, unaware that night had passed to day. He grew cold as the storm layered him in folds of snow. He listened dazedly as it guttered around his flimsy shelter. In moments of snatched sleep the sounds dimmed as if the world outside his refuge was leaking away from him. Each time he awoke he had the sensation that his ears had filled with water. He yawned and stretched his jaw but the muffled, distant timbre remained. He slept again, resting his head against his hand.

He thought of her falling and dreamt his hand had gone with her. He watched his fingers release and let her fall. He saw her hand clenched tight

43

round his hand as it painlessly separated at the wrist. Waking abruptly, he felt an icy paralysis in his hand, deadened by the sleeping weight he had pressed upon it. He shook it vigorously until the heat of returning blood flushed fiery life into his throbbing fingers.

Angrily hitting out with his arm, he felt the clinging weight of the surrounding nylon sag away from him. The snow was burying him. He struck again and again and kicked out with his swaddled legs. The taut nylon slackened and hung limp in the torchlight. Motionless? He peered around, listening intently. The wind had ceased.

Fumbling for the draw cord, he pushed his head from the sack and blinked in the softly bleached light. Snowflakes settled on his cheeks, melting like tears. It was warm. He strained to hear the storm winds harrying the summit ridge. Silence.

Peering up, he saw dark, scattered patches of rock above the snow-crusted slings and handrail rope. Beneath him lay a world of idly drifting snow. The snow he sat upon merged with the moving cloth slipping past him. He seemed to hang suspended in a cloud. He had no idea of how much time had passed. The fresh, cool air cleaned the nonsense from his mind and he peered around with relieved wonder. He smiled at the shifting white silence, feeling calmed.

A dislocated feeling unnerved him as he stared at the lazily drifting walls of cloud and fog and slanting snow, wondering where all the violence had gone. He was light-headed; his breath, shallow and hesitant, smoked in the windless air. He felt tempted to step calmly from the ledge and walk away across the spectral clouds.

He pushed out an arm, watching the snow eddy and swirl, ripples undulating softly away. He shook his head, puzzled by what he was seeing, wondering at the fragility of his mind. Time stilled. The tranquil, nomadic cloudscape wrapped him in its winding sheet. He felt disembodied—haunted.

He should have felt elation, yet sensed instead a low menace, a tense disquiet. He glanced above him, momentarily unnerved. Snow fell alluringly. From far above he heard a muffled thump as an avalanche fell into the soft clouds with a concertina ripple. He tensed, awaiting the deluge. There was only silence and the velvet caress of snowflakes. He felt them melt and slip weeping across his face and a part of him wished for the return of the wind. It was too calm.

The sense of being stalked by an implacable predator filled his mind. A vulnerable anxiety spread through him. He felt the breathless tension like a living thing tighten around him. A suffocating fear surged through him. He nervously scanned the enveloping clouds. An ancient, vestigial awareness crept sharp and familiar into his mind. He was being hunted. Alone in this immense hostile landscape, he had become prey. He licked his cracked lips, tasting fear.

4

The stove purred with a busy, comforting blue flame. He settled the snow-filled pan carefully onto the flames, checking that the base was securely lodged against the rock wall. He watched the snow settle in the pan, darkening as the heat ate into the aluminium. Droplets of condensation ran down the sides and hissed in the flames. He turned away and lay on top of the bivouac sack, feeling the still-warm sleeping bag inside.

An hour had passed since he had sat bewildered in the shelter, peering out at the softly drifting snow. The sense of menace had gradually left him and he had watched as the flakes had thinned and the clouds had lightened. Rising stiffly, he had swept the ledge free of the accumulated drifts of powder, shaking down the slings and the handrail rope, listening to the steel chatter of ice screws and pitons and stove against the rock. The metallic din sank into the clouds. Each time he glanced down he could see more of the ice field, now pristine with fresh snow. A sinister rock buttress began to loom massively through the thinning mists above the ledge. The cracks and grooves were choked with snow and the smooth sweeping walls disappearing into the clouds glistened with the treacherous glaze of verglas.

He had busied himself clearing the ledge, checking the pitons and the safety slings clipped to his harness. Standing on unsteady legs, he had held up the bivouac sack spread wide between both hands and flapped it free of its dusting of powder snow.

Now as steam rose from the stove he picked through the contents of the food bag, occasionally looking up to study the weather. He felt unnerved, quietly intimidated. The speed at which the ferocious assault of the storm had dissipated confused him. He thought of the long wind-wracked night with the tight knot of fear balled inside himself, and the moment when he saw his light eaten by snow-laden darkness, and knew then he wouldn't get through. The storm had blanketed off the world as it went about its business of extinguishing him. He looked at the pale light glowing around him and wondered how it had all come to this.

At one moment in the night when a madness had held him he felt himself falling. He had the sensation, crouched in the wind-hammered bivi-bag with the rush and hiss of the snow, that he was hurtling down through the clouds, severed from the ledge and the slings in one long free fall through the night. He felt that he had been lifted by the wind, flown out far clear of the face and spun and tumbled in his dark cocoon. It was a comforting sensation, a kindness, even, that he accepted gratefully as he fell weightlessly to the waiting glacier. He had stretched out a tentative hand to check that it was happening—that it was over.

Then he had slipped into an exhausted sleep feeling oddly perplexed, waiting for something, a little lost. He woke later, throwing out an arm as he fell from his bed with a cry. He fumbled for the table lamp, muttering in the darkness until abruptly the air seemed ripped open, an ugly

47

noise, and the memory of the fall and the storm came flooding back and all around him the shelter convulsed to the rhythms of the wind.

He glanced around him. It had been dark, now it was light. He had fought a storm and now there was this calm, this utter placid silence, as if the storm had stopped a moment to survey its handiwork. It was hard to understand the sudden transformation of states as he watched the mists and clouds shift sluggishly in front of him. He raised his right hand and examined his wrist, finding the three scratch marks above his watch band. The blood was blackened and crusted. It had a bitter metallic taste.

A skein of thin damp vapour blew across his arm. Water bubbled in the pan. He ripped the top from a foil packet and poured water into the powdery contents. He poked and stirred, scenting the aromas of beef and burnt wood and something identifiably sweet. He blew on the food and gasped as it scalded his palate. He chewed with wide-opened lips, rolling the hot doughy mass with his tongue, cooling it with sharp exhalations. The heated lump tasted of sweet gritty soil. He forced himself to chew the crusty, partially hydrated wads of beef. It tasted like nothing he had ever eaten.

When the water came to the boil again he added a tea bag, four spoons of sugar and squeezed half a tube of concentrated milk into the pan, stirring the mix with the spoon and watching oily gobs of stew floating on the surface. The tea was heavenly. He sucked greedily at the syrupy fluid, alternating it with spoonfuls of stew. When he was finished he leaned against the wall and looked up at the sky.

The light was diffused, brightening by the

minute. There was a strange directionless opacity to the gleaming clouds. It was impossible to discern the angle of the sun. When he leaned forward and looked directly down the ice field it was as if he were looking into the depths of a white, unsettled sea. It reminded him of light in the oceans, cutting through the depths like fractured glass, splitting the water into a shifting kaleidoscope of colours. The sense of plunging spaciousness made him giddy.

Looking down, he watched as slanted angles of shade criss-crossed each other as the clouds and mists swam past. The shifting, form-changing clouds cast languid shadows, pale planes of luminosity gliding over swathes of grey-white shadows mesmerising him. He stared fixedly, a pulling, longing sensation. Then in a sudden burst of light far below, as if at the far end of a distant white valley, he saw the thin ribs of the crevasses on the white sheath of the glacier a thousand feet below.

Looking up, he saw a blue opening lined with towering white cloud walls. He watched as they were sliced open by blades of sunshine that silently burnt off the fog. More and more patches of blue appeared as the wind teased apart the clinging tendrils of disintegrating cloud. It happened with remarkable silent swiftness until the sky was cleared but for dying puffs of shredded mists.

The mountains suddenly materialised, indistinct nebulous forms at first, then they came into crisp focus. Stately ice-rimed peaks piercing an azure sky, dark icebergs above a fog-bound sea.

It had happened with such quiet speed that for a moment he questioned his sanity. The memory of the storm still left him trembling as he watched the clouds vanish. Like mist burnt away by the sun, the storm dissipated in the silence of sublimation, the quiet of transformation of solid to vapour. He felt grateful to have survived and to have been given this unexpected gift of life. Beneath him the undulating contours of the glacier were revealed, snaking valleywards in a serpentine curve, its covered crevasses marked out by scaly shadows thrown by the long evening sun.

He checked his watch, astounded to see that it was late afternoon. He had no memory of the morning passing. Had he been hidden all that time, cowering within the shelter as the snow had moaned wetly from the clouds? Was the storm really over? He shook his head, wondering at the deception of time. After making another sweet brew of syrupy tea he lay on his side on the balled-up sleeping bags and bivi-bag absorbing the warmth of a pale winter sun, sipping reflectively at the steaming liquid.

There was little left in the day. A shallow, crepuscular glow spread across the sky. There was a shimmering light in the air and the cloud line on the horizon was an ice-blink reflection from the vast snowy expanses. It stung his eyes to watering.

Below and to the left of the ice field a hanging glacier jutted out from the west ridge. Great slices of ice, separated by deep shadowed chasms, had been cut into the cliff as if some giant knife had carved down from above. It led his eye to her fall line from the ledge to the glacier far below and he tried to shake the half-formed thoughts and strained emotions from his mind. He was worried by his fractured thinking, the fragility of his mind.

He had been alone too long.

As he studied the glacier he found himself searching for a distinct shape, a defined shadow that would act as his guide. Even as he recognised what he was doing, the idea came to him, clear and immediate. He would find her. He looked to each side of the wide glacier basin lapping the foot of the face but there were no open crevasses to be seen. Glancing to his left, parallel with the ledge, he tried to find a distinct point in the structure of the mountain that he could use as a guide. The buttresses above and the irregular tide line of the rock band meeting the ice field were veiled in powder snow. He knew at once that looking up from a thousand feet beneath him everything would appear different, foreshortened, distorted. Distinctive pillars, corner systems and crack lines, so apparent from where he sat, would blend into the soaring acres of rock and disappear. He needed some mark, some point to guide him.

Looking directly above and then swiftly down, he tried to fix in his mind's eye the exact position of the ledge. He knew at once that it was hopeless. Approaching the foot of the face from the glacier, he would have to envisage an imaginary plumb-line dropping straight down the ice field if he was to have any chance of finding where she lay.

He sat back and stared blindly at the horizon of ice peaks. A mark! Two marks. He needed a bearing. Why hadn't he thought of it earlier? He rummaged in his rucksack, glancing anxiously at the sky, judging how much daylight he had left, until his hand felt the hard, plastic edge of the compass. Looping the thin cord around his neck, he leaned forward excitedly over the edge of the

51

ledge and followed the line of the west ridge down in a series of jagged rock towers to its junction at the right edge of the glacier. He quickly found what he was looking for. A sharply cut shadowed notch at the foot of the ridge, delineated by the low evening sun, marked where they had crossed over from the hut to reconnoitre the foot of the face. He would use it to make his first back bearing. Holding the compass flat, he pointed the direction-of-travel arrow directly at the notch, making sure that the red end of the magnetic needle was pointing to North and the orientating arrow in the compass housing lay underneath the needle. He read off the bearing, repeating it in muttered chants until he felt certain he had memorised it. Looking out from the face, he found a distinct, jagged peak breaking the horizon directly in line with the ledge. Again he took a bearing and memorised the numbers.

Satisfied, he sat back and surveyed the scene. He had a plan, a purpose. Tomorrow he would abseil directly down the ice field from the ledge, following her down. He should reach the bergschrund exactly in line with where she lay. It would then be a simple matter of searching out from the face on his second bearing. He thought of the heavy storm snow piling drifts onto the glacier. She would be buried deep. If he kept on the line he could minimise the search area. *Just keep digging on that line and you will find her. You will take her home.* He glanced across at the notch on the ridge. He repeated the bearing aloud. It was his fall-back bearing. If for any reason he could not descend directly or was forced to return to the hut, he could use the first bearing to retrace a direct line from the notch to the point where it bisected the foot of the face. He could then resume his search on the second bearing.

He felt energised, strengthened by purpose. He could act, where before he had simply endured. He reached for the sling of ice screws and unclipped them from the handrail rope. They jangled in his lap as he carefully examined the teeth of each screw, discarding those blunted beyond use. He was left with five good ice screws and he arrayed them on a sling to carry around his neck. He calculated that he would be about one hundred feet short of the glacier by the time he had abseiled from the last sharp screw.

He felt he would try to fix one of the three damaged screws for the last swing down over the bergschrund; or he could use one of her axes as an anchor, or dig an ice bollard. He ran the possibilities through his mind as he sorted through the remaining hardware. He methodically racked the gear, clipping wired steel nuts and camming devices and bunches of pitons to a sling and pushing them to the base of his rucksack. He wouldn't need them descending the ice field.

He threaded the shafts of her ice axes in the loops on the back of his rucksack and pulled the retaining belts tightly into place. When he had prepared the rucksack he placed it carefully to the side of the stove to act as a wind-break, making sure to clip the shoulder straps to the handrail rope. He chewed spicy sausage meat as he worked. There were ice crystals in the meat and hard nodules of fat. When the second pan of snow melted he filled his water bottle and set more snow on for tea. He wished he had a cigarette. He would smoke again when he got down—if he got down. Everything was ready. He would wake early in the morning darkness to make the first abseils. He didn't need light to slide down the ropes or fix the anchors.

In the time that he had taken to prepare for the descent and make his food the weather had begun to change. He watched the horizon warily. Beyond the distant ice-capped peaks a dark-faced bank of cloud had formed. It was coming on again, he thought, coming on with the night, and he cringed at the memory of the wind.

Scanning the nearby peaks still bathed in an eerie evening glow, he watched as the snow and ice took on the colours of the dying sun. The ice cliffs had changed in the waning shades of dusk. Where before they had been sharp-lit and bright-edged, they now glistened in faceted aquamarine. The colours had intensified, highlighting the dark, deep blue caverns yawning at their feet.

The encircling mountains threw up a snow-capped palisade to guard the glacier bay below him. Sinister layers of bruised purple veined the advancing storm front. In the shadowed valleys beyond he glimpsed the sheen of a distant lake, bright-sparkled by a flash of weak sunlight.

He sat sipping his tea, watching the mountains stand sentinel around him. They had the serene, understated power of startling beauty and deadly menace. The power unmanned him. They had an aura of absolute permanence: silent; inviolable; hypnotic. He knew at once it was why he always came back. There were mysteries in this strange landscape, a transient, dream-like quality that called him.

For a moment it seemed to him that on a mountain you can sit for a long time with the story of a man, like a stone, in your hand. In the stillness and the pure light and the sea of silent peaks enduring through the pulsations of time you can, if you are lucky, find something irreducible within yourself, utterly alive.

He watched the day die before him as he huddled, chastened, on his exposed ledge of adze-marked ice. A slipstream of cool air flowed by and he shivered. He threw the dregs of the tea at the urine-yellow snow below the ledge, tucked the pan into the rucksack and pulled open the neck of the bivouac sack. As he shucked his legs into the damp warmth of the sleeping bags he saw the outriders of the storm sweep over the encircling mountains. The cloud wall had breached the dam, and snow stormed silently in a grey dust across the distant peaks. He pulled his head inside the sack, drew the cord tight and lay on his side with a coil of coldness in his belly, anticipating the night. Sleep snared him before the first snowflakes settled on his curled form.

5

She had sunbathed one long sunny afternoon lying naked by the hut. She had taken the long planked lid from the wood-box on the porch and laid it flat in front of the steps, sheltered from the wind. He had come out from the hut to sit on the sunlit steps only to find her lying there, eyes closed. Her head tilted towards him and she slowly opened her eyes, squinting in the sun.

'What are you staring at?' she had asked quietly.

'Nothing,' he said.

'Liar,' she'd murmured and closed her eyes.

He held to that memory as snow fell gently, insistently, dusting the mountains, lagging the folds of the bivouac sack as he hugged it tightly around himself, trying to sleep, remembering.

The air bent around the contours of her body, cascading across the flat sweep of her belly and he followed, winding around her, rolling like mercury off itself, tingling up in whorls across the ridges of her ribs. Sliding beneath the arch of her back, he lay briefly in the space between her and the earth. He flowed and ebbed, pooling in her belly, running with a whisper round the curve of her hip to settle coolly in the pockets of her throat, a chill prickling as he evaporated with a shiver from her skin.

He felt like the weight of sunlight as he talked to her, whispering over her skin. He watched her at his passing, skin tightening at his touch. She had a natural benevolence that softened the strength of her jaw, he thought, studying the curve of her mouth. Her face had a kind authority, lending her an appraising, defiant look. She was a woman of strong, high cheek bones softened by the fiery warmth of her hair, making a good face, a fine-looking face. He had trusted her at once—not because of her beauty but because she accepted him with such direct honesty. Her eyes and the extraordinary width of her smile were beautiful. When her eyes and smile worked together they transformed her. She rolled her face to catch the sun. She smelled of wild ginger.

Her eyes opened to a lustrous smile and she

56

looked at him with impish humour, radiating happiness. He was entranced, trapped. Life seemed muted when she left.

He never knew why she loved him, only that she did—and he accepted the blissfully unexpected gift. He held a certain knowledge of their shared future. It infused his life with an unfamiliar calm.

Sleep drew the memory away, the dream fading, and he felt his life ebbing, the past blurring, left behind, the betrayal of his dreaming mind. He shuddered to an abrupt wakening.

'I wasn't . . .'

He heard himself speak to the darkness of the shelter and snow slithered from the nylon walls. '. . . dreaming,' he muttered dispiritedly, a trough of bewilderment welling dully in his chest. '. . . dreaming,' he repeated quietly, breathless with regret.

He heard the faint movement of his blood and his thoughts were incomplete. He struggled to regain his composure, breathing steadily, listening to the thudding of his heart—aware of the eerie silence left in the wake of his dream. His thoughts scattered, seeking answers, back and forth, blindly accepting his loneliness.

He tugged at the draw cord to peer, blinking, uncomprehending, at the night sky. The snow had passed. A gloomy wash of clouds lurked on the edge of the moon. High in the stratosphere, wind-shredded streamers back-lit by the moon formed a long, pale ghost fire. He felt the last breath of the storm, a slipstream breeze against his face. Stars, carelessly scattered diamond dust, glittered bright against a sable sky. The peaks were bone in the moonlight. Snowfields glowed in the starlight. The

57

silent immensity filled him with apprehension just as the sound of the wind had led him to a place of madness.

The moon shone a sickly light, tinting the clouds with a unearthly gleam. As they were chased across the horizon, the mountains dissolved and re-formed with startling rapidity, veiled by wraith-like mist, then laid open by gusts of wind. They had a strange beauty, mutable. Everything in front of him felt a little thinned; too cold, too vast, to feel exactly real.

Hours drifted by unnoticed as he watched. He was surprised by the clear light, the silence and the pull of the wind under an immeasurable sky. It made him faint with vertigo. He felt the suck of atmospheric tides in the limitless space above him, an endless moon-ruled ebb and flow. Gaunt-faced, he watched it unfold with eyes that glinted feverishly.

He imagined his meanings draining away in the deafness of the mountains. Pinned on this eyrie, he had the fleeting notion that he had been there before, would be there forever, that this had always been waiting for him, like an inherited memory. Loneliness, he realised, becomes obsessive. He was losing everything.

As the moon flushed its light through the night sky he thought he could hear the distant wind chattering like glacial water over rocks. When at last the moon rose and the clouds cleared from the last few, suffocated stars the land was bathed in harsh brilliance, the peaks carved from bleached skeletons, the glaciers like washed-out salt lakes beneath an ashen sky.

He looked to the horizon, searching for the edge

of dawn. Checking his watch, he was taken aback by how long he had slept.

'Sweet Jesus!' he said, surprised at the sound of his voice, feeling bereft and light-hearted at the same time.

While the stove purred by his side he shuffled out of the bivouac sack and pulled her sleeping bag from his legs. Still encased in his own bag, he raised hers to his face and breathed through the fabric to her faint, musky scent. He pushed the bag away. He had no further use for it.

Pulling the food bag and his boots from the bivi-bag, he searched for her rucksack, pushing his head into the opening and turning his head torch on. As he pulled the rucksack out he noticed the open zip on its top pocket. The soft brown leather of his tobacco pouch shone in the beam of his torch. He remembered her mischievous, smiling eyes. She must have hidden it away as he slept.

When he had stuffed the sleeping bag into her rucksack he strapped her sleeping mat to the side and then emptied the bivouac sack onto the ledge. Spare socks, a stuff sack with film and sun cream, a woollen balaclava, gloves and a pair of glacier glasses lay by his side against the rock wall. He dropped them into the rucksack and then unclipped the slings of hardware from the handrail rope. He selected a few pitons and five wired chocks and dropped the rest into her rucksack. He wouldn't need rock gear to descend the ice field. As he pulled the straps tight, closing the rucksack, he glanced down at the ice field. It glowed a dull pewter, grey-shaded in the moonlight. He looked up at the horizon and saw the first pale colour of dawn. It would be light in an hour. He would drop the rucksack when he could see clear to the glacier and watch as it followed her fall line. It was all that might lead him to her. He sipped his tea and he smoked and he waited for the light, waiting for the end game to play out, wondering where she was now and whether he would find her. He flicked away the glowing butt to spin firefly-briefly out over the lightening snowfields. The ember flared in the last vestigial gloom of the night as he followed the tracer line of its flight until it disappeared and he saw the glacier come clear in the flat early light.

He stood on the ledge, staring down the fall line, holding the rucksack out over the abyss. Leaning forward so that the rucksack lay against the snow-covered ice, he let go his grip and watched as it slid swiftly and smoothly away. The dark shape quickly gathered speed and he stared intently, concentrating on the shrinking dark speck speeding towards the glacier. In an instant it vanished and he fixed the point in his mind. It had fallen in a straight line. Slowly, he lifted his eyes to the horizon, finding the distinct peak that he had taken the bearing on. With luck, the light rucksack would not be deeply buried in the accumulated powder snow.

When he had shoved the bivouac sack and his sleeping bag into his rucksack he sat up and struggled to pull his boots over his fleece-lined inners, tightening the laces and flexing his ankles to test his circulation. Satisfied, he reached for the rock pitons and wired nuts and clipped them to the gear loop on the back of his harness. He rolled his insulation mat into a tight tube and strapped it to the side of the rucksack.

A sharp, icy breeze gusted against his face as he

sparked the stove into life for one last brew. The snowfall had clothed the land, its contours like an undulating winding sheet flowing down to the still dark valleys. Ice fields gleamed like ancient, rippled glass. As the pale morning light strengthened, the mountains seemed to grow, expanding to fill the sky. The fickle mutations of light made them look austere, implacably beautiful, their ridges starkly etched.

He knew he was making excuses: he was scared. His plan to descend in the dark of early morning had leached away into idleness. He didn't want to start down the ice field, to leave this last place they had been together. He was frightened of finding her—frightened of not finding her. He thought of the snow hardening around her, holding her trapped between worlds, and he turned the stove off and rose to his feet. It was time to leave.

There was a sudden strangeness to the atmosphere, a breath-held sense of danger that stopped him reaching for the food bag. He paused, arm outstretched, and glanced to his side. He exhaled slowly, spine stiffening. It was as if the air had subsided. He almost spoke aloud to question the silent landscape and the hushed, expectant tension. Nothing happened and he relaxed warily.

Unclipping the sling of bunched ice screws, he leaned down and stirred the pan with one of the screws. The pan was too hot to hold so he laid the screws down on the ledge and searched in the top of his rucksack until he found one of his thickly insulated climbing gloves. The temperature had dropped hard with the coming of dawn. He could feel it all around him in the crisp air plumed with his breath and the edgy rasp of his boots on the

61

ledge. Settled weather after the storm, he thought, and the air slumped again and he dropped the cigarette with a jolt. He stared fearfully above him.

The summit cornices shuddered along their length, hung still for a moment, then began to peel slowly from the summit ridge line. Blue ice gleamed as the cornices fell away, exposing the sheer ice walls clinging to the ridge. Tons of ice and snow lumbered forward, then inexorably began to accelerate.

For a distance of two hundred feet on either side of the summit the cornices slid with gathering speed down the upper slopes of the north face. A frontal wave of powder snow billowed ahead of the surge. The heavy, knocking sounds of colliding ice blocks merged into a deafening, thunderous reverberation. Fresh, dry granular snow and heavy slabs of old snow pack shivered into motion. The heavily laden snow slopes slithered away in sweeping outriders to the leading mass of the ice avalanche.

It was subtle at first, a low-frequency trembling. Then the air began to roar and spindrift swept back like white horses gale-torn from a breaking sea. The concussion of disrupted air created a back-blast of exploding powder squalls as the disintegrating, pulverised blocks of ice lifted up and the avalanche seemed to leap forward, accelerating in bounds, overtaking itself in ground-eating surges until the amphitheatre of the face resounded with its thunder. The air turned white.

6

Crack! The sound punched through him, the world moved, something split the air and he sensed the mountain tremble, its surface sinking beneath him. He seemed to shrink into himself and even as he puzzled at the strange movement, the avalanche burst over him with explosive savagery.

Like a wave that has built its power over thousands of miles of open ocean, fountains of snow burst over the ledge to crash past with horrifying force. In the white bomb-blast of concussed air he was thrown from the ledge. The avalanche diminished him until he was conscious only of a tortured inferiority; he knew that this was death. It was all he knew.

As the ropes and slings snapped tight his head battered forward, chinning his chest with great, thumping hammer blows. The colossal force of streaming rivers of snow scooped under him, lifting him up light on his anchors and his heartbeat skipped, scared and erratic, until he was smashed brutally back down onto the ice. Ropes whipped his face as his knees thudded painfully against the ledge.

Great blows pummelled his back and the coarse sandy texture of ground ice particles flayed his skin. The thundering torrent increased in weight, crushing his face into the jagged axe-adzed ice ledge, rattling his head in a sharp juddering tattoo until his vision faded. He opened his mouth to breathe and snow jetted in, packing solid in his throat. Through barely opened eyes he registered dark, bulky shadows moving within the white torrent. Then a ferocious impact battered him away from the ledge until he hung horizontal, his body streaming out in the current of snow. He was acutely conscious of the vibrating rigidity of the safety sling holding him to the handrail rope. The sling shuddered, slackened, then whipped tight-hard again as a piton flew free. There was an unbearable pressure in his chest, the burning acidic heat of starved lungs, then the noise subsided to a distant rustle as consciousness faded.

For a moment he was filled with a wild exhilaration. He saw the rivers of snow spurting past him as if from a distance and the vicious, jabbing blows to his body as he swung in the fierce current seemed strangely disconnected. His eyelids fluttered over staring eyes as violent white swathes trembled across his vision. He watched cascades of luminescent ice particles stream past to hang in the air like vast sheets of suspended airborne waterfalls. He saw it all through glazed eyes, his mouth slackly opening and closing tremulously, a banked fish flapping spasmodically, retching silently.

A vaporous chasm engulfed him and he would have screamed but for the blockage in his throat. A looming shadow lumbered into his helpless body, smashing him sideways against the ice field. The impact vomited the plug of compacted snow from his throat and he sucked a scant breath of thin, powder-filled air. Water formed instantly in his lungs and he coughed and tried to breathe at the same time. Then, skull-crushed, instant blackness flooded silently around him.

He awoke hanging head-down the slope.

Blinking his eyes open, he saw a spray of red misted snow, thick globules of blood dotting the crimson stain. When he opened them again he looked past the blood and straight down the ice field, a sheet of rippled grey dropping to the glacier. Twisting to look over his shoulder he saw that he was hanging ten feet below the ledge. He saw the sling stretched tight from his harness and a length of rope, but the handrail had gone. *What was holding him?*

Swinging his legs below him, he saw the karabiner on the end of the sling jammed sideways in the belay loop on his harness. It wasn't clipped into the loop. Panic swamped him as he grabbed the sling, feeling his legs scrabble across and down the ice with a sickening lurch. He struggled to force his fingers between the rigidly closed tape of the slings, gripping the karabiner hard with his spare hand to prevent it slipping through the loop, but it was to no avail. Reaching up, he grasped the sling and pulled as hard as he could, kicking with his legs and pulling the slack through the loop as his body rose a few inches. He gained enough loose tape to twist the karabiner down and clip it through the sling. He sank onto the sling, breathing heavily. Blood dripped steadily from his face.

Pulling on the sling with both hands and ramming his boot caps against the slick ice, he hauled his body back onto the safety of the ledge where he knelt, coughing and gasping. When his breathing had steadied he looked at the handrail rope. Two pitons had been torn from the rock wall and the remaining steel peg was bent over at the eye. He quickly swept the ice chips and drifts of powder snow from the ledge until he discovered his ice axe. He found the two pitons hanging on the handrail rope, unclipped them and hammered them hard into cracks in the rock wall. Tying the handrail rope into two loops, he clipped each to a piton. Only then did he relax and slump, exhausted, onto the ledge.

He touched his face with numb fingers until blood smears appeared and he felt the ragged edge of the laceration running across the left side of his eyebrow and up into his hairline. Pressing a handful of granular snow against the wound, he waited until the bleeding subsided, checking and replenishing the bloodstained snow-packs. By the time the bleeding had been staunched his hand had lost all feeling. He pushed it weakly through the zip opening in his jacket and clamped it in the warmth of his armpit. As he did so he saw the leather tobacco pouch lying loosely within. He stared at it dumbly. His last memory was of holding a cigarette and a pan of tea—then violence and darkness.

Leaning forward from the ledge, he saw the avalanche debris field spread like paralysed surf across the glacier. He could make out the blue sheen of ice blocks scattered amidst the tumbled white trail of rubble. He sagged back against the wall and fumbled with his bloodied fingers to roll a cigarette. As he inhaled a thin stream of smoke he began to giggle and then to cry.

It was silent. It was as if nothing had happened and, but for the blood and the avalanche debris, there was nothing to show that it had.

He had been brought down to the raw edge of life, felt the cunning instinct that makes men live and now sat humbled at simply being there. He smoked the cigarette and shivered convulsively.

A small dark shape span into view from the north. It hovered on the light air, rising up the ice field, dipping its wings to swoop closer to where he sat, then swinging away to examine him from a safe distance. The bird appeared tired. He wondered whether it had suffered in the storm. It flew above his head and circled lazily, then, as if coming to a decision, it swept down towards the tangle of ropes piled on the far side of the ledge and landed. He had never seen a chough land in the mountains. Their forte was taking insects on the wing and giving acrobatic displays simply for the sheer pleasure of flight. The bird watched him intently as he slowly blew a thin stream of smoke into the air, dipping its head to one side, a dark beady eye fixed on him. It stepped sideways, gripping a knot in the rope with its claws where it was more comfortable. It remained still and watchful. He found himself breathing lightly, tensing himself to make no sudden movements. He liked the bird. It gave him courage.

Without thinking, he raised his fingers to the cut on his forehead. The bird flew up from the ropes and was gone. Saddened, he searched the sky, spotting the tiny dot skimming the crest of the rock ridge bounding the east side of the face. He sat quietly staring at the point on the ridge where the bird had vanished. There was something familiar about it.

As the nicotine slid through his veins he became aware of a compressing pain across his forehead. Feeling dizzy, he again lifted a bloodied hand tentatively to the ragged gash, exploring a raised

67

swelling with deadened fingers. He pressed hard against the bone and was rewarded with the spiny pain of fractured bone. He closed his eyes and saw blood swim across his eyelids and sensed the pressure building beneath the skull. Grasping his head in both hands, he pressed gently at first, then with increasing force, wincing with anticipated pain. The ache centred on his forehead close to the wound site. He shook his head from side to side, feeling the pain surge as it swung. Peering through squinting eyes, he found that his vision remained focused. He found himself staring at the front points of a crampon protruding from a drift of snow on the ledge.

Glancing around, he noticed for the first time that there was very little equipment left on the ledge. He reached for the crampon, relieved to see that its companion was attached. He clipped them securely to the repaired handrail rope next to where he had hung the ice hammer. A sweeping search through the grainy snow revealed the ice axe, a spoon and the stove—but no pan. With increasing concern he widened his search, brushing snow and ice chips from the ledge until he was down to the bare surface. His rucksack was gone.

He checked the handrail, convinced that he had clipped the sack to it, but there was no sign of the sling he had used: it had snapped. Whatever had severed the sling so easily would have killed him instantly. He thought of the headache and the stunning blow into unconsciousness and the blood on the snow.

Then he remembered the ice screws. He had been holding them in his hand, stirring the tea with one, watching tea leaves floating on the surface where the sharp points had torn the tea bag. Then he had put them down on the ledge and used one of his thick gloves to hold the hot pan. He searched the ledge again with a leaden feeling in his stomach. They, too, were gone.

No rucksack, no sleeping bag or bivouac sack, no gloves and no ice screws. He would not survive a winter storm unprotected. Instinctively, he scanned the horizon, studying the clouds for signs of a front moving in. A low graduated grey mass rimmed the edge of the sky. He swore softly. Without shelter he would not survive the night.

'Anyway, you can't just sit here,' he said aloud, surprising himself. 'No one knows you're here. No one will come for you.' He stared at the ridge. A sheet of ice rimming the lower edge of the rock band undulated in grey corrugated waves for three hundred feet before washing up against the rock walls rearing up to the crest of the ridge.

Without the ice screws he couldn't abseil down the ice field. His only option was to down-climb, but even as he thought of it he knew it would be suicide. On the ascent they had struggled to climb the iron-hard winter ice, teetering on millimetres of crampon steel as their axes splintered the brittle, glassy surface. He glanced again at the treacherous line leading across to the ridge.

Both rucksacks had gone and with them any chance of escape. Glancing at the handrail rope and the cat's cradle of slings clipped to it, he saw only the three pitons that he had fastened to the rock wall. Looking down the ice field, he searched for rock outcrops protruding from the ice. There was only a sheet of blank greyness.

He picked up the stove and hurled it angrily into the cold morning air, watching as it fell swiftly away. He sat disconsolately on the ledge and rolled another cigarette. His head throbbed with a dull, pulsing resonance. He felt nauseous and gulped cold air to clear the sensation. The roof of his mouth was dry with the sour, metallic taste of blood. He recognised the flood of fear ebbing back into his mind and thought of surviving the night coming on.

A high-pitched cry echoed across the silent face and he jerked his head, seeking the source of the sound. *Was there someone there?* He scanned the buttresses and then looked down at the glacier, searching for tracks left by the diminutive figures of his rescuers. The cry came again. Spinning above the ridge, cavorting on an up-draught of wind, he saw the bird holding station above a notch in the ridge. Its shrill caw sounded again and soon it was joined by a companion.

There was something about the notch that he recognised, an old familiarity. He looked across the ice field away from where the birds hung on the wind, level with where he sat. He had seen this view before. They had sat in the afternoon sun and looked across the face at the rock wall where they planned to make their first bivouac. He remembered leaning out over the crest of the ridge to look down a steep, ice-glazed rock gully capped with a short, viciously steep rock wall. He remembered thinking that the gully might be a good escape line from the face.

Sitting back on the ledge, he stared at the notch on the ridge where the birds flew. Things were as bad as they could get, yet he could feel the excitement beginning to rise in his chest as his mind ran through the options. If he could use the few pitons and wires left to him he might be able to traverse the edge of the ice field towards the gully. It was hidden from him but he knew that directly below the notch the ice ran up in a sharp, narrowing cone until it petered out in the overhanging rock wall that guarded the exit onto the ridge. He could use his two ropes tied through pitons and chocks placed in the rock band to protect him as he edged towards the gully. He wished now that he had studied the final moves leading towards the ridge.

As he freed the ropes he let them slide down the ice field in two loops until the knots were free, then he dropped the loose ends to snake swiftly down until they were dragged straight by the grip of the pitons.

He checked the pitons, tapping with his hammer to listen to the sound of steel seated within rock and watch for any movement. One knifeblade shifted, so he unclipped the handrail rope, hammered it free and clipped it to his gear loop. He tied the blue rope to his harness, feeling the weight of it as it hung down the ice field, then stopped as he reached for the red rope.

'Be careful here,' he said. 'How are you going to do this?'

He sat and smoked his cigarette, staring at the ropes and the traverse line and the anchor pitons buried in the rock wall, and wondered if there was enough rope to reach the gully. He could back-rope it but it would take time. He looked at the sky. He didn't have time. The birds cawed and flew high above the ridge; a speckled cloud against the sharp morning sky.

'It could work,' he said, exhaling the smoke. The ice traverse did not look so hard now that he could think calmly about the problems ahead. He could see the lipped edge of the ice field running into the rock band. Axes hooked over this rim of ice between the rock and crampons kicked into the ice field below—that was the way to do it. He glanced anxiously at the handrail ropes. The crampons hung, scraping the rock wall. Still there. 'At least you did one thing right,' he muttered.

He quickly knotted the two ropes together, then threw the heavy loops from the ledge with practised ease. They whipped out in a welter of unzipping coils before twanging tight to hang in a three-hundred-foot loop, one end tied to his harness and the other to the pitons.

As he knelt on the ledge to fasten the crampons to his boots, pulling hard on the straps and feeling the leather compress around his feet, he noticed the blue-black marks of frostbite staining the fingers of his left hand. His right hand felt stiffly wooden—the fingers a dull grey-white. He clenched the fingers into a fist and released them. There was no pink glow showing the return of flowing blood. He examined the wet slick of plasma and thin blood on his fingers. Blood throbbed in his temples. He grimaced and rubbed the stubble line of his jaw, a rough beard now coated in rime, burnt and blistered. His lips were dry and cracked and he wiped a scum of lip cream and food from the corners with fingers smelling sourly of urine, nicotine and blood.

'I've been better,' he muttered to himself.

As he stood to reach for the axes he spotted a

72

patch of black at the far edge of the ledge. Brushing aside the snow, he uncovered a thick, heavily insulated glove. It was for his right hand. He searched in vain for the left glove. His left hand was in bad shape. He pulled the glove onto his numbed hand and flexed the fingers, feeling the constriction of the insulated liners within the tough leather and nylon exterior.

Looking across the traverse line, he saw how his hands on the axe handles would be pressed hard against the ice. The wrist loops would cut the blood flow to his hands. It was a problem that he could not ignore but could do nothing about.

He tucked the tobacco pouch into his shirt pocket and zipped the down jacket closed with his ungloved hand. He couldn't feel the ice-cold metal zipper. Warmth was building within his only glove and he moved his fingers, luxuriating in the returning blood. He felt the soft liner slip against his skin. Pulling the glove from his hand, he eased the liner from the glove and thrust his left hand into it. He tugged the glove onto his right hand and made fists of both hands, flexing life into the fingers until he was satisfied. It was the best he could do.

There was something missing from the familiar ritual of preparing to climb. He glanced around him. He looked at the great loop of rope hanging down the ice and checked the knot at his harness. There was nothing more to do. He had no rucksack to tighten onto his hips, no rack of pitons and screws to arrange—no one to hold his rope. The familiar chinking of metal against metal and crisp clicks of the gates closing on the snaplinks soothed him. He clipped the pitifully small selection of wires and pitons to his gear loop. There was nothing more to do but climb.

He felt his stomach clench at the thought of what lay ahead. He had become accustomed to the solid comfort of his ledge and didn't want to leave it.

It was early-morning cold with a brittle alertness to the air, a gloss to the light. He shuffled on the ledge, hearing the scrape of his crampon points and the creak of his boots. Nervous, acutely aware, standing silent on the ledge planted to the ice, he felt benumbed and isolated. The air seemed thin and stretched as if he were peering through fractured crystal. A cool wind blew against his face and his eyes watered. He wiped them and breathed deeply.

He hefted the axes, checking the wrist loops, feeling the balance and weight of them. He rolled his shoulders, stared fiercely at the piton and then at the traverse. He swung with the axe, felt it bite hard and firm. He felt the pull of the abyss and forced himself to look down and kick his front points into the ice. Splintered glass tinkled below. Gingerly, he transferred his weight, feeling his calf muscles tighten and hold. The second axe crunched into the ice and held. He eased away from safety, hearing his sharp, fast breaths.

He took slow, measured inhalations, tiptoeing sideways, the rope rising in a shallow arc, methodical, exaggerated and scared. His muscles were cramping, stiff from the long hours on the ledge. Then the blood began to flow and he relaxed, feeling the lithe sense of the dangerous dance seduce him. Anxiety became movement translated into elegance. He was not urgent, only consciously precise. Occasionally he glanced back at the ledge, checking on his belayer. She was gone and he stopped looking.

He stood alone above vast emptiness. It excited him. Colours seemed intense, more solid, shapes perfectly realised, densely defined. He watched for air bubbles in the ice, white seams revealing softness, then killed them with his axe pick: a thud of satisfying accuracy. He traversed tentatively below the rock band, splits crackling through the brittle skim of ice under his feet. Occasionally sparks and a cordite smell revealed the rock beneath. The rope stretching to the anchor piton tightened, pulling him from the reverie of his concentration. He searched for fissures and cracks to take a piton or a wired chock. The rock above him was blank, rolling up in a smooth rounded pillar, a flying buttress braced against the ice field.

Reaching down, he chopped steadily at the ice until he had carved a foot-sized ledge that he could step onto, releasing the tight strain on his calf muscle. Then he let out another fifty feet of rope, thumb-knotted a loop in place and clipped it into his harness. The rope slid in a graceful curve across the ice. If he fell now he would swing in a one-hundred-foot arc. He would not fall. After an hour, he had extended the blue rope to its full length from the ledge. Above the ice he saw an inch-wide crack splitting the rock. Moving within reach of the rock felt thinly precarious, exposed.

Breathing shallowly, he flipped his ice hammer so that he could catch the handle and reached tentatively for the piton. He perched on the points of his crampons, feeling uncertain without the comfort of hand holds, nervously off balance, as he placed a piton lightly in the crack, hearing the rock

75

grinding tight against the metal. Two sharp blows and he was rewarded with the high, ringing sound of well-set steel. The hammer blows rang loud and sharp in the quiet air. It was a strong piton, he thought, as he clipped the rope into the snap link at its eye. He rested at the piton as he considered the way ahead.

The sudden security made him aware of the electrifying height around him, great spaces of empty air inducing a tense hollowness in his stomach. While he climbed he ignored the earth, the fall line, even forgot about breathing, forgot his entire world. Now, motionless and bereft of that cocoon of concentration, he tried not to think of falling. The sky seemed so cold and vast and blue. He dislodged a fragment of ice and watched it spin away beneath his boots with disturbing velocity. Far below, the glacier squeezed between its mountain walls above the valley. It was as if he were held above it all, suspended. The ice, so recently a fascinating puzzle of decisions that had engrossed him totally, now seemed treacherous. Smooth as oiled glass, it slipped away in a giddy sweep of wetly polished silk. He looked fearfully at his crampons. They grated scratchily.

He felt weak, dizzy and his head pulsed with a steady ache. A sticky fluid leaked from his hairline. He was ill. He wanted to rest, but if he stopped he knew he might not move again. He must keep moving, he told himself, and unhooked his axe from the piton and lowered himself onto the ice. Pushing away the panic, he forced himself to repeat the steady, calming patterns of climbing.

He crabbed sideways across the ice and the rhythms of the axe work soothed his nerves. Fear settled and he relaxed. He felt light on his feet and smiled as he watched his delicate footwork on brittle fragility and used just the necessary pressure to make the points stick. He listened intently to the crazed, splitting noises as he transferred his weight, judging the required pressure meticulously. The ice curled around a toe of rock jutting into the ice field. He, too, moved down, following the creased grey ice until he spotted another fine crack splitting the rocky pillar.

The thin knifeblade of the piton sank half its length with the first blow of his hammer. He leaned out to swing again, hearing a singing resonance as the blade cut into the crack. When the eye bedded hard against the rock he let the hammer dangle from its wrist loop as he pulled in slack rope ready to tie a loop. There was no noise, just the minute slippage that made every muscle in his body clench tight and hard. He watched himself drop a few inches, then the hard grey ice was gone and rock flashed by his face.

Swatted from the wall, he became airborne. He heard the ice sheet grinding and slapping, then saw it lift on the wind, a great ashen wing stalled in flight. Then it exploded into a corona of shattered particles. The fall threw him down, arms to either side, axe picks bouncing uselessly off the skidding stone-hard surface. He arrowed across the ice, facing out and down, absorbing the galvanising chasm below him.

He tried to scream but his ribcage had gridlocked. Something snagged violently at his hip. He flipped sideways and his helmet hit the ice hard, forcing a grunt from his lips. He was

77

astonished by the acceleration, wind beating his ears, ice flashing past and the rock ridge stark against the sky. He glimpsed the glacier, crocodile-backed with crevasses. Twisting, worming on the hook of his rope, he hurtled through the pendulum arc of his fall as he pirouetted dizzyingly, his belly emptied. The rope stretched hard against the piton, pressure building. *Don't rip, don't rip.* Then he was falling into the sky, weightless, escaping gravity. He shut his eyes as he crested the rise, hung half-swooped in frozen animation, then fell back in a rip-rolling scythe, thrumming across the corrugated ice.

When the swinging stopped he hung whimpering, both hands clutching the rope, head resting prayerful against them, waiting for his breathing to calm. He heard ice chips rustle by, then silence. Lifting his head, he stared at the piton eighty feet above, its eye winking against the sky.

'Thank you, thank you,' he muttered and lowered his forehead to the ice in relief. A surge of chemicals flooded through his body and he listened to the adrenaline babble singing through his brain.

Gathering his scattered wits, he tip-tapped shakily up the ice to perch on trembling legs below where the piton protruded from the rock. Beneath it a wide expanse of bare rock was exposed. The ice sheet had detached in one piece, tobogganing into space as he rode it down the ice field. A crampon point caught a thin, sharp-edged crease, held and he steadied himself. He clipped a loop of rope to a karabiner and sank back onto the piton's taut, comforting security.

Far to his right, yellow urine stains revealed the bivi-ledge some two hundred and fifty feet from where he hung. He studied the way to the gully cutting up towards the ridge. Another two hundred feet to go, he decided. A stream of powder snow abruptly swept past in a weightless torrent. He flinched at the bite of the stinging crystals, staring fearfully at the buttresses looming above him and anticipating the roar of another avalanche. He paused, waiting, hunched protectively against the wall. The knifeblade piton looked fragile.

Nothing came down. Above him, white streamers bannered the clear blue sky. He heard the distant wind hammering at the cliffs far above him with a dull moan. It was sheltered on the face but the wind had changed direction and was building in force. Bad weather would come from the direction of the wind, from the lee of the mountain, invisible to him until it struck. Time had swept quickly by. The sun, now high in the sky, gave only an illusion of warmth. He needed to hurry before darkness set in. He glanced at the joined ropes arcing out towards the distant ledge. He would have to abandon one of them.

Climbing back along the crest of the ice, he reached the knot, untied it and let the blue rope fall. It swept across the ice until it hung straight down from the ledge. There was no return.

Tying the two ends of the rope to his harness, he formed a seventy-five-foot loop which he clipped to the piton. He would climb the traverse in seventy-five-foot sections, placing one piton at the end. Then he would pull the rope through, leaving a karabiner and piton behind.

After two hours had passed he had gained a

further hundred and fifty feet. Only four pitons and two wires now hung from his harness. The hardest climbing lay ahead of him. He studied the ground ahead. The gully lifted to a narrow ice cone, its sides bounded by steep rock walls, sunless and gloomy. At its head the ice was pinched out and the walls surged upwards in a vertical shield capped by an overhanging groove. A crack about the width of his fist cut through the overhang but the lower wall looked disconcertingly smooth, hard, unrelentingly steep and intimidating.

There would be little light left for him to reach the safety of the ridge. The prospect of a long, freezing night hanging on anchors without sleeping bag or shelter began to weigh on his mind. If he survived such a night he doubted whether he would be in a fit state to climb the headwall the following morning. No warmth had returned to the wooden fingers of his left hand. He spat away the cigarette butt and reached for his axes.

7

As he neared the head of the gully the ice grew thin and brittle. He found himself tapping the picks of his axes gently against it, just hard enough to hook the edge of the hole the pick had made. His crampons bit, flexed and cracked. He thought nervously of the sleigh ride he had taken earlier. A flake of rock protruded from the left bank of the gully and he draped a sling over it and clipped himself to its karabiner. With the security of the sling to bolster his courage, he moved higher,

80

until, standing on the last vestiges of ice smeared onto the rocky headwall, he placed a solidly seated wired chock, hammering it into the crack, watching as the alloy steel distorted under the sharp blows of the axe pick. He knew it would be impossible to remove, but it would also form his main anchor for the climb out over the headwall.

Within an hour he had abseiled to the foot of the gully, recovered the wires and pitons and returned to his high point. He studied the rock rearing above him. Silvery creases of ice seamed through its folds. A tracery of thin fissures rose to a widening crack cutting into the roof above. A serpent of blue-black ice glimmered at the back of the crack.

There was no way to avoid the roof. It would have to be climbed directly. He counted himself fortunate to have the crack to help him. Without it he would have been trapped. The walls on either side of the roof were blank shields of rock blocking all sideways progress towards the ridge. There was only one possible line to climb. He felt pleased: at least he had no more decisions to make. It was simple: climb the crack and escape the face or die in the gully.

He pulled hard on the rope, watching as the karabiners jerked tight with metallic clinks. The battered wire chock remained stolidly unmoving in its rocky cleft. The knifeblade that he had hammered into an adjoining crevice flexed slightly and held. He removed the sling and draped it over his head. Clenching his bare fingers, he checked that his axes dangled securely from their wrist loops and reached up with his right hand to grip a slight edge on the wall. He watched his fingertips curl tight over the hold, but he couldn't feel it. If his fingers began to creep or slip he would get little warning. Letting go, he tried again. He winced. There was only a hard, numb sensation of pressure.

He committed to the move, leaving the ice by placing the front point of a crampon carefully into a glazed groove. The point seated and held firm with a splintering crunch and he stood up in a smooth, watchful movement.

He exhaled slowly. Reaching high, he drove an axe firmly into the crack. The plastic ice shivered and fragmented, yet held firm, and he pulled and stood in tentative balance.

His locked bicep began to weaken and shake and he leaned back, arm straight, hanging on bone. The muscle relaxed and the shaking eased. The climbing was steep, intricate, commanding his attention so that he became aware only of the next few feet of rock above him. The great fall of the ice field, framed by the enclosing walls of the gully, was behind him, out of sight and concern.

He forced himself to breathe calmly as he moved, listening to the small sounds in his world— the click-clicking karabiners, pitons chinking at his waist, ice crackling past, picks thudding home. Crampon points screeched, steel talons raked rock, then caught. He teetered, balanced on nothing, trying to breathe.

Composed rhythm returned, defying gravity, and he felt a sense of weightlessness permeate through him. He hooked tiny edges, moving weight onto them and leaving instantly as if movement alone would keep him alive. Making delicate placements, he could see space plunging beneath the soles of his boots to the avalanche-scarred cirque of the glacier. He ignored the view.

Ice glimmered, a platinum ribbon in the depths. He glimpsed sparks in the darkness as his picks struck rock. Placing his last piece of protection fifty feet above the gully, he jammed the largest wire he possessed deep into the rock. Above him the wall became an imposing blank slab glazed with sheets of rime.

He hadn't noticed that his knuckles were skinned raw and bleeding. The creeping poison of lactic acid cramped his forearm muscles, loosening the grip of his fingers, making him acutely conscious of the chasm inviting his backward, sailing fall. It was gloomy where he hung, bat-like, in the shadows of the gully.

As he hung slumped on the sling he shook his splayed fingers, trying to force the lactic acid from the cramped muscles. He knew that progress to the roof would have to be made in a single, unprotected push. The crack thinned down to smooth blankness as it ran into the roof. Where the lid of rock pushed out into the sky he saw only darkness in its depths. If he could get close up, crouched under the roof, he might be able to reach around with one arm. What he would find, groping blindly with waving axe or numbed fingers, was anyone's guess.

Then he heard it—a low whistle at first, rising to a regular deep hum. Powder snow suddenly engulfed him. A thin white stream bloomed busily down the gully. He looked up. The edge of the dark crest of the roof was starkly outlined against the sky by ragged, white streamers like a gale-shredded sail. The wind had returned, blowing hard from the far side of the ridge. Loose storm-laid powder snow swirled into the evening sky. He ducked as a frosted vortex swirled around him and then stared anxiously at the scene unfolding above him.

The ridge line exploded in wind-borne crescents of ice crystals lit up by the sinking sun. It formed a bursting corona of sheeted silver and for a moment his fear fled and he was intoxicated, blinded by the beauty. The snow spurted skywards in a dazzling spray and he watched as crystalline banners rocketed vertically up before spreading out into mists and sparkling haze. Everything seemed bright and fiercely alive. Even the singing of the wind with its lethal menace seemed like a musical accompaniment to the bursting halo of frozen, silvered spray.

He grinned, feeling revived. The risk and exertion elated him. He thought of the avalanche survived and the swooping fall across the ice field and her body lying coldly immobile far below and felt incoherent rage at the injustice of it all. A grim determination settled into his mind. He would do this thing and do it well. Purged of guilt, regret, sorrow or hope, he was left with a great and furious intent. Then, looking at his fingers showing the blue-black burn of frostbite and feeling leaden tiredness in his arms, he knew just as keenly that he was nearly beaten.

He grasped the axe handles, unclipped himself from the sling and began to climb the vertiginous ice-rimed wall, moving determinedly towards the shadow of the roof. His fear vanished. He would climb it or die trying, he told himself, as his axe bit into the rime.

It was so dark under the roof that he could no longer see what was below him. It felt as if he was at ground level. He accepted the delusion gratefully and kept up his momentum, moving steadily, struggling along a network of thin finger-cracks glazed with verglas. He vigilantly hooked the picks of his axes, moved up, then edged crampon points into the nicks his axes had made. With the illusion of continuous movement he became fixated solely on the next move, and he moved so lightly he scarcely needed holds as solid as he might if he had paused to rest. He muttered words of encouragement to himself, sometimes swearing in a litany of obscenities as he scuttled insect-like towards the roof.

He had a detached awareness of rasping breaths, his muscles quivering, and knew that soon he would drop from the mountain. His forearms, stomach and calves felt wire-tight, pumped with lactic acid. Gravity dragged, the abyssal centrifuge hauling at his back. His weight doubled with every move.

Falling might not finish him, but a crushed limb would be a long slow killing like an abattoir victim squirming on the rope. Death would flow in on the icy tide of night, a fact, nothing more. It did not trouble him: only the next move mattered. He reached high with a weakening arm, the axe wobbling in his hand, and pushed it deep within the crack that split the roof. He could see nothing. Would it hold?

A shower of ice chips sprinkled his eyes. He blinked away tears and pushed his wrist deep into the rock, swung hard and blind, hearing his fraught swearing from a distance. As he began to relax into the fall he felt the thudding, chewy grip of a firm placement. He sagged his weight onto the axe, choking on retching gasps for air, too tired to care if it ripped free. It held.

He clung, a dark arachnid shape suspended in the black underbelly of the roof. Shadowed silhouettes of his axes clawed upwards into the evening light above the darkness; spasmodic, desperate movements. Torn metal noises, grunts and whimpered curses and still he searched with the outstretched axes, willing something to hold, to catch an edge, to stop this endless downward pull. A pick stopped abruptly and held. He went immediately silent, focused on the feel of the edge, tentatively pumping on the handle. It held.

No time to rest and plan the next moves. Leaning out over the drop, left arm fully extended, he pushed with his legs until he hung horizontally under the roof. His stomach trembled, rigid with the strain of keeping his upper body parallel with the roof. Pained grunts and yelped curses spat from beneath the roof as his other axe flailed blindly. His back curved down. He couldn't hold the position. With a convulsive upward surge he reached around the lip of the roof, a slab of rock no more than six inches thick. The pick skittered across the flat upper surface of the roof and he scraped it from side to side, praying that it would jam in a fissure or lodge against a build-up of ice.

Ten seconds more. Ten seconds, less, and he would fall. His stentorian breathing was amplified in the confined space. Five seconds of futile scrabbling passed by. He hadn't fallen. He pressed his face to the crack, seeing the glare of the sinking sun, a corona of blown ice crystals and then, at the back of the crack, he glimpsed a sheen of ice. Calves vibrating, crampon points creeping from their rock edges, he stretched upwards again, breath held.

His stomach muscles were burning and his legs trembled in spasms. He felt resignation flood through him, embracing the end, feeling his body imperceptibly slacken, accepting the fall. He glanced over his shoulder into the gully. How would he impact?

He dropped lower, swore again and anger flooded hotly through his mind. *This was not going to happen.* Strength ebbing swiftly, he made a last convulsive thrust, straightening his knees and throwing his arm out and over the roof. The axe swung down, feebly blind—and held. The ten seconds were up.

His body began to swing out from the roof, crampons torn free by his lunge. He kicked hard, steel spitting sparks in the dark as he pushed with his last vestige of power. He swung out of the dark, his legs hanging in yawning space. With the curled spring of his body he had converted the fall to a leap.

The fall stopped. He hung vertically from his hand, pinioned painfully by the axe wrist loop. The pressure on his twisted wrist, trapped above the roof, dragged a cry from his throat as the slender bones hovered on the edge of splintering.

Kicking his legs vainly in the space below the roof, he tried to pull his body up on his right arm. Exhausted, he slumped back—having risen no more than a few inches. Once more he doubled up his legs, frantically slamming his boots against the underside of the roof, hoping to find some small purchase. His left foot bounced uselessly from the rock and he heard the screech of crampon points. The boot stopped and held—on what he had no idea—and he gave a despairing thrust, stomach muscles snapping his torso to full stretch, reaching out towards the lip of the roof until his chin came level with it and a low sun burst across his retinas. There in front of him was his right axe lodged in a bulge of water ice little thicker than a matchbox.

He reached around the roof with his ice hammer and hooked the pick over the head of his axe just as his lower body skipped out and swung into space. Not daring to think about the strength of the pick placement, he pulled hard with both arms, twisting and swinging his legs to gain momentum until he had dragged himself high enough to get his shoulders and upper chest over the lip of the roof. He lay balanced precariously, see-sawing on the lip of rock, canting up and down on his belly as he struggled to inch his body onto the flat smooth ledge. Mewling with fright and pain, he shuffled himself forward.

He breathed in choked gasps, tears filling his eyes as he pushed himself into a kneeling position and blinked in the sudden brightness. The wind blew with such ferocity that for a second it pushed him backwards and he would have lost balance but for his firmly hooked axe. In front of him, the rock stretched out in a flat ledge bounded on the left by the steep, knife-edged plunge of the ridge. Ahead lay the open, snow-plastered sweep of the east face.

The eye of a piton protruding from a wall above the ledge was silhouetted against the sun. A loop of abseil tape flapped in the wind. At full stretch, he hooked the loop with his pick and then wrenched free the axe that had saved him from falling. As he stood up and straightened his shaking body he heard a splintery sound and felt the rock tilt beneath his feet.

It seemed to happen with cartoon-like speed. With the grating noise of pulverised rock the slab that had formed the roof dipped down and began to topple from the ridge. He pulled hard on the abseil tape, running on the tipping slab, watching as his crampons kicked sparks from the rock and he made a despairing lunge. His chest pounded painfully against the ledge as he felt the roof fall away below his thighs and his legs plunge into emptiness. There was a heavy wrench on his harness as he heard the boom of the rock exploding against the gully wall below. He scrambled his legs sideways onto the ledge and lay face-down, stupefied with fright and fatigue, spasms shuddering his muscles. With hurried, fumbling fingers he clipped the eye of the piton and collapsed on the ledge, sucking air into his lungs as the crazed whirl of his thoughts settled.

When he lifted his head and opened his eyes he noticed a delicate pattern grooved into the rock where his cheek had rested. A perfectly preserved fossil lay drawn in surreal detail in the stone. He stared at it in disbelief. He traced the fossil with his hand, edging a numb, blackened fingertip tentatively around the shape of the ancient marine creature.

Having shakily rolled a cigarette, he dragged deeply on the flame, feeling the acrid, unpleasant burn as he exhaled through his nose. Wiping a shaking hand across his face, he examined the snow-laden east face, noting the towers jutting from the crest of the ridge dividing it from the north face.

The sun, now low on the horizon, sank with the temperature. He had no head torch for a descent in the dark but he knew that he could not stay where he was, exposed on the windswept ridge. They had left abseil points fixed when they had descended to the hut after the reconnaissance, but they had been abseiling on two fifty-metre ropes and he had only the single red rope left to him. There were large sections of the ridge that could be down-climbed without abseiling but to do so after a storm and at night would be risky. He rose to his knees, wearily preparing to abseil back down the gully to untie the red rope and retrieve whatever pitons and wires he could remove.

He pulled in the slack rope, expecting it to tighten against the anchor. It kept coming. He leaned out over the edge where the roof had sheared away to see the tail of the rope flick into view in the gloom of the gully. Moments later he held the frayed rope end, remembering the wrenching impact on his harness when the roof had crashed down. The slab of rock had sheared through the anchors, slicing easily through the rope held tight by his straining body. He thought of how close he had come to falling with the roof, not knowing that his self-belay system had been severed.

Threading the rope through the abseil tape, he threw the coiled loops far out, watching them snaking down to slap against the rocks. A stream of snow jetted against his jacket, making his bare face and hands smart. He fumbled to cinch tight the hood of his jacket over his helmet. Then he searched inside the jacket, relieved to find that the liner and the outer glove were still inside.

Moving as fast as safety allowed, he abseiled the seventy-five-foot rope length to a ledge perched above a vertical wall. Peering down, he could see the red flash of their abseil tape at the foot of the wall. A wire hammered into a thin crack enabled him to reach it. He threaded the rope hurriedly through the tape, conscious that the light was fading fast. To follow their original line on the ridge was the most direct descent but he did not have enough anchors. He peered out across the darkening east face, which dropped away in a series of interconnected ledges and rock walls. A diagonal downward traverse out onto the face would lead him away from the steep cliffs of the ridge. There was a chance that he could down-climb unroped by zigzagging through the maze of walls and snow-covered ledges.

He abseiled out onto the expanse of the face, testing the depth and strength of the snow, leaning sideways on the rope, studying the terrain falling away beneath him. The lower face of the mountain was already bathed in darkness. He caught a glimpse of the notch in the ridge where the hut lay a thousand feet below and thought he saw a flash of light glinting from a window. It lifted his spirits as he pulled the rope down and coiled it neatly around his shoulders.

He traversed further out onto the face, taking care to bury his axes deep into the banked snow, searching for layers of hard ice. He knelt facing the mountain, sweeping powder snow from the rocks until he found enough holds to climb gingerly down each short wall he came to, slanting sideways, searching for an easier line. Within hours he found himself stranded, unable to see far enough below him to continue safely. Excavating a hollow in a bank of snow pushed up against an overhanging rock wall, he burrowed in under the rock until he could huddle, protected on three sides from the wind.

He brushed as much of the powder snow from his clothing as he could, then removed his helmet and sat on its rounded, slippery surface. It provided some insulation from the snow. He rolled a cigarette blindly and smoked quietly, rocking gently, as he watched the red end flare and glow bright with each inhalation. It was a long cold night coming, waiting for the moon, praying the clouds would stay away. He was shivering by the time he stubbed out the cigarette.

8

He fought the urge to sleep, aware that it might be the last thing he would be conscious of, but, as the wind whipped eddies of driven snow around his shelter, he felt fatigue eating into his core. He had forgotten how long he had been on the mountain, had lost the reason for being at this new place. Hunger and thirst were pains that momentarily kept sleep at bay, but even as he licked his dry lips his eyelids drooped, closed and he lowered his chin to his raised knees.

The wind blew hard as he slept and the snow drifted in deep folds, gradually closing the open side of his shelter until a hole near his head, little bigger than his face, was all that was left. Feathers of snow settled on the stubble of his lips and became dribbled icicles in his breath. An icy carapace formed around the tightly cinched hood of his duvet jacket.

A dream slipped in and out of his mind, hovering on the edge of his consciousness. The sudden gust of wind and the hustle of snow across the hood of his jacket became the rush of air over feathered wings as a bird swooped past his shoulder. He stirred and muttered. He saw a solitary bird rising in swinging thermals, hanging above a familiar ridge line, then diving straight at him, shrieking its attack cry, talons extended. He flinched at the odour of carrion, recoiling in horror. Filled with a sense of dread, he tried to wake, to rise and leave the dream. He wanted her back, needed her in this terrible place.

Feeling the raking grip of the talons as they settled on his shoulder, he turned to look at the bird and saw her face close to his. He appeared to be observing from the outside. He saw that they lay side by side. An uneasy stillness smothered them, a sense of permanence, of unending sleep. When he looked again he saw that they were not sleeping. They had a deathly pallor. He looked closely at her face. Her eyes were open, looking into him, with a distant, troubled gaze—from far back in her mind it seemed, afraid of where she was, trying to tell him something. She mouthed inaudible words, inarticulate impulses of love that he strained to hear, unspoken, dislocated sounds drifting on the wind. They suggested a great loneliness.

93

He was caught in a trough of bewilderment, her words whispered in rolling, tormented eddies around him. He could hear the tears in her words, imagined a great, wide, uncreated sea separating them. Her sorrow washed around him, forbidding, a paralysing emptiness.

She looked stricken. He smiled, trying to console her, gazing into her eyes with desperate intensity. He felt old, cold as stone. He stared into her eyes, imploring, and her face calmed. He nodded in affirmation, encouragement, reading her thoughts, although they had said nothing. They no longer needed words.

He should have felt blessed to have her back, yet he stared at her longingly, filled with apprehension. Then something deep within her eyes changed. She was staring through him now, out to a bleak northern emptiness, at something only she could see, making him shiver. It was a strange moment, sombre, almost frightening, when he should have been joyously exultant. The horror of these past days was becoming clear to them now. *We shouldn't be here in this awful place; we know how much we have lost.* He turned to look at where her gaze was fixed and heard the barest hiss of feathers beating the air. Turning quickly, he found that she had gone.

The apparition looms into his dream, a cold, fearful awareness. The shadow bird haunts his distracted mind, malice in living form. It is a hooded crow, a terrible thing winging past, fixing him with malevolent, evil, lidless eyes. Then it flashes by his lonely eyrie, stealing an indefinable part of him.

It must be a portent, an omen, a harbinger of

death? This inhuman thing holds him in thrall as it sweeps across the surface of a winter sky, a blazing vision skimming the shimmering air. When its eyes fix on him the depthless stare brings on an absolute certainty of death. There are no such things, he chides himself. Maybe it is a trick of the light, a mirage perhaps, and he shifts uneasily in his sleep. Yet he believes in it, his dreadful arbiter. Suddenly filled with a frantic need to act, he tries to wake—to no avail. Something holds him down, a ferocious pressure, and he is crouching helpless in the gloom as a sinister black northern sky calls down another blizzard and there, sweeping from side to side, his harbinger wings the air, emotionless eyes boring through him.

You will die in this place. Her words drift into his mind from far away, as if hovering on the wind. He listens, bird-like nervous, to the sound of her voice, urgently gentle. He stirs, trying to respond. What must he do? The voice, a blessed, delighted memory, repeats the warning and he answers silently that he is coming, but he cannot move. He seems fixed, immovable, frozen in this dream place, trapped on this unsafe, quartered shelf. He must act.

Far above where he crouched on the snow-laden mountain side, locked in the gloom of his dreams, the sky had come alive. As the hours drifted by pale colours swept the winter sky, barely visible at first, then increasing in tone and intensity until hanging veils banded the moon-brightened sky. High in the atmosphere above his huddled, shrouded figure, a hundred miles above the earth, a long spectral cloud seeped steadily across the heavens.

The long, moonlit, orographic cloud capping the distant peaks slowly unfurled, lacing the night with a gentle delicacy of light rarely seen in such latitudes. It moved up and across the sky in great lateral sheets of pale luminous smoke. Rolling across the stratosphere in graceful motions, inward-turning, pulsing and rippling in the night air like a wind-drifted curtain of silk, the light wall grew until it hung, in the silence of the mountain night, draped across the sky, never quite touching the earth; energy released as light.

Out, far beyond the corona of the sun, on the dark side of the earth, the solar wind surfs the magnetosphere, a plasma shield wrapped protectively around our fragile blue world. Plasma, electrons, atoms and molecules collide, energise into light, colours distinctive by element—oxygen glowing red through yellow and greens, nitrogen shimmering blue. Auroral ovals formed by the continuous stream of charged particles form the greatest natural light show on earth. An expert might sagely explain this phenomenon with the cold, exacting perspective of a scientist. A mute, awed layman peering heavenwards might take a more spiritual view. A grieving, exhausted man on a storm-swept mountain face remembered that three days previously, when that solar storm sped from the surface of the sun, he let his love fall— time's arrow outrunning the sun.

He came to wakefulness with a swift immediacy. It was as if he had been resisting some immense force intent on pressing him down, which had abruptly let go its grip. He blinked in the gloom of his shelter, disorientated, with the dread of the dream still hovering in his memory. As he felt the long fingers of cold knifing his body he remembered the harbinger and her voice and her troubled eyes and the joy of watching her face. He became slowly aware of a sharp light flashing weakly through the opening in the drifted snow. Struggling into wakefulness, he felt that he was rising from a drugged sleep, his head heavy and clogged with fumes. He peered at the patterns of light, feeling the cold bone-deep within his spine. For a time he had no idea of where he was or what he was seeing.

There was a soft, soundless sensation. Raising his head broke the fragile bonds the crystals had formed and snow cascaded down his chest to be blown away by the wind. Before him, the mountains lay revealed. The unfamiliar eastern view confused him. Jagged peaks thrust sharply into the night sky, their black crests silhouetted by starlight and moon, snow ridges raked by the wind into bladed edges of burnished steel.

The moon was high in the sky, stars shone hard as diamonds and the mountains seemed silver-plated, acid-etched. He remembered the ledge and the climb out and the darkness and he came fully awake. He thought of the dream and the portents and shuddered. He must use the moonlight while he had the chance. How many hours had he wasted in dull sleep? He shook his head and turned his face to the sky. He gasped.

What he saw was so strange and so beautiful it made him afraid. Anything of such perfection, he reasoned, must be the last thing he would see, and a part of him quailed even as he stared. The sky was alight, flickering in a way he had never seen. It was strangely brilliant, beautiful beyond measure.

The dusted snow crystals on his jacket glowed with the glimmer of phosphorescence as he shuffled frozen-footed on the ledge. As he looked again at the heavens he became aware of a silence so profound that he swore he could hear the pulse of the earth. He peered at the sky, and a diaphanous transparency of light unfolded before him, drapes of pastel hues meandering down the sky in undulating, rippling colours. Winding sheets like oiled silks hung waving in a windless sky, leaking pallid blues and sea-worn, glassy greens. They formed wave upon wave of pulsing, tremulous colours suspended in a blue-black sky. Stars glinted behind this shrouded brilliance, scattered diamonds on black velvet. The ice beneath his boots seemed to shiver and crack as if on a lifting tide, as if the earth had released a vast exhalation of breath.

He had heard of these translucent banners of the aurora being likened to a gaseous form of lightning, a long, pale ghost-fire arcing across the sky. These flushed, gossamer veils of layered colour melted in and out of each other, delicate and fragile and perfect. They were to him the passing of a soul, a celestial brushstroke, a sense of the divine. This startling, unimagined loveliness gave him a feeling of frailty, a sense that he had no right to be there, an intruder, a voyeur. He could feel the beauty sucking him upwards out of himself towards a remote dimension in the sky and felt afraid.

The Inuit people believe the lights are torches carried by spirits drifting towards their heaven. Dazed polar explorers have heard the lights, describing a gentle swishing sound, a soft, musical

98

fluting, sometimes the flapping of a heavy flag in a stiff breeze. Others say gentle whistling brings the lights nearer. They throw the sky into a third dimension on such an immense scale and with such profound beauty that one is left with a yearning sense of awe and tenderness.

He shook his head slowly, trying to understand the gently swinging lights above him. Strange, strange days, all silence and darkness, light and noise and fear. This winter mountain with its iron indifference had almost destroyed him. Somehow, he had become an intermediary between darkness and light. He knew there was one last task to do, yet was weary beyond measure before he had even started. As he stared at the streaming lights he sensed the feeble core of anger fade within like doused embers, and was filled with a miserable, bewildered sadness. He tore his eyes away from the lights, half-expecting the bleak shadow of the hooded crow to come winging across the sky.

He thought of the past days, the winter darkness, the fall and the storm and the hunted fear; all had beggared his language. The sight and feel of it all would never leave him. Hell will be dark, endless, empty and black, and icy cold—cold as Dante's hell—like watching her fall, like these last days. He sank slowly to his knees watching the heavens' light wash the surrounding moon-lit snows, unable to understand what was happening to him. It had become too much to bear. He did not believe in God and yet he squatted on a mountainside with no other explanation for what he saw. He did not believe in fate or omens, harbingers, devils or angels of light. He had believed in her with a reverence. It had been a comfort of sorts, now

99

gone.

The storm on the ledge had been more than he had thought possible to endure. He had been thrown into a cold so brutal it had silenced him, shocked his mind. The darkness made it terrible. It had arrived without warning at a moment of grieving stillness, in silence forewarning of death, as if the world were holding its breath. The bedlam of the wind had almost torn his mind away. Then, when it was over, and before his senses could recover, there was that ripping sound, steel tearing, as the avalanche came down on him, black snow punching against him in waves, buckling his knees, battering him to black insensibility. And now this strange coloured sky with its whispered resonances.

There was a dizzying madness around him now, an unfamiliar sense of space and movement as if the horizons were retreating at speed away from him in all directions, as if he were wandering on a vast treeless plain with the sky rising endlessly without any lines of compression and his mind unbound. *I am a dead man. I will die here now.*

His clenched hands felt wooden, lifeless. He blind-fumbled in the drifted snow on the ledge until his wrist knocked against the sharp adze of his axe. Threading his hand through the wrist loop, he stood and swayed unsteadily on numb feet. While the lights played out their spectral dance and the moon still shone he had a chance to descend. If he stayed he would succumb. He wasn't sure that the things he had dreamt and the sky he stood beneath were not one and the same. Bitter cold, isolation, hunger and thirst had chipped away at his defences. He remembered the gentle insistence of her whispered voice in his dream urging him to leave.

Moving stiff-legged, he followed a path of drifted snow which delineated the upper edge of the steep wall. As the path narrowed, so the height of the wall lessened and he found himself descending in switch-backs down the open face of the mountain by the glow of the gibbous moon. The light, shifting between the ivory moon and pastel hues, tricked his eyes until he had to stop and wait patiently for the moment when it became moonlit clear again and he saw the direction he should take. Once, as he moved cautiously towards a shelved ramp of snow, he stumbled, crampons catching some protrusion beneath the white surf lapping his ankles, and he fell, unresisting. He bounced three times, falling from wall to wall, rolling in the snow, arms swinging through the drifts, then accelerated in a rush of powder. He made no effort to stop himself, just rode the fall with a blank, fearless indifference. When he stopped he rose to his feet and glanced curiously up the slope to see how far he had fallen. He saw only gaunt, bleached slopes glimmering above him. Looking down, he saw that he was close to the foot of the mountain but far out in the centre of the face. Following a weaving connection of ledges he tottered forward, watching the bow wave of powder foaming at his ankles—unrestrained and drunken.

Hours later, he stood, dazed, swaying, on what seemed to be flat ground. There was something strange happening around him. A glacial wind harried his face and he thought he could hear water flowing nearby. It was too cold for water, he

101

knew that, yet he could sense it, smell it in the snow around him. It was darkening fast. Glancing at the sky, he saw that the light-show was over. Part of him felt relieved, part grieved. He had lost her. Stars and the waning moon gave just enough light for him to see the way ahead. The angular shape could only be the hut. He looked at the sky and whispered thanks, then continued his inebriate, snow-muffled footfalls.

When he stumbled against the balcony steps and collapsed to his knees the moon had gone and he had to feel with deadened hands in the gloom to confirm that it was the hut. For a while he knelt on all fours, breathing heavily, head hanging between his arms. The glacier was close. He thought he could feel the rivers of cold air flowing from its bowels, the thunder-like cracks, the deep rumbles of its digestion. With a groan, he pushed himself upright and lurched forwards, colliding heavily with the door. It burst open, hurling him abruptly to the floor. He crawled towards the shadow of the bunk-bed, illuminated by weak starlight from a snow-spattered window. Exhaustion pooled around him and he remembered the hooded crow, her gently urgent voice, the spectral lights, and murmured in his gathering sleep. Pulling the blankets in a twisted curl around him, he let himself down and slept.

9

A thin light gleamed through snow-coated
windows. His eyes flickered open to register dawn
rising in the shadows of the hut. He rolled onto his
back with a groan, feeling the bruises sustained in
the fall down the east face. He stared blankly at
the wooden beams and planks of the ceiling, trying
to adjust to the strange sense of security. Rolling
onto his side, he swaddled himself in the damp
blankets and lay watching the door of the hut
through his frosted breath. There were no wind
sounds against the hut. It might be snowing. He
still had to get down to the safety of the valley, but
he no longer cared.

Sleep took him back into uneasy dreams, of a
wide, morning-misted lake, fringed with russet
reed beds against a bank of dense woodland. He
knelt to drink water warily, watching the far bank.
Drifts of mist clung to the oil-slick surface of the
lake. As he raised his head, still gulping down the
water from his cupped hands, the tendrils of mist
rippled apart and a black shadow skimmed the
surface. It turned its blazing eyes to fix on his. He
moaned in his sleep.

When he awoke several hours later it was with a
confusing, abrupt immediacy. He sat up, letting
the blankets fall to the bunk, and looked around
for the reason for his sudden wakefulness. It was
quiet: no one had called him. As he pushed
himself from the bunk to stand unsteadily he
noticed the complete lack of feeling in his left
hand. He tugged the thin, sodden liner from his

hand with his teeth and examined the fattened fingertips bulging with blisters and tinged an ominous inky blue-black. Biting the glove from his right hand, he was relieved to see a lack of blisters but the first joints of each finger were also a dull, deathly colour.

He shuffled wearily towards the door, tripping as his crampons tangled in the blankets. Kicking them free, he pulled the door open and stood blinking as the white light glared into the hut. He raised a hand to shade his eyes as sunlight filtered through an overcast sky. To the east a jagged profile of rocky peaks was visible beneath the lowering clouds. He gazed blearily at the bleached surroundings, unsure of what he should now do. He turned to peer into the gloom of the hut. On a warped wooden shelf near the window he saw the supplies that she had carefully sorted and packed neatly away. He remembered her laughter as she saw the mess of tins and packets that he had shoved lazily into the corner of a bunk.

As he stared dumbly at these luxuries he became aware of the gnawing, hollow ache of hunger in his stomach and the foul taste in his mouth. He lurched towards the shelf, noticing the large gas cylinder by the stove. Water. He desperately needed water. On the stove top she had placed two pans filled with water and by the side a tin box of teaspoons, tea bags, instant coffee, dried milk powder and sugar.

Treading heavily across the floorboards with his crampon points splintering into the wood, he reached the shelf and sat on the bunk beneath it. Leaning forwards, he tried to free the buckles on the tightly cinched straps but his stiff fingers could not grip the waxy material. Resting a boot across his knee, he bit hard on the strap, pulling his head back and watching the steel pin ease slowly from its retaining hole. He unlashed the criss-crossed straps from around his ankle, then leaned forward to repeat the process with the straps fixing the toe of his boot. He pulled until his teeth hurt, gasping for breath between attempts, but the buckle refused to release. Even using the leverage of the ice-axe pick could not break or stretch the strap enough to release his boot. He lay back on the bed and swore in frustration.

He began searching the hut, pulling open cupboards and drawers, strewing the contents on the floor. The small vegetable knife was in the last place he looked, a box of opened food cartons and salami sausages—exactly where she would have stored it if only he had bothered to think. The blade cut easily through the straps and he kicked the useless crampons across the floor in irritation.

With mutinous fingers he struggled to connect the pipe to the stove, then fumbled to spark the gas lighter with his deadened thumb. The water in the pan formed a solid block of ice, expanded above the aluminium rim. Everything had been done so that making the first hot, sweet reviving brew of tea would be as effortless as possible. She hated inefficiency and mess. He guiltily surveyed the chaos he had created in his search for the knife.

He balanced the lid on the pan, then sat heavily on the bunk and made a quick inventory of the food they had stocked in the hut. The tins of fish would be frozen solid and unpalatable. He could defrost the salami on the lid of the pan. Packets of

105

soup powder and dried noodles would be the easiest to prepare, as well as providing vital liquid for his parched body. As soon as the water boiled and he had made tea in a plastic cereal bowl he added more snow to the pan, scraped from the window ledge, and sprinkled tomato soup powder onto the surface. It reminded him of the spray of blood that he had woken to after the avalanche.

By the time the soup had begun to simmer and bubble he had set a fire in the squat wood-burning stove using the bark, kindling and firewood stacked by the door. The torn pages of a book they had both enjoyed served a last useful purpose as the flames licked against the logs he had carefully arranged on top of the kindling. He crouched by the open grate, feeling the heat of the flames on his face as he examined the cover of the book. It had been her choice and she had smiled when he had grumbled about having to read it. He could scarcely remember its contents now, less than a week after reading it, but he had devoured it avidly, perched on the hut steps in the sun, trying to ignore her amused glances. He flicked the cover into the flames and watched as the artwork bubbled and curled in the heat. He closed the metal door and set the vent fully open. The rush of air fuelled a roar as the logs flared up and fire glowed red through the glass panel in the door.

He slurped noisily at the soup, crunching through the poorly dissolved lumps. Gnawing at a half-frozen salami, he searched through a pile of tins and packets that he had swept onto the bunk. Searching with numb fingers was a messy business and he became more fretful with each clumsily dropped article. Only when he had finished gorging himself did he lean back on the bunk and survey the devastation he had wreaked. He fumbled items back to their appointed places on the shelf with remorseful haste.

The hut had warmed considerably and he closed the stove vent after checking that the logs were glowing fiercely. He noticed the cigarette packet with one missing that they had found in the hut. She had left them openly on the shelf, tempting him into smoking them. He had sneaked outside to quietly roll his own. He looked at his blackened fingertips and realised that rolling cigarettes was no longer an option. He flicked one from the packet and lit it against the glowing ember of a twig poked into the flames. Pulling the cork from a bottle of cheap brandy, he drank from the neck, coughing at the harsh burn of the spirit.

Closing his eyes, he raised his hand to suck on the cigarette, feeling the warmth of the brandy flooding through his chest. He knew what he had to do, what he had promised to do, but the weariness permeating every muscle in his body and the luxury of lying in warmth and comfort in the hut was too strong a temptation. *I will find you.* Even as he said the words he felt the ache of guilt returning. He remembered the grip of her hand on his wrist and the intense, determined expression in her eyes as she fell away. He saw the deliberation in her steady gaze and it puzzled him. He opened his eyes and stared at the smoking cigarette poking between the blistered fingers of his left hand. He tried to remember if it was this hand that had let her go. Maybe the frostbite was his due. He had failed her. Was he going to fail her again?

He sat up and threw the butt on the floor,

stubbing it out with his boot. It occurred to him to remove the boots and check on the condition of his toes. They, too, felt numb and lifeless. He tried to wiggle them and thought he could feel the movement in the damp slip of his socks. He remembered the struggle to remove the crampons and decided against undoing the laces.

When he pulled the door open he felt the cutting bite of the winter cold. The rocky peaks had been swallowed by clouds and only the dark mass of their lower buttresses was visible. There was a blue-grey cast to the sky. Another storm was setting in. He glanced at his watch: midday. He had five hours, six at the outside, to reach the foot of the face, find her and return to the hut. There was no chance of him dragging her back that day, but he could mark where she lay and return after the storm had passed.

He retrieved the axe from the floor, picked up the glove and the liner and then stepped out onto the porch, blinking in the glare. He turned to look at the dark wooden walls, trying to adjust to the brilliance of the surrounding snow slopes, wondering how long he would last on the glacier without becoming snow-blind. Stepping from the porch he knelt in the snow to peer under the planks where he had seen bundles of wooden staves stored by the warden. He pulled two free from the bundle, sliding the red and white painted stakes out into the snow. They stood head-high when placed point-down on the ground. He tucked his ice axe into a gear loop on his harness and, using the staves as crude ski-sticks, he headed for the notch in the ridge.

At the notch he could look down onto the sweep

of the glacier two hundred feet below, a steep snow-covered slope of rock slabs and boulders. All trace of their tracks had disappeared. He felt relieved. Suddenly the thought of what he was about to do overwhelmed him. He almost turned to retrace his steps, then straightened his back and made the first faltering steps down the slope. The deep snow cover enabled him to make quick, sliding progress, occasionally tripping over hidden boulders and tumbling into powder-filled hollows. Within half an hour he had reached the glacier where headway slowed as he ploughed through thigh-deep drifts of powder snow, grateful for the support of the staves.

As the glacier began to rise towards the foot of the face he stopped and turned to look at the facing horizon, searching for the distinctive summit he had marked with his compass. The bearings he had memorised were useless with the compass and rucksack now buried in avalanche debris. He spotted the peak and glanced back at the face. He studied the faint shadow line of the bergschrund, the crevasse, marking where the glacier had cracked free from the flanks of the mountain.

Staring up the ice field, he traced the line of their ascent and the leftwards traverse they had made towards the rock band. He looked at the ridge line, searching for his escape line up the gully. Then he saw a familiar prow of rock. He recognised it as the protecting wall of their bivouac ledge. Traversing slowly to the right, he kept glancing up the ice field and across the glacier to the marker peak behind him. He thrust one of the staves into the snow as a marker and began to climb. He was breathing heavily when he reached the bergschrund, a gaping crevasse running along the entire base of the ice field. It pushed out in a wall of overhanging ice some forty feet above him and he knew that she must have hurtled clear and plummeted down the steep slopes below.

He sat facing the glacier, shielding his eyes with his hands, examining the surface of the snow for the slightest irregularity. He saw nothing. The ferocious speed of her fall would have slammed her deep into the snow, and avalanches would then have swiftly covered her impact crater. Further down the glacier he could see the softened mounds of snow-covered ice blocks where the avalanche had slowed to a halt. He cursed himself for being stupid. There was no hope of finding her, never had been. He gazed at the deep tracks leading to the hut, mocking him. He slumped back in the snow, raising his hands to his head, bone-cold weary, beaten.

Pulling the liner from his left hand he flexed the swollen, blistered fingers. They were getting worse. Reaching into his jacket pocket for the cigarettes, he struggled to hold the packet in his inert grip. He pushed himself upright and looked down the slope to where he had left the marker stave. He would zigzag down the slope searching a wide grid with his legs and prodding deep into the snow with the stave.

After two hours' fruitless searching he reached the marker stave. Looking at the slope above him, he could see the swathe of disturbed snow ploughed by his legs and the constant jabbing stabs with his stave. The one solid contact he had made with a thrust of the stave had caused his heart to race as he had dug frenziedly into the deep powder, only to find a large chunk of blue water ice.

Now he stared up the ice field at the prow of rock and doubts crowded his mind. He had not seen her hit the glacier. She could have been catapulted from the lip of the bergschrund in any direction. He slumped down by the marker stave and noticed the feathery touch of snowflakes on his face. Clouds hung low over the path back to the hut. It was noticeably darker. Night was coming on and, with it, another storm. A steady wind blew a veil of snow across the glacier. He had no torch and his tracks were filling in. Pressing his hands to his face, he closed his eyes and wearily accepted defeat. To reach the hut before dark he knew he must leave at once. He looked bleakly at the rolling expanses of snow wondering where she had gone, wanting to apologise, needing to say goodbye.

He stood and, taking a stave in each hand, began to heel down the tracks he had forged up the slope, the poles now relegated to holding his exhausted body upright. As he approached the point where his tracks veered to the right, the stave in his right hand snagged something soft and dragging beneath the snow. He would have trudged forward uncaring but for the flash of yellow material that broke the surface as he tugged the stave free.

He stopped and stared mutely at the small patch of yellow fabric, then sank slowly to his knees and reached tentatively to touch the shiny nylon. He gently brushed loose drifts of snow to the side to reveal the shoulder and upper arm. As he swept

111

the snow clear he was careful to touch her as lightly as possible, scared of what he might find. Resisting the urge to run, he became aware instead that he was quietly calling her name. She was found. He tucked his fingers beneath the exposed elbow and began to lift the arm free to turn her onto her back. His hand shot upwards in a flurry of snow and the sleeve of the jacket slapped against his face. He flinched, then gaped stupidly as the empty sleeve flapped back onto the snow.

As he pressed the back of the duvet jacket, he felt the material sink softly into the snow below. He grabbed the empty sleeve and pulled the jacket free, shaking the loose powder from the slick nylon. Sitting with the jacket in his lap, he thought back to the moment she had fallen, remembering the distant speeding speck, the feral scream rising shrill on the wind and the sudden blossoming of the spread-armed jacket. It had been ripped from her by the wind: he had not found her.

He saw smears of blood on the yellow cuffs and winced. Holding the liner of the jacket to his face, he breathed deeply but cold storage had erased her scent. As he pressed the jacket he felt a small hard lump against his cheek. Examining the black liner, he saw the zipped inner chest pocket. Pulling the zip open with his teeth, he turned the jacket upside down and shook it gently. He saw a flash of gold as the small shell fell from the pocket and disappeared into the snow. He knew at once what it was and stared in dismay at the dimple in the powdery snow where it had vanished. Pulling the glove from his right hand with his teeth, he carefully leaned forward and pushed his bare hand down into the snow. He knew that if he got it wrong it would sink and tumble through the deep layers, lost forever. When his hand was a foot below the surface he curved his palm into an upward-facing position and slowly lifted it towards the surface, directly under the entry hole. The moment he felt the slight hardness touch his palm he clamped his fingers tight shut.

When he opened his hand, resting it in the safety blanket of the outspread jacket, the delicately marbled sea shell with the broken pin and the fine thread of gold wire rimming its opening lay in a dusting of snow. A pale pink tinged the creamy colour of the inner surface; a sudden intimate reminder.

He remembered her laughter in the sun outside the hut as she had pulled the shirt over her head and the squeal of pain when the pin clasp had caught in the thin material and pulled sharply from her ear. It had bounced onto the ground by his feet where he sat on the porch steps, watching her impromptu striptease. He had reached down to pick it up as she clasped her bloodied ear between thumb and forefinger and cursed in pain and frustration. He remembered placing it in the pocket of her jacket, assuring her as he zipped it closed that it could be easily mended. He rolled the shell between his fingers, letting memories slide quietly through his mind. Snow whipped across his bare hand and he looked up to see that the notch on the ridge had faded into the leaden clouds. Pushing the earring into his jacket pocket, he pulled the zip closed and then thrust his arms into her jacket. He shucked it across the tightly compressed down of his own jacket and left it unzipped as he rose to his feet.

Taking hold of the staves, he took two strides forward and fell. He saw his foot step forward onto a flawless section of smooth snow, watched as the boot sank from sight and then rolled his weight forward, expecting the thickening pressure of compressing snow beneath the foot. Nothing happened. His boot met no resistance and he plunged vertically down as thin slivers of snow filled the air around him and ice crystals blew against his face. He felt neither fear nor anger—a mild, surprised disappointment perhaps, but he made no effort to resist the fall, to throw out his arms and thrust desperately with the staves. The blurred blue walls of the crevasse flashed past. He braced for the impact, then found himself plunging into soft snow, knees collapsing as he came to a halt.

He heard the blood ringing in his ears and registered the soft thumps of the crevasse roof collapsing around him. Intact, unhurt and bemused, he was amazed to find himself fifty feet below the surface of the glacier. He began to laugh and the sounds echoed in the shadowy chamber. Above him, glistening walls of water ice curved up to the roof. An eerie light flooded into the chamber and a dusting of snow sifted down. He was relieved to see that ahead of him the floor of the crevasse sloped upwards between narrowing walls. As he stepped towards the slope he felt something hard against his boot, tripped and fell face first. He rolled sideways, choking on the inhaled powder. Something rigid and unyielding lay beneath his hip and thigh. Sitting up, he moved to one side and began to sweep the drifts.

He worked in silence—only a sharp intake of

breath breaking the rhythmic noise of his sweeping hand as the jagged bone end was suddenly revealed, punched through the fabric of her trousers. He worked methodically down towards her feet. The broken limb was twisted cruelly back on itself so that her foot lay on her buttock, pointing up the line of her back. Her other leg was bent at the knee as she lay in a foetal position. When he uncovered the heel of her foot he paused and sat back in the snow, staring mutely at the bared limbs.

The sight of the bone had hurt him. He had brushed with exaggerated gentleness, desperate not to hurt her. He turned towards her head, unable to bear the sight of her mutilated leg. It was as if she were sleeping, waiting all these days for him to come. It comforted him and he began to talk, reassuring her, reassuring himself. She lay on her side, one arm buried beneath her chest—the other bent at the elbow, hand laid, child-like, with her thumb near her chin. The tears began when he saw the terrible damage to her hands. Her nails had gone—the fingertips torn and shredded, ravaged by the ice. He carefully hid them in a pillow of mounded snow.

He blew softly on her face and its fine powdery shroud flew away to reveal a deathly grey skin. Without thinking, he brushed snowflakes from her eyebrow with one finger, a tender, unconscious grooming. A faint pewter line coursed down her cheek, a frozen tear, and he sat back stunned, staring silently at the ice-raised weal and the opaque, staring eye. With her frosted shroud removed he lay by her side. There was no softness there. He slid his arm across her huddled shoulder, pulling himself into an embrace, drenched in sadness. Closing his eyes, he let her voice run through his mind and wept salt. He lay, unaware of time passing. At first he whispered to her, begging forgiveness. He strained to see her face, even as it faded into the shadows of the night. He leaned his face away to give her the little dying light remaining and watched it fade. Snow settled, finely sifted. He gently blew it aside.

He felt consciousness floating away into the shadows. Life had become vague sensations and, as he peered hopelessly at her departing beauty, he realised he no longer wanted it. In the shadows of this cold coffin dying was easy. He had fought to reach her—why leave? It was calm with her in his arms. He would slip into an endless sleep, his body hardening with hers until, locked in their embrace, they would begin their journey to the uncreated sea. Night moved in on them dreaming, falling snow unheard.

'I love you,' he murmured, looking for some affirmation in her shadowed face. The words sank into the cold shadows, slid away on glass walls and he grew colder. 'I'm sorry.'

Much later he revived, slowly, too tired and ill and beaten to care. It was the sound that called him back. It came low and insistent from above, like wind soughing in the branches of high trees. He bent his senses to the whisper and glanced at the lighter opening above. When he turned back he had lost his night vision and she had gone. He stared frantically into the darkness, feeling cold skin in his hands, searching for her face. He found her hand and clasped it tightly, remembering the last time. The sound came again, distracting him.

You must go now. It was insistent, female.

'I must go.' He said it loudly for courage and felt his hands slide free of their hold on her.

The feeling in his left hand braced around her shoulder had long since died. He couldn't move his legs or his arms. He closed his eyes, feeling sleep stealing in, and opened them in sudden panic that she would be gone. Another heavy blast of snow funnelled into the crevasse and the sound of the wind fluted over the exposed maw. There was a familiar siren call to the wind and a memory came to him of a wintered dream when her voice had called him to wakefulness and sent him down to safety; enchanting, pulling him back to hold her, yet insistent, commanding, telling him to go. He had to leave. If he was to survive the night he had to leave at once. Cupping her face in frozen hands and kissing her he promised to return, vowed to come in the morning to take her home.

Yet when he tried to push himself upright he found his legs had deadened in the biting cold and he staggered, almost falling, as he rose to his feet, bracing himself against the smooth ice of the crevasse wall.

Hours of darkness seemed to have passed as he fell again in the deep snow. He had marked the crevasse with one of the red and white staves and, clutching the last with both hands, he had blundered drunkenly across the glacier. It occurred to him that he might fall into another crevasse but the thought caused no anxiety. Sensing the looming bulk of the mountain on his right side, he faced the wind and kept shuffling forward, waiting to feel the slope rise beneath his feet. For a long time he swayed unsteadily in the

117

wind, wondering whether he had walked around in circles, whether the wind direction had veered, then sank to his knees, confused and lost.

There was a silvery glimmer in the black velvet of the sky and then for an instant the wind tore a rent in the clouds and moonlight streamed through the craggy notch in the ridge directly above where he crouched in the snow. The light lasted long enough for him to scramble halfway up the slope; then the clouds slid across each other and the darkness seemed ever more impenetrable. One hundred yards of blind falls and insect-crawling progress in a welter of blown, black snow found him suddenly prone, facing the full fury of the blizzard. The wind, compressed and guttering through the notch, blew with fierce power and he found it difficult to peer forward into the blinding ice crystals. He rolled and tumbled down the short slope to slither into a crumpled heap by the sheltered porch of the hut, feeling as if he were suddenly in a lull between the gales.

The abrupt silence after he crashed through the door of the hut and collapsed on the bunk swamped him in the darkness. He pulled the blankets around him with thickening fingers, shivering in uncontrolled spasms rippling through his body. Beyond pain his body was inert, a leaden weight dragged there in the wake of his will. He lay wide-eyed and sightless in the empty room, scarcely able to comprehend where he was.

*　　　*　　　*

The road running through the village was polished ice. It came down in a meandering line, cutting through the brightness of the snow-covered fields. It was swallowed by the lowering outline of the forest. Squat wooden barns dotted the fields, their roofs thickly laden with snow. The Inn, a long weather-beaten building with low eaves, stood on the outskirts of the village. Snow-filled flower boxes hung from dark window recesses. Yellow light gleamed through cracks in the carved shuttered windows. Six men trudged down the icy road, kicking their nailed boots into the icy footing. They were woodcutters. As they stood by the door they laughed and joked, knocking snow from their boots on the stout wooden door jambs. When the door was pushed open there was a flare of warm firelight and the sound of singing. The men hurried inside, their shoulders hunched against the knifing wind.

Inside it was smoky dark despite the firelight. A low-beamed ceiling, stained dark by smoke and tobacco, hung over high-backed benches around a long wine-stained table. By the wide hearth two old men sat contemplating the flames, contentedly smoking their pipes. Beer glasses, fresh-pulled, foamed on the adjacent table. They raised their eyes to the newcomers and nodded in greeting. The men chorused their respects in muttered voices as they took their places around the long table closest to the fire, reaching gratefully for the beer. They stood stamping their boots and steaming, shrugged off jackets and took their places, pulling thick gloves from their hands and reaching for the beer.

One man called loudly to the back room. He had the air of a leader. The singing stopped and a girl in an apron came through the door.

119

'Yes, Peter?' she asked and the man ordered wine. Tobacco pouches were produced and a buzz of conversation came from the table.

'Did you see the stranger yesterday?' the man who had ordered the wine said to the group.

'I heard he came here,' the youngest of the men answered.

'He was carried here,' another man said curtly.

'He was dying, they say,' the boy said.

'When they found him, yes,' Peter agreed. 'He recovered. They took him to hospital.'

'He will lose his fingers, I hear,' the boy added excitedly.

'On one hand,' the girl said as she placed two bottles of wine held in one hand on the table. 'I saw him.' She placed six glasses beside the bottles.

'You only need one hand, eh?' The boy laughed. The girl frowned and turned away. The older men smiled. 'Was he really done in?' the boy asked and reached for a glass.

'Yes . . . he was bad.' The girl wiped her hands on the apron. 'We could not understand him. He was a sick man.'

'He had been climbing the peak,' said the leader.

'His woman is dead.' The girl pushed through the door. It swung shut behind her as the group digested her words.

'She fell,' explained the leader. 'He wanted us to recover his woman. When we said no, he insisted, was cursing and shouting. Then they took him away.'

'We shall find her in the springtime,' one of the old men by the fire said quietly and tapped his pipe against the stone mantle.

'No. She fell to the glacier. She is lost.'

'It is sad.' The girl pushed the door open and placed a large platter of strudel on the table. She dropped the forks in a jangle of metal-ware and the men reached for them. 'To lose your wife like that.'

'His wife should not be climbing on the face,' the old man said. 'No one should be on the face in winter.'

'It is the new way,' Peter shrugged and the men nodded slowly in disapproval.

When the wine bottles were empty and the platter cleared they stood abruptly in a clatter of heavy boots and pulled their jackets onto their shoulders. They opened the door and the cold burnt. They stepped outside and followed the road up towards the pine trees, the snow crust crunching under their feet. Ashen steam hovered above them as they breathed heavily in the sharp air.

The boy hung back in the doorway and the two old men eyed him curiously, smiling knowingly when the girl came out of the kitchen.

'Will they find her?' she asked.

'No,' the boy replied. 'He said she was buried deep. The glacier has her now.' He nodded to the leader who was striding up the road at the head of the group. 'He is the guide; he knows,' the boy added.

'Do you want a brandy?' she asked quietly and the old men nodded.

'No. I will be drunk. I have work to do.'

'After work, have a brandy.'

'I will.' The boy pulled the door shut, ignoring the expressions of the old men, and followed the woodcutters towards the trees.

121

PART TWO

PART TWO

10

Patrick had risen early. As he lit the hurricane lamp he watched as it threw a wash of soft light through the window, illuminating the handrail on the porch beyond which nothing was visible. He settled at the table, glancing at the stove to see if the kettle had boiled. Only the crackling of burning logs broke the silence. The windless quiet did not deceive him. He had read the weather in the sky the previous evening—mottled, wind-rent clouds streaming high in the stratosphere and birds circling down from the summit heights, the front moving swiftly through, heralded by the birds and now the ominous quiet. The storm was coming.

As he finished the bowl of bitter coffee he saw the flicker of light flash in the rapidly lightening gloom beyond the porch. He rose from the chair and moved towards the door, taking his jacket from the hook as he swung the door open. The man turned at the sudden flood of light from the hut. He saw the lean figure shrugging into a jacket and held his hand up in acknowledgement, not breaking his stride as he followed the weaving beam of his head torch up towards the ridge. He heard the hut warden's shouted query and in reply he pointed towards the dark silhouette of the ridge.

Patrick flicked his cigarette out onto the stony ground as he watched the bobbing head-torch light shrink into the distance, then blink out. Glancing at the sky, he could see dawn was fast approaching.

The man was alone and moving fast. He could reach the summit within two hours, Patrick noted admiringly as he turned back into the hut. Reaching for the logbook, he carried it to the table and opened it to the last entry page. Writing the date neatly at the top of the page and leaving space for any other entries for the day, he noted at the bottom of the page, '... *lone male, solo attempt, east ridge, departed 5 am.*' As he was closing the ledger he heard the sound of voices and the thump of boots on the wooden steps. The door flew open and Patrick looked up to see a man, red-faced and breathing hard. He attempted a smile but it seemed like a grimace to Patrick.

'Doctor Johannes Stern,' the man said in an abrupt tone, glancing at Patrick self-importantly. 'I lead a party of four—two men, a doctor and a lawyer, and one woman.' The latter said dismissively. 'We are for the ridge.' He nodded towards the door where a portly, balding man was peering curiously into the hut. 'The book, please,' the doctor added curtly and, opening it at the day's page, Patrick slid it slowly across the table towards him. The man bent over the page, writing with busy precision. As he straightened from the table he pressed a forefinger to the bottom of the page and tapped at the note Patrick had only just entered.

'He passed us on the path, very fast, too fast and he goes alone.' The doctor closed the ledger with a knowing look at Patrick. 'I can assure you, sir, there will be trouble.' Before Patrick could comment the man had turned on his heel and was strutting out of the door, issuing unnecessarily loud instructions to his companions. By the time the party had roped themselves together and headed towards the start of the ridge, Patrick noted that the man who was too fast was two-thirds of the way up the ridge. 'Trouble perhaps,' he said studying the disorganised party, 'but who for, I wonder?' Thirty minutes later, he observed the lone climber again. He opened the logbook and wrote beside his initial note, '... *summit reached 6.30 am (approx.)*'.

Karl sat on the rocky summit and watched the horizon as the dark band of night above the eastern skyline was eaten away by the light blue flush of dawn. His gaze was occasionally drawn down from the jagged peaks by the sound of thin, shouted voices of the roped party struggling up the lower rocks. He smiled at the memory of their muttered irritation as he had swept past them on the path up from the village. 'Doctors,' he thought, 'they're all the same.'

He inhaled deeply, then held himself still as the hollow feeling invaded his chest. He felt the blood rush in a hammering pulse at his temple and he raised protective fingers to the side of his head. It was coming, just as they had said it would all those months ago. He rose to his feet and swung the small day-sack onto his shoulders before moving swiftly down the summit snowfields to the crest of the ridge top.

'Bloody doctors,' he muttered, 'always so damned right.'

*   *   *

Karl had only agreed to the tests to please his wife. She had been so concerned for his health, yet her own body held her trapped, bedbound, dying. The last months had seen such fast deterioration he could almost see the change on each waking dawn as she seemed to shrink into the bedding.

'Go, Karl. Get the check-up,' she had said and weakly pressed his hand in hers. He smiled and looked at her. Where had all her youth gone so suddenly? 'Please.'

He bent and kissed her proffered cheek. 'Of course I will go. It will do no harm, eh?'

'Exactly,' she replied. 'And it is all paid for. It is part of the company plan.'

'We don't need the money,' he said, a little sharply.

'No,' she smiled. 'No, we don't, but you always worry about it.' With that she lay back amongst the pillows, looking exhausted as if from some strenuous battle.

And now he sat and watched the doctors consult and explain and point at the scans and glance uneasily in his direction. He knew immediately from their body language that the news would be bad. The first one, alone with his expectant patient, had made a hurried explanation of the test results, speaking loudly and with false appreciation of the general good health of the patient. Strong, fit, blood pressure excellent, low cholesterol, blood tests good, liver and kidney function as expected. He slowed, seeking refuge in his paperwork, shuffling rapidly through sheets of printed scans.

'Problem?' Karl asked calmly.

The doctor looked up from his papers and held Karl's gaze. 'There is a problem, yes ...' The man's air of studied professionalism was undermined by his obvious disquiet. 'These CT scans.' He held up the sheaf of papers, nodding and removing his reading glasses. 'They have shown up something really quite unexpected.'

Karl held his hand up, his expression calm, trying to set the man at his ease. 'Perhaps it would be best if you simply told me what is wrong.'

'Yes, perhaps you are right.' He glanced at the door and Karl slowly followed his gaze. The doctor noted his wry, quizzical smile and nodded. 'I am waiting for my colleague. This is his field, you see. I would prefer his opinion first.'

'You would prefer he told me the bad news, you mean?' Karl thought, as the door opened abruptly. The doctor's colleague entered the room and smiled awkwardly at Karl.

It didn't take long for them to consult and come to an agreement—some minutes bent over the scans, murmured conferrings, grave expressions and sagely nodding heads and then they straightened from the table and the second doctor pulled back his shoulders and addressed Karl, staring determinedly at his left shoulder.

'It would appear that you are suffering from a cerebrovascular disorder.'

'It doesn't feel like suffering to me,' Karl replied.

'No, quite so,' the doctor agreed. 'Often the case with these things, I'm afraid. The CT scan, entirely routine of course, has revealed a serious complication. Here.' He held a sheet of paper out for Karl to examine. He registered a vague skull-like shape, brain-lobe patterns swirling on the paper, but did not look too closely. The doctor poked a long pianist's forefinger at the paper. 'You have a cerebral aneurysm, here.' He pecked the paper with his finger again.

129

'Is that serious?' Karl asked, knowing the answer.

'I'm afraid so, yes, very serious. In fact, you see, because of the position of the aneurysm and its size,' he tapped the paper again, 'there is nothing that we can do.' He looked up at Karl's face, then hurriedly at his attentively silent colleague.

'Nothing you can do, you say?' Karl said, amused at their gravity. The doctors exchanged glances and then looked back at him with fixed expressions, each waiting for the other to answer.

'It is in a very awkward place,' the second doctor said quietly and held his hands out in a placatory manner. 'It is also a large, complicated aneurysm, a cluster of them in fact, like grapes. As is so often the case, this type of aneurysm is commonly found on the anterior communicating artery.' His finger pecked the scan again, making an odd, dry, tapping sound. 'Unfortunately, these arteries are situated at the base of the brain.'

Karl tried to look interested, but the words *'nothing we can do'* ran insistently through his mind. *How would all this detail help his wife?* The doctors continued to talk among themselves, a plethora of complicated medical detail. The more complex the detail, the more relaxed they became. He registered the words, white noise in the background, but all he could see was his wife's gaunt, grey face. *What could he say to her?*

'. . . normally we would perform a supraorbital minicraniotomy for such intracranial aneurysms, but not in this case, I'm afraid . . . or maybe we can reinforce to reduce the risk of rupture . . .'

'No, too large, I suspect . . . the size is the problem.'

130

'As diameter increases, wall tension increases, which leads to increasing diameter. As tension increases, risk of rupture increases. A vicious circle.'

'Quite,' his colleague nodded enthusiastically, pointing at the scan and then at Karl, realising they had left him out of the discussion. He lowered his hand.

'So, you can see, this is why our hands are tied, sir.' He checked his companion, who nodded gravely. Karl stared blankly at the pair of them. 'We see the problem, but whatever we do will make no difference.'

'Aneurysms can be tricky things,' the other doctor continued, determinedly avoiding Karl's gaze. 'As this systemic hypertension continues, so pressure increases . . .' Karl stopped listening until he heard '. . . such an advanced aneurysm would undoubtedly rupture, but if left unattended all aneurysms will rupture anyway . . .'

'And when that happens?' Karl asked quietly. They fell silent and appeared discomfited.

'With a rupture, the escaping blood within the brain may cause severe neurologic complications.'

'Severe neurologic complications?' Karl asked with a faint smile on his face. 'By which you actually mean . . . I die. Yes?'

'I am afraid so, yes.'

'Will I know . . . in advance?'

'Possibly, but I suspect in your case it may be very fast. Some patients speak of a strange sharpening of the senses, an increased awareness, light-headedness, leading to an acuity of consciousness. We don't know exactly why but it may be caused by the aneurysm creating pressure on the brain. It may simply be because of the awareness of the existence of the aneurysm but in truth we do not know ...' The doctor tailed off, then added, 'It really depends on the state and size of the aneurysm itself.'

'In an aneurysm as large as yours such a rupture would result in massive fatal bleeding,' his colleague interjected. 'I suspect it would be very quick, almost painless. In the meantime there is no reason to think that you cannot lead a perfectly healthy life. Almost as if we had never told you,' he added lamely as he realised what he had just said.

'But you have,' Karl stated bluntly and stood up. 'And now I have your "acuity of consciousness" to look forward to. Well, thank you for your clarity. It must be difficult for you.' Karl reached for his coat hanging on the surgery door.

'Would you like counselling? We could refer you.'

'Not much point really. I must leave now. I also have someone who is afraid and she needs me.' Karl swung the door open and began to walk slowly down the bright, white hospital corridor.

*   *   *

It was fully light when Karl reached the ledge. He was pleased at the speed of his descent from the summit where he had stood watching the thin streak of dawn silhouetting the serrated peaks of the eastern skyline. He had remembered the ledge from his ascent. There was an old, rusting piton winking from a crack in the wall above. He swung his body around the wall bordering the open

132

broken ground of the east face and stood on the ledge. The wall formed a secluded eyrie partly sheltered from the east face and perched on the craggy knife edge of the ridge bounding the north face.

He stepped forward to where the rock appeared to have sheared away, revealing an exposed fracture line in marked contrast to the smooth, water-worn ledge. He leaned gingerly out over the edge, conscious of the hypnotic depths, suddenly anxious about the cause of the fracture. He glanced back at the piton protruding from the wall above the ledge, stark against the sun. Then he turned and leaned out.

He found himself looking into the depths of an intimidating gully, cutting down through the vertical rock walls until it spread out into the ice field of the north face. He waited for his eyes to adjust to the gloom. An icy fillet reached up towards him, narrowing to a shining, wet sliver. White scratch marks scarred the rock on either side of the ice: crampon marks. He was surprised. He hadn't known of anyone climbing on this side of the north face. At the foot of the gully he saw a spike of rock protruding from the edge of the ice field. An ancient sun-bleached tape draped around the flake fluttered forlornly in the cold wind rising up the ice field—evidence of some desperate moment in the distant past. Someone had climbed there once and climbed for his life. Ice glimmered in withered cracks, dank rock walls spread out on either side, impending vertiginous shields of blank stone blocking progress towards the ridge above. It was an inhospitable view.

He saw ochre stains discolouring the rock,

133

betraying hidden, rusting, abandoned hardware and, higher still, the thin loop of a buried wire glinted at him from the depths of a stony fissure. *'Why climb here?'* he thought, as his gaze was drawn across the sweep of the upper rim of the ice field. He peered again at the gully. Escape. Someone had escaped up the gully to the safety of the ridge. It must have been a desperate struggle.

He moved back and settled himself upon the ledge, leaning his back against the wall, impressed with the difficulty of the climb. Glancing at the piton in the wall above his head, he wondered if the climbers had made it to the sanctuary of this ledge. They would have been mightily relieved to escape that gully.

There was a clear view across the north face from where he sat. The steely ripple of the ice field lapped against the steep rock bands of the upper mountain. Far below, he could see the serpentine line of the bergschrund cracking the ice field from the glacier and the snakeskin pattern of crevasses running down its crest towards the distant valley. Now in its dry summer coat, only the upper basin of the glacier was snow-covered, while below the dark lines of rubble and moraine carried upon the surface of the glacier gave it the reptilian appearance of a dragon's body filling the valley floor with its scaly folds.

Leaning against the wall, feeling its cold solidity through his shirt, he waited for the sun to clear the skyline. It did so in a gradually expanding halo of light shards piercing the serrated mountain peaks. Then the ridge above him changed from the muted shades of dawn to the red glow of the new day and he immediately felt the heat on his face as his eyrie was abruptly bathed in sunlight.

Once again the hollow feeling spread through his chest. His eyes closed as his mind explored this invasive sensation. He knew what it was. He had known for many months now. The doctors had completed their endless tests, spoken countless words, theories meant to give him hope, but only to assuage their own guilt at their helplessness. Ultimately, there was nothing they could do, they said. Too deep within the brain. Impossible to reduce the steadily expanding bubble. He had not asked for their excuses. He had felt detached as he watched their uneasy postures and overly polite words. It was their problem, not his. He had gone home to watch his wife die.

The emptiness spread and his chest felt cold. It was as if he held dusk within. He pressed his palms to his forehead as he always did when the coldness came, unable to understand why the feeling was in his chest and not his head. How many years had it been since they had told him? Almost three. Two years since she had slipped away and he had stepped desolately from the withered shadows of her room. Perhaps that was when the empty feelings had begun. The company job had been quickly abandoned, the house sold, pension schemes, life insurance, shares and savings cashed in, and he had walked away from his former life back to the mountains where it had all started, where they had met and loved and married and then drifted away from the very places that had given them meaning.

He climbed alone these days. Freed from the weight and constraints of ropes, hardware and companions, he had returned to the landscape that

135

had always defined him. He climbed with a careful fearlessness; longevity no longer shackled his mind. It was no suicide bid, no desire for the swift plunge into the abyss. He had discovered a previously unknown freedom, relishing the utter concentration of the moment, moving in a separated, almost trance-like existence of simple movements, the delicate pressure of a thin edge under a finger, the imperceptible shifts in balance, the tiny, vital things that kept him alive. When a summit abruptly interrupted the reverie of his progress or the sight of a hut signalled the end of the climb it left a bitter-sweet regret, a longing to return to the freedom of that suspended landscape.

As he inhaled a long, measured breath he felt the vacuum in his chest ease and as he breathed out he looked at the rock upon which he sat. Partly hidden by his thigh, he saw the fragile shape of an ancient marine creature sketched in the smooth rock. A fossil. He stared fixedly at it, surprised to be staring at an ancient seabed. The distinct whorls of polished rock patterned out the living form of a creature that had died millions of years before. He brushed his fingertips wonderingly across the delicate outline, stroking the rock-frozen life within his hand. A picture of her against the pillows came to mind and then the days so many years ago when they had moved laughing amongst these very hills. He remembered her smile, caressing the fossil, as a dusting of snow-like grains of mica came spinning on a sudden up-draft from the ice field, glinting in the sunshine.

His father had spoken of the need to last, although we never last, not even him. It was one of those talks he had often given to his wearied son, hoping that his infatuation with the mountains would eventually wane. It did, of course, much to Karl's regret, as he dutifully tried to do his father's bidding.

'The thing, boy, is to learn from others and to last,' his father would announce after another heated debate about his future. 'Other men are lenses through which we read our own lives ...' And Karl would nod, having heard it all before. '... The main thing, for all of us, is to tell our stories, to be noticed in some small way so that we fit. Our memories are lives and you cannot make a life story in the mountains ...' He talked forever of the unchallengeable unity of a life, the fearful symmetry of all our lives, and then he died and his story died with him and no one ever told it.

So Karl buried him and thought, *where was the challenge in that life, or the symmetry, for that matter?* He had never had talked to his father about mountains. They were not his father's story: they were his.

He loved mountains. They existed through all of time, acquiring in the process a haunting presence, an enigmatic immensity both exhilarating and terrifying. They overwhelmed his mind with their vaunting cathedral forms. He loved their edges and interstices, their numbing verticality, the summits in serried thousands marching towards a curved horizon. Monolithic, immense and unknowably wild, they were brought alive by weather, cloaked, shaped, made motive by passing clouds, stripped by wind, ice-carved, illuminated by each changing season, fatally beautiful.

Karl always knew they could only be understood

by being on them. They were so beautiful they could make him cry, so beautiful it made him afraid. They sought him, drawing him in until he was lost in the landscape of his own memory.

In the mountains he cut the bonds of time— living, it seemed to him, in a suspended place where time and memory and imagination formed the landscape of his life. It was the landscape he most adored, where he felt he came closest to finding his place.

If he was lucky, he might find something pure within himself among the mountains even if he could not understand it. Then he could walk away utterly alive.

Perhaps it was all consciousness ever allowed. Desires and dreams were as much part of the landscape he inhabited as they were part of his imagination; in the end he always returned to the same landscape, to the one that fitted. He lived within both. He had tried to find his place in this world, yet the landscape never seemed to be what he intended: forever changing, baffling in its subtle complexity, it changed as swiftly as thought, as mysterious as the rock-bound fossil he was stroking.

And he had never once been able to describe this to his father. He would not have listened and Karl was never sure, until now, whether he had the words. Since his wife had died the words had come thick and fast and true and he had wondered where they had come from. No matter; only he was left to care now. He realised all this as he began his dying.

With his hand on the long-dead sea creature, Karl wondered about the stories we tell. What had this creature's story been? It didn't amount to much, the life lived and quickly left, the stories made, told once and then forgotten. Karl knew that he, too, had spent a life looking for something unknown, some way of fitting in, like a deep unfilled hunger.

He felt the shadow cross him again, the abrupt spreading chill, and he inhaled, trying to drive it away. It receded like an ebbing tide, hanging on the edge of his awareness, ready to flood. He looked at the sun-pierced horizon and the emptiness within subsided a little. The mountains were his comfort, the only landscape that made him whole.

At the moment of his dying he became aware of the hiss of air over wings. A flight of choughs danced on the uplift. He saw an age-greyed raven settle slowly on the nearby ridge with a primitive alertness and it immediately sought a bond with his eyes. The bird moved from foot to foot and nodded its long beaked head. Its eyes never left him. It was as if it knew.

The hollowness came again. Turning his eyes from the bird, he settled his gaze on a mountain that stood alone, remote, on the edge of the range, a proud and dominant pyramid. His vision blurred and he wiped a hand across his eyes. The hand, he noticed, was shaking. The peak sprang back into sharp focus. He sank back against the rock, feeling the sudden stillness around him as if life had paused. It was happening at last. He stared fixedly at the distant peak, feeling surprisingly tranquil.

He thought of the fossil, so long dead, up here at this place of his own dying. Things change up in these places, he thought, even time which seemed to hover in the stillness, almost stopping. He concentrated on the fossil. The mountain had carried it high into the winter sky, into a world of frozen, lifeless movement. It was an ageless print of ancient life, fixed in the final movement of its death. It lay in bas-relief below the skin of the mountain. He traced the spiral turns of the fossil with his fingertip as if drawing its shape in the rock.

The emptiness in his chest had always brought with it a feeling of restriction, as if being overtaken by some other entity. The doctors had said this was normal. Now, however, something different was happening. He tried to breathe—deeply, calmly—but gasped instead as a surging pain lanced through his head. With the strident, fizzing crackle of shorting electricity an intense light erupted across his brain. From a distance he heard someone groaning.

Then his head jerked back as the pain rushed in. A blood-red flash blazed across his clenched eyelids and he knew instantly that it was happening. Agony flooded his skull with a bone-splitting sensation and then abruptly faded. As the pain contracted he felt strangely separated. He was still conscious; everything was as before. Nothing seemed to have changed except the disembodied sensation: a lightness of being as if he were hovering above everything, not quite touching the ledge upon which he sat or the rock at his back. He no longer felt the sun on his face, although he could see its strong, bright light. He tried to breathe but nothing seemed to happen. It was as if he had forgotten how to. He placed the palm of his hand on the ledge and looked down at the fossil.

He sensed rather than saw himself falling, with no impression of movement. The sky, the rocky ridge and the raven swam across his sight. As he toppled sideways he felt happy that it was happening in this of all places.

He heard the impact as his temple thumped hard against the rock ledge and his head bounced up from the stone, then settled until he was staring directly at the raven, which spread its wings and jumped skittishly into the air. As it alighted again on the rock, slightly closer to him now, it cocked its head to the side and looked into his eyes, then hopped forward a few more feet.

Dimly he registered that he was not breathing and knew it no longer mattered. Thoughts and sensations jangled through his mind in chaotic consciousness. Dying took the briefest of time, seconds, minutes at the most, yet it seemed infinite. It began as a moment of great intensity, the light-brightened pain as the aneurysm detonated. The taut, weakened artery burst like a shattered dam deep within his brain. As he toppled sideways there were flashes of light, exquisite pain, the thrumming blood roar in his ears, the inchoate sounds of his extinction. With a fixed stare he watched the raven edge from foot to foot, flapping up to land near his leg, watching his eyes.

A fiery pain built to an agonising binding pressure around his ribs. He made tentative movements of his fingers, tremulous shudders, low-key vibrations running through his body. There was a power to this dying; a power he recognised and accepted. It was time. The mountains were fading from his vision, the light of the sun now only vaguely glimpsed, but he felt reassured that they were with him—and the pain had gone. He was still, unperturbed by breathing, the layers of his memory a shower of past emotions distilled into this one endless release.

He felt the abrupt pressure of the raven's feet alight upon his shoulder, smelt his musty feathered smell and knew the brush of his flapping wing feathers against his cheek. The long, heinous beak, streaked with grey, carrion-scented, quested forwards warily. Darkness spilt slowly around him like the sun sliding behind the mountains.

The raven hopped forward onto his shoulder and, delicately, with great precision, plucked out an eye. The choughs screeched and wheeled as if offended and abruptly dived into the shadows of the ridge line. The raven threw back its head, beak opening and closing, as it swallowed. Then it let out a triumphant caw and bobbed forward to pluck out the remaining eye.

11

Two parties had descended the ridge to tell him about the dead man. Then they had hurried for the valley, carrying his note for the guides to come up the next day and fetch down the body. Now, twenty-four hours later, Patrick was worried. The storm was approaching too fast. It would soon engulf the rescue party working far above him. Glancing up at the second tower on the ridge, he saw that it was in shadow. He thought about the body laid out on the rock ledge alone during the previous night and he thought about the birds. Tracing the line of descent down the ridge, he eventually spotted three small figures grouped at the top of a steep rock wall. Below them he could make out the shape of the stretcher with the corpse lashed tightly to its sides. Another tiny figure swung precariously beneath the stretcher, guiding it down the wall. The sound of a distant voice floated down from above; a sharp, urgent command.

He thought of the birds sweeping down from the heights and wondered if it was only the storm that was calling them down. He knew the stories of mountain birds being the reincarnated souls of fallen climbers and he looked again at the milling choughs soaring above the ridge line and wondered whether they had done their grisly work. He grimaced and shook his head at the stupidity of these tales. People would not believe such stories if they saw what was done to the eyes of climbers. It was said that this was their way into men's souls— through the eyes. He chuckled and examined the ridge as the dying sun lit the summit slopes in a wash of pale rose Alpenglow.

He glanced at the horizon, noting its ominous colour. The wind speed was increasing steadily. Snowflakes scurried across the stony ground and flitted past the hut's wooden balustrade. A white lacework pattern edged the dry wood of the handrail and did not melt. The storm would soon be on them. Patrick had been monitoring its advance as the afternoon had progressed.

A sinister lenticular cloud, lying like a great grey disc over the summit of the mountain, had gradually massed out over the entire range and had begun to sink, smothering the surrounding peaks. The sky was darkening as heavy, snow-laden clouds came lower and lower, pushing in against the icy vastness of the north face. By four o'clock only the grey-streaked ice field and the dark crags of the mixed ground a thousand feet above the glacier were visible. As night approached the barometer showed a steady drop in pressure. Patrick already knew the storm was imminent; the birds had told him.

The previous evening a jostling flock of choughs had appeared briefly above the tin roof of the small hut perched at the foot of the east ridge. He heard their bickering, high-pitched cries and went out to study their spinning and swooping acrobatics as they played on the lifting wind beneath their wings. They had swept down from the heights and he knew what it meant without even a look at the barometer. The sky was clear of cloud and the day had been sunny and warm. There was no evidence of the approaching storm front, but the birds had sensed it.

The choughs wheeled impatiently, their cries raucous as he watched their frantic, circling flight. They seemed to be hesitating; hanging in the turbulent wind that streamed up from the glacier beneath the north face. They were unwilling to desert the hut and abandon the mountain to the storm. A few brave individuals drifted down towards the valley, then came swiftly back to the strident calls of the impatient flock. Patrick watched their ecstatic flight. They were not feeding on the wing. Their wild and swooping curves and loops were just an elemental delight in flight. A few hung in the strong wind, legs dangling comically, wings crabbed to slow the air as they hovered unsteadily above the hut. They cawed and screeched and eyed Patrick warily as he leaned against the rail. Then, as if on some silent signal heard by the entire flock, they rose high into the sky—a dark speckled vortex like spiralling, wind-scattered leaves—then turned to swoop as one into the valley depths. They could not compete with the storm.

As he scanned the mountain, searching for the rescue party, only the foot of the ridge was still visible, a great broken buttress of splintered limestone, part-swallowed by dark clouds. It wasn't a rescue, he reminded himself—it was a body retrieval. A heavier gust of spindrift raced across the lower rocks and he realised his fears were coming true. The storm would be on the men before they reached the safety of the valley.

'Heart attack,' the lead guide had said when he had passed by that morning. 'Up by the second tower, you say?' he added, and grimaced as he swallowed the last of Patrick's strong coffee from the enamel bowl. He threw the dregs on the ground and spat and glowered at the phlegm on the stone. It would be a hard day for them to get the body down, tough work on the ropes.

'He was a big man,' the guide added with a scowl. 'A big German man,' he said, as if it made any difference to the task in hand. 'Red in the face and so fat.' He held his hands curved in front of his stomach and bulged his cheeks. The hand gestures were disdainful. 'Why so fat on the mountain?'

Patrick remembered the man heading up the ridge in the dark of the previous morning: big man, but not fat. He had moved with surprising grace.

145

Patrick had watched as he had climbed purposefully towards the ridge and dispatched the first awkward rock steps with a calm, proficient technique. He noted that he carried no rope on his small rucksack. Seeing the way he moved over the rocks in the gloom of early morning, Patrick did not doubt his ability. He was experienced and confident, moving quickly out of sight, rapidly pulling away from the two roped parties that had left the hut just behind him.

When the same roped parties returned, grim-faced, in late afternoon to inform him of their discovery they were subdued. They said that he had been found on the level area at the top of the second tower with his back against a rock buttress. There were fossils on the ledge and an old piton. It was on the edge of the ridge looking over the north face.

'Yes, I know the place,' Patrick replied quietly and nodded encouragingly as he listened to them. They thought the man was resting—or, perhaps, sleeping—when he did not reply to their greetings. They saw the carelessly spilled coffee on his trousers and the cup lying forlornly on the rocks, but they did not see the unfilled gaze of his eye sockets. It crept into their worried minds that he was dead. They gazed silently at the body and could feel the lifelessness. They did not touch him. Yet even now, chattering out their news in nervous, fevered explanation—even justification— Patrick could see that they were still not persuaded. They were not comfortable with death in their day.

The man had reached the summit many hours earlier and had passed them as he moved agilely down the crest of the east ridge. He was fast and fit and confident and it made them unsure, intimidated. They disapproved of his solitariness. He should have had a rope. He made them feel less capable and they agreed that he was irresponsible, whispering so that he did not hear. Then he was there, alone, on the rock ledge— dead—and they still couldn't quite believe it.

'He should have reached the hut by midday,' one man said.

'Maybe earlier,' his wife added, and looked at Patrick with wide, searching eyes as if he alone could somehow undo this shadow on their mountain day. They crowded around him, twittering like the choughs, wanting to tell him, wanting to be away.

'Was he dead? Are you absolutely sure?' Patrick asked firmly, at which a portly, slow-moving man stood up and somewhat stiffly announced that he was a doctor, then glared accusingly at Patrick before he sat down again on the wooden porch of the hut without a further word. He seemed insulted by the question. They were keen to head down to the village, eager to put distance between themselves and the tainted day. Patrick gave the doctor a note for the rescue guides, telling him where to go and who to talk to. The man strutted importantly away from the chattering group.

'Go to the bar in the centre of the village. It has green shutters and flower boxes in the windows. Ask for Maurice. He is old and has bad eyes. Give him the message and they will come for the body tomorrow!' Patrick shouted and the doctor waved without turning back.

'You have no radio?' the woman demanded

147

querulously of Patrick. She was tired from the long day on the mountain and angry that the death had marred her day and made her fearful.

'No,' he replied. 'This is a small summer hut. It has no warden. I volunteer. I am not paid.' The woman sniffed. It was not her concern. 'There is little money and no funding for such a small hut,' Patrick explained. 'Normally, there would be no one here.'

'But what about the man on the mountain?' Her husband, a stout balding man, stepped up beside her and pointed at the ridge, bathed in late afternoon sunshine. 'You cannot just leave him up there, alone.' He glanced nervously at the retreating doctor.

'You said he was dead.' He met the man's eyes. 'He is dead, isn't he?'

'Well, yes, of course. The doctor told you so. We all saw him. He was dead.' He looked at his companions. His wife scowled. 'He is dead,' the man repeated with a dismissive wave of his hand and he sat on the porch step with his back to the wooden wall of the hut. He looked drained.

'Of course he was dead!' the woman added sharply. 'We are not fools, you know.'

'No, of course not,' Patrick replied and smiled. 'So he will not mind a night on the mountain, eh? It is not a problem for him any more, is it?' The group looked perplexed at his casual acceptance of the death. They did not meet his gaze as he waited for their answer. 'By the way, did any of you cover him?'

'Cover him? Why should we cover him?' the doctor snapped irritably.

'The birds—' he muttered and then cut himself

148

off.

'What birds?' the woman demanded. 'What are you saying?'

'It's okay. There is nothing to worry about.' He held his hands out, palms upwards, reassuringly friendly. There was no point in upsetting them. 'He will be safe where he is now.' As he said it he remembered the choughs sweeping down from the heights and hoped fervently that they hadn't investigated the body.

'The weather is stable,' he added, 'and the guides will come early in the morning if you get this message to them tonight. They will bring him down off the mountain. He will come to no more harm. Now go, before it gets dark.'

He had watched as they hurried down the path which curled around the crested remains of the mountain ridge below the hut, filing down into the darkening valley. They clustered together, he noticed. They were silent with their thoughts and no longer chattered. They stayed close, moving with sharp nervous strides, as if proximity would protect them. One of them stopped to look back, not at the hut, but high up at the second tower still glowing in the rays of the setting sun. He searched briefly for the dead man and then he turned to see the group far ahead of him and hurried to catch up.

Patrick thought of the dead man: mid-fifties, a tall, heavy-boned climber, powerfully built with broad shoulders and strong, muscular legs. He had seemed contained and composed, as if he rarely released the full force of his strength. He had smiled at Patrick when he had rested by the hut steps and drunk from his water bottle. He didn't

149

speak. There was no need and Patrick understood. The lead guide had grumbled that the man was fat but he was angry at the hard work to come and there was nothing for them in it—only a long and arduous carry.

There was no one to save—only a body; a big, heavy, awkward, stiffened corpse that they would curse and wrestle, a body they already resented and would dislike by the end of the day. In their minds it had neither name nor identity. They had decided the corpse was a German. Maybe they didn't like Germans. They certainly did not feel friendly towards this unwillingly adopted one. It was a dark thing weighing heavily on their minds—difficult work to come. They had seen too many dead to feel much sympathy.

When they reached the ledge the man lay with his back to the rock wall of the Second Tower, staring, eyeless, across the northern glacier. They sat beside him to smoke and share watered-down wine from their flasks and chew at tough, peppery sausage. The young guide looked at the ravaged face and then spat out his sausage and took a hurried swill from his flask while his companions laughed, but were careful from experience not to look to long or too closely at their silent companion.

They struggled to rig the twin-wheeled stretcher and the eldest guide stood back and gave commands. It was a new design and he was proud of it. He hoped some day he could make a good living selling his prototype stretchers to mountain rescue teams across the world, but for the moment his three companions cursed him and laughed at each other as they attempted to bolt the axle to the stretcher and fix the big wheels securely. They liked the new design. In fact they admired the old man's constant stream of inventions that they were forced to carry up onto the mountains, but they never let him know this. Instead, they swore and criticised the stretcher and the wheels and smiled among themselves when they saw the irritation and hurt on the old man's face.

Then they heaved the unwieldy corpse onto the stretcher, complaining about having to lift it above the tall wheels. They lashed it with ropes and slings and took no gentle care as they roped it down over the rock walls and short, vertical towers. The youngest guide was elected to lead the stretcher down; a task he accepted with muttered displeasure. His companions grinned and played to his vanity by praising his youthful strength and acknowledged prowess as a climber and, before he knew it, the flattered young man was stepping backwards down the walls, fighting to steady the handles of the stretcher while his cheerful companions controlled the speed of the ropes. They let the individual ropes slide out evenly, so both guide and corpse were kept safe and in line.

The young man did his best to make sure the stretcher wheels kept in contact with the rock. The wide-diameter wheels turning on either side of the lashed-down corpse helped to stabilise the stretcher, but often he would slip under the torque from the handles, and corpse and stretcher would spin over and twist the ropes and he would howl with anger and a tremor of fear. His gleeful companions shouted ironic encouragement, enjoying the distress in his voice, until a gruff, barked command from the old guide silenced them.

After a while he decided that he would not fight so hard to steady the stretcher and if it writhed free he sprang away from it, swinging out on the rope at his waist and watching as the stretcher slithered and scraped across the rock. After all, he told himself, corpses can feel nothing. Still, he felt bad watching the impacts and winced and turned away. His companions looking down on him became solemn and held him tight on the ropes and nodded to him, making eye contact, telling him to be strong, they were with him in this business. Resigned, reassured, he would breathe in deeply, exhale with a shudder and then reach forward for the handles once again.

At times, as it bucked onto its side, the stretcher would bounce and swing heavily and thump the body against the rocks and he was not fast enough to jump clear. He would try to ward off the worst of the blows and keep his rope free from the spinning axle and wheels. Once, when he came to a breathless stop, he found himself lying awkwardly across the corpse. The hood of the man's jacket had become loose and for a brief, nauseous moment the young guide felt his cheek pressed to the man's cold, grey skin. He recoiled in disgust and pushed the stretcher away with a heavy, angry kick of his legs, wiping his cheek with the side of his arm, expletives spat out with furious revulsion. He heard his companions' merriment and he glanced up at them angrily. They wrapped the lolling head well to protect it from further injury, but he would not take the handles after the fall and insisted that one of the others took a turn with the troublesome corpse. None of them would try too hard to prevent the blows. They could move faster that way and there would be no cries of pain or pleading, frightened eyes to slow their progress. Sometimes it was easier with the dead.

Patrick studied the guides through his binoculars as they shepherded the body down the ridge, the stretcher swaying between the struggling men and the body convulsing as they juddered the wheels over the rocky terrain. Flurries of snow brushed across his cheek as he watched the grim procession through his binoculars. The men looked tired and withdrawn. No one was speaking. They appeared not to acknowledge the dead man's presence. He was a heavy burden.

That morning the lead guide had shrugged his rucksack into a more comfortable position and tipped the peak of his cap in salute to Patrick, then turned away with a resigned curse and a call to his three comrades.

'Only us four,' the last and youngest guide had complained to Patrick as he trudged gloomily past, laden with the trussed and heavy-wheeled stretcher. 'Only four and we have a fat man.' His companions continued towards the shattered rock buttress, heads bent to the ground under the weight of their rucksacks.

Now, ten hours later, Patrick watched from the balcony of the hut as the group of struggling men and the stretcher passed in and out of view between heavy snow squalls. He ducked into the hut, hanging the binoculars on a hook by the door, and moved to light the single gas ring beneath the kettle. He hefted the kettle from the ring and dipped it into the large plastic barrel of water by the side of the stove.

When he returned to the balcony to check their progress there was no sign of them. The wind buffeted the wall of the hut and whipped stinging ice particles across his cheeks. He blinked and stared into the storm. Glimpses of grey rock appeared, rapidly whitening under settling snow. Occasionally the wind tore rents in the snow-laden clouds and vague, shadowy figures seemed to appear uncertainly in the distance. They, too, were grey, frozen into the mountain terrain by the storm. They disappeared just as swiftly. The initial buttresses of the ridge were shrouded instantly from sight as if the mountain had vanished. There was no sign of the little group. It was appreciably darker: night was no more than an hour away. He stared again into the storm clouds, then stepped back into the hut. He had no worries about the guides. They had known the mountains since childhood and in all conditions. They would soon appear.

He reached for the gas lamp hanging above the small trestle table, turned the switch and lit the mantle. He hung it back on its hook and the delicate mantle heated quickly, pulsing a warm yellow glow onto the balcony outside the window. He looked around the tiny hut. At twenty feet by fifteen feet square, it was little more than an emergency shelter, to which he had added a few comforts. The table by the window with the gas lamp hanging above it was his domain. His books were stacked neatly on one side. The notepad and pens and a dirty coffee cup proclaimed his possession of the table. To the right of it there was a partially walled-in bed with book-laden shelves lining the wooden walls. A blue sleeping bag lay on the mattress and a bright yellow down duvet jacket hung from a nail on the wall by the foot of the bed. Two basic wooden chests beneath his bed provided all the storage space that he needed.

Above the bed, a weak light glimmered through the hoarfrost-coated window. He could hear the rising note of the wind as it swept over the ridge on that side of the hut. Ice rattled against the glass. He leaned over and rubbed steam from the window but there was nothing to be seen. Beneath the window lay a drop of several hundred feet down to the broken rocks bordering the glacier beneath the north face. On fine days he could see the face from his table by the window, looking out across the foot of his bed.

Another long table stretched along the opposite side wall with two lamps hanging above its rough surface. There were windows on three sides of the hut and along the back wall there was a single bunk bed, crudely built from heavy timber beams. A thick foam cushion mattress lined the plain wooden planks and a few stained blankets, damp from lack of use, were folded neatly at its foot.

The gas stove near the door was braced in a basic wooden frame that he had built the year before. A man-high red propane gas bottle was strapped to the outside wall of the hut by the door and a heavy rubber pipe led through the wall, connecting to the back of the stove. He had fashioned a sideboard to prepare food on and an assortment of plates, pots and cutlery was racked on the wall. In the centre of the hut a squat pot-bellied stove sat beneath its black tin chimney which rose to pierce the ceiling planks into the poorly insulated attic space, exiting through the sloped wooden shingles and

155

corrugated iron of the roof.

He leaned over the long table and lit the two rusty hurricane lamps. He had a plentiful supply of paraffin but resented wasting it. It was hard work carrying the big gas bottle up to the hut. At the start of each season he spent the quiet early weeks hauling supplies. The heavy propane bottle, jerrycans of paraffin and sacks of split logs were the toughest loads. At first the guides had remained silent and unhelpful, unsure what to make of this foreigner changing the emergency shelter into a warden-occupied hut. He had asked neither for permission nor help. He was courteous to the guides, free with cigarettes and coffee as they came through with their clients. He was fit, strong and clearly a powerful climber.

He asked nothing of them and gradually he commanded a grudging respect. It was never openly acknowledged, but bit by bit the silent deposits by the hut door became a regular event. A stack of logs or a can of paraffin would appear by the steps as a guided group passed through. A bottle of wine or some sausage wrapped in greasy paper might be left on the table. This year when he had carried down the gas bottle and ordered fresh propane from the small garage in the village he had been surprised to see two young men bringing it up the path to the hut two days later. He smiled to see them sweating under the awkward weight. They knew he had regularly carried it up the path on his own without complaint.

He watched the snow lashing against the windowpane, hoping that the extra light might lead the guides to the hut. Perhaps they had already passed and hurried down to the valley with their burden. Moving over to the stove, he hooked the heavy hot plate from the top with a tong hanging by the black tin stove pipe. A gust of hot air rushed against his face as he dropped a log into the hot embers. A burst of sparks flickered out of the stove and settled in a dust of ash on the metal. The log basket was nearly empty. He dropped in two more split logs and tipped the accumulation of bark and chippings into the flames before replacing the hot plate. The kettle began to whistle, so he switched off the gas and placed it on the hot plate. The lid rattled as the contents simmered gently. He picked the basket from the floor and headed for the door.

As he pushed it open he was surprised at the amount of snow that had already built up on the balcony. He looked to his right around the corner of the hut where the balcony led down to some rough-hewn stone steps at its furthest end. The two lamps by the long table lit the snow-covered balcony and the railings. There was no sign of the guides or even of the mountain beyond. He pulled the door closed behind him and walked to the left where the long box barred the furthest end of the balcony. From the darkness beyond, the wind came howling up from the glacier hundreds of feet below. It funnelled through the notch in the ridge with a low, eerie whine.

He lifted the heavy lid of the box and, bracing the basket between his knees, leaned deep inside to reach the logs stacked neatly within. It usually held a four-foot-deep layer of logs several feet wide and stretching the entire width of the balcony. Now he was almost unbalanced by how far he had to reach to grab the few logs left on the

157

second layer. It was near the end of the season. Once the basket was full, he stepped back to let the wind slam the lid down hard and flicked the bolt across to hold it in place.

As he turned towards the door he became aware of the snow-dusted figure of the lead guide standing at the far end of the balcony. He smiled and nodded his head at the door and the guide turned to speak to his companions before trudging along the balcony.

12

Patrick busied himself with the kettle, the enamelled tin bowls for the coffee and the glasses. He reached up to the shelf above the stove and brought down the bottles of brandy and red wine. The guides shuffled gratefully onto the long benches at each side as he placed them on the table. No one spoke. The men steamed as the snow darkened on their jackets. Cigarettes were lit and a fug of smoke rose above the steam. Four glasses were swiftly filled with shots of brandy and dispatched without emotion or pleasure. The youngest guide pulled the top off the plastic wine bottle and the glasses filled again.

Patrick poured boiling water into a large tin jug and the aroma of fresh coffee rose into his face in a steamy rush. He swirled the contents and left the jug to stand on the edge of the hot plate. He placed a cardboard box of sugar lumps on the table whilst waiting for the coffee to brew, then dipped a cup into the barrel of icy water and splashed some into the coffee jug. The coffee grounds swirling on the surface disappeared with a hiss and sank instantly to the base of the jug as soon as the cold water hit. He filled the four bowls and left the jug on the table. Sugar was added, along with generous shots of brandy, and the guides bowed their heads to the bowls and sipped the brew in silence.

'What about the man?' Patrick nodded at the closed door. The bolt rattled in the latch as a gust tore along the balcony. 'Did the birds get him?'

'Yes . . . of course.' The young man hesitated and looked at his companions. 'They always do.'

'Yes, that's true,' Patrick grimaced.

'We think it is late now to get him down tonight.' The young man glanced at his companions, as if seeking support.

'Yes, I know,' Patrick agreed. 'And it will be slow in the dark in this weather.'

'Yes.' The man looked at him uncomfortably and then away.

'Do you want me to help? I can come down with you.'

'Oh, no, that is not necessary.' The guide held up his hand. 'Anyway, four is the best number with this stretcher and with the wheels it is not so difficult, not down from here when the path is good. But now there is too much snow.'

'Yes, getting worse too,' Patrick said as the window rattled and the wind thrummed, coursing over the roof. The younger guide stood up from the table and went to the door. A torrent of icy air rushed into the hut as he pushed the door open. The storm was increasing in intensity. He leaned his shoulder against the door and looked at

159

Patrick.

'We must leave him here.' He shrugged his shoulders apologetically.

'This will be bad, this storm.' The lead guide stood and finished the wine in his glass. 'It will come in harder now. Strong winds and heavy snow, they say. Two days, maybe three. Who knows? It is the *Föhnsturm*, no?' His companions shrugged and nodded agreement.

'We must leave him.'

'He will be fine. It is cold. He will not bother you, I think, my friend.' The young guide looked at Patrick and laughed.

'Okay, but where?' Patrick asked and the young man looked relieved. A broad smile creased his tired face for the first time.

'We can wrap him in canvas. The snow will cover him.'

'Yes,' the older man interrupted. 'Let the snow cover him. He will come to no harm. We will return when the storm has cleared.'

'Do you have canvas to wrap him in?' Patrick asked. The man shrugged and looked away.

'No. It is not needed,' the young guide answered. 'The snow will do its job. There is no problem with the birds now the storm has arrived.'

'Rats? Marmots?' Patrick asked.

'No, no rats. They will be safe inside with you, eh?' The man smiled. 'Unless you want to come down with us? He will not be such good company as us, eh?' He nodded towards the door which rattled in its frame. 'This is a bad one, no? Come down with us. Have a good hot meal, some cards, some company, a young lady for you, eh?' The group grinned, nudging each other and chorusing

160

encouragement for Patrick to join them.

'No. I will stay.' He looked at the storm-lashed windows.

'I knew you would not leave your precious rabbit hutch. Why do you stay here? Always alone, every summer. You never explain.'

'He doesn't like the ladies,' the young guide chuckled.

'It doesn't matter,' Patrick said brusquely and stood up. 'I have a better idea. Come on, where is the poor man? You will have to hurry to get down before the snow is too bad.'

Patrick shrugged into the yellow duvet jacket and then pulled open the door, flinching as the fierce wind stung his face. He turned left and strode across the balcony, buffeted by flurries of snow. When he heaved up the lid of the wood box he had to push hard against the power of the wind blasting over the railings.

'Come on,' he yelled, struggling to keep the lid open. 'He'll fit in here. Bring him over.' He heard the ribald banter of the guides as they went to the edge of the steps, crouching over the stretcher and quickly unlashing the corpse. They carried it awkwardly at waist height along the balcony. The body had lost the rigidity of rigor mortis and it required little manoeuvring to lower it into the wood box. The man's broad shoulders were pressed tight against the sides; his head rested on a raised log. The face had lost its red glare and appeared grey and waxen in the light from the window. The gaping, bloodied sockets gave him a look of horrified surprise. Patrick flinched at the obscene expression and looked away, nauseous with shock. He busied himself with arranging the cramped arms so the cold, grey hands were clasped across the stomach, careful not to let the guides see his revulsion. The guides stepped back, amused at the easy solution to their problem. Patrick lowered the lid slowly, resisting the pressing wind. It seemed discourteous to let it slam shut on the staring face. He slipped the bolt across the latch.

'We will return when it is over. The stretcher is stored at the side of the steps.'

The small group were hitching their rucksacks tight, pulling hoods up against the wind and tightening waist belts and arm straps. The bright beams of their torches cut into the swathes of snow rushing past the hut.

'The young couple will be here soon,' the young man said, as he cinched his belt and nodded towards the mountain but the storm muffled his words. 'You will hear them first!' another called and the group laughed and huddled companionably together, backs to the wind.

'They know how to fight, those two!' the old man muttered but Patrick was not listening and the storm stole their words. He glanced towards the end of the balcony, preoccupied by the man in the log box, remembering the bird-ravaged face with tendrils of dried blood vessels creeping, worm-like, from the gory cavities. The young man waved and stepped from the balcony, followed by his jostling companions. The drifted snow covered their boots.

The elder guide stepped forward and stretched his hand towards Patrick, who reached out and clasped it in warm affection.

'Thank you, Patrick,' he said with a grizzled

frown. 'Go with God.' He looked down at Patrick's ravaged hand with its stunted, thickened stumps. 'You be careful, eh?'

The guide looked fiercely into his eyes, reluctant to release his hand. He looked again at the truncated fingers and back at Patrick.

'And one day you will tell this story, eh?' He raised Patrick's hand to his companions and grinned. He turned swiftly away and stepped into the storm.

The tired group turned to Patrick with curt waves and nods and strode briskly down the broken ridge below the hut. Their tracks showed darkly against the deepening snow in the pool of light spilling from the hut. He watched the lights bobbing away into the night, flickering and fading as the snow clouds swallowed them in gusted waves. He glanced in the direction of the ridge. The light from the windows glowed brightly in the streaming snow. Beyond the cone of light, shadows seemed to shift in the darkness.

*　　　　*　　　　*

For the third time in an hour Patrick looked up from his notebook and listened to the storm. The window glass vibrated at another heavy volley of snow. He checked the shopping list he had been making in the book against the stores he could see ranged on the shelves. There might be some food rationing needed if the storm lasted more than four days. Fuel stocks were fine—plenty of gas and he could damp down the stove to conserve his dwindling wood supplies. He should have given the list to the head guide when they arrived with the

163

corpse and had cleared the mountain. He shook his head, irritated at his forgetfulness. It was unlike him.

'Cleared the mountain?' The words sounded harsh in the empty hut. He sat back in the chair and pushed the notebook away with his hands, '. . . cleared the mountain?'

Patrick stood up, pushing the chair back across the rough floorboards and reached for the large red ledger hanging by the side of the door. He lifted the looped cord from the hook and carried it to the table, opening it in the middle and hurriedly flipping through the pages, each one dated in his neat handwriting. Pages of scribbled names flicked by, some scrawled untidily in garishly coloured ink, other entries neatly scripted with comments below the listed names of the climbers, the date, the route climbed, observations on conditions, snow cover, weather, the occasional complimentary note to Patrick for his hospitality. Near the back of the book, he came upon the most recent entries—the sparse formality of the doctor's group, names and notes written the previous morning—the tight neatness of the script reminiscent of his haughty self-importance as he had querulously demanded the hut Logbook from Patrick earlier that morning. Beneath the entry Patrick recognised his own handwriting. The lone climber had not bothered to make an entry but Patrick had written '. . . *lone male, solo attempt, east ridge, departed 5 am . . . summit reached 6.30 am (approx.)*' Patrick reached for the pen and added '. . . *died above 2nd Tower on descent between 8 am and 9 am (approx.)*'

He had left enough space to add a few comments once the guides had descended with the corpse. A

164

few lines beneath the entry were the words '. . . *young couple, mid-twenties, late start 12 am on east ridge, ignored weather warnings, male (apparent leader) impatient and argumentative ...*'

Patrick slowly closed the book and pressed his palm against the battered cover. He should have remembered the young couple; should have asked the guides to wait. It hadn't even registered when the young guide had joked about their arguments. It was the dead man. Patrick had let the eyeless sockets distract him. It was unlike him. He had seen enough death in this place over the years, become inured to the sight of broken, lifeless bodies. Perhaps it was the storm? There was something familiar about it—a bristling, unearthly, almost electric atmosphere combined with the shrieking dissonance of the wind. He thumped the book angrily and turned away from the table, trying to marshal his thoughts.

Within hours the path down to the valley would become impassable—too late to recall the guides for a rescue. He looked at his boots, crampons and ice axe hanging from a wooden peg by the door. *What could he do alone? Could he even climb in these conditions?* He unclenched his fist, staring at the frostbitten stumps of his fingers, and cursed his stupidity. The storm was well set. The big one, the old man had said. How big? Three days, four even? Waiting until the light of morning would not help in these conditions and by then they would be weakened by a night in the open. *God forbid if one of them were injured.* The thought decided it for him. He would climb as high up the lower reaches of the ridge as was safely possible. If they were above the First Tower then they would have to

165

fend for themselves, but he felt confident he knew the mountain well enough to find them below that point.

He dragged the wooden crate from beneath the bunk-bed and rummaged hurriedly through the contents, throwing selected items towards the wall where his boots and crampons hung. A small First Aid kit, a Thermos, a gas stove, a pre-prepared bag of soups, energy drinks and spare batteries, a light rope, a nylon survival bag, sleeping mat, spare clothes. The pile of gear quickly grew as he stuffed the sleeping bag into its sack and pushed it to the base of his rucksack. He packed the sack with practised efficiency, slung the rope across the top and cinched it tight down with the straps.

As he stepped from the porch and moved through the edge of darkness into the full force of the wind, he shielded his eyes with cupped hands from the light glow of the hut and studied the ground above him. It was a blur of racing snowflakes, grey, mottled buttresses looming in and out of focus and the disorientating buffeting of the wind—but gradually his vision adjusted. He began to make out darker shapes against the night sky: the broken edge of the lower ridge showing black against the small snow patches of the east face. He searched the slopes to the left of the ridge, scanning with his peripheral vision, trying not to see what he was looking for. Just as he was preparing to abandon the search and set off towards the ridge, something flashed in the corner of his eye. He kept his head still and waited, staring straight ahead. It came again—a momentary blink of light, swallowed immediately by a cloud of snow. Then again—the intermittent

166

bobbing, telltale flash of head-torch lights, moving down painfully slowly, but moving. The lights sparked again, well below the First Tower.

Ten minutes later, as Patrick was preparing to re-fill the coffee jug, he heard their heavy steps on the balcony and the sound of voices raised in tired anger. He pulled open the door to see a man shaking a woman by the shoulders. Whey-faced and almost immobile, she had a vacant, unfocused stare.

'Come on, Cassie! Come on!' the man yelled in a hoarse, exasperated tone. 'We just need to keep going and we can reach the village. I saw the lights of the guides. There will be tracks. They're not far ahead.' He was shouting in frustrated anger. There was no reaction in her dulled eyes and she muttered something inaudible in reply. She looked shocked by the sudden opening of the door and the sight of Patrick holding the coffee jug in his hand.

'Come in. Come in,' Patrick waved the jug at the two young climbers. The man glared at him.

'No, it's okay,' the man answered curtly. 'We must follow the guides while we have time. We can still follow their tracks. It will only be a couple of hours to the village.' The woman swayed in the doorway, her face waxy and drawn, her lips quivering. Patrick studied her deathly pale complexion and noticed the lack of shivering. Reaching forward, he gripped her elbow and for a moment she swayed, almost losing balance. 'Come inside,' he said gently. 'It is warm.'

'No. We must go,' the young man insisted and looked irritably at Patrick who was leading the woman into the hut. 'What are you doing? We

167

have no time for this.'

Patrick pulled the door shut after the woman had stumbled inside and turned to face the man, who pulled angrily at the straps of his helmet and dragged it from his head, swinging it threateningly. He ignored the snow whipping across his face as he stared at Patrick. He was shaking. Patrick couldn't tell whether it was from anger or cold. He leaned close in towards the young man's face and said, 'You go if you must. She is staying. She is in no fit state to go on. I suggest you—'

'Who the fuck are you?' the man snapped and jutted his face towards Patrick as if about to butt him. 'This is not your business.' He pushed Patrick aside with one arm. 'Come on!' he shouted at the closed door. 'We have no time for this, Cassie. Get the fuck out of there. We have—'

His words were cut off with a grunt as Patrick's open palms punched heavily into his shoulders and he staggered backwards. His left arm caught the handrail, preventing him falling, and he sprang forward, a curse on his lips as his right arm swung towards Patrick's head. The punch was easily ducked and the curse cut off as Patrick's fist jabbed forward to crunch against the gristly cartilage of the man's nose. As he reeled back, Patrick grabbed his throat, swung him round and pressed him hard against the hut wall.

'Don't even think about it,' Patrick said in a calmly menacing voice. The man slackened beneath his grip but Patrick kept pressing hard against his throat, feeling the cold wet skin against his fingers and the ribbed outline of his windpipe. 'She is exhausted and dangerously cold. I will not allow her to leave in these conditions. Do you

168

understand?' He relaxed his grip and the man pulled his head to the side and stepped away from Patrick, reaching to massage his throat and coughing in abrupt, rasping breaths. Blood trickled from his nostrils.

'Bastard,' he spat between coughs, then, regaining control, he straightened but did not move towards Patrick. 'She's fine,' he muttered, 'it's only a few hours to the valley.'

'Not in these conditions it isn't,' Patrick replied. 'And she is not fine. Another hour and hypothermia will set in. Your pace will slow. Even supporting her, you would be lucky to get her to the village in time. If you leave her and fetch help, you had better be sure of getting back to her within hours. You'd better hope the snow doesn't cover her and you can find her on your return. Do you want to take that risk?' Patrick met his angry gaze and the man looked confusedly at the door and then back at Patrick.

'She's fit, you know? Stronger than you think.' Patrick shook his head. 'She doesn't like it when it gets hard, that's all, gives in too easily. I've been telling her—'

'I'm sure you have,' Patrick interrupted him. 'And fitness has nothing to do with cold resistance. She stays. I suggest you do so as well.'

'Let me talk to her.' The man stepped forwards and Patrick nodded and gestured with his hand towards the door.

The words were harsh and belligerent, even above the noise of the wind. At one point as a crash emanated from within, Patrick moved towards the door, then hesitated as the voice was raised again—his voice. Hers was barely audible.

Suddenly the balcony was bathed in light as the door flew open with an inrushing flurry of snow. The man pushed roughly past Patrick and grabbed the shoulder strap of his rucksack. He swung it across his shoulders and furiously tugged the straps tight. He pulled his helmet onto his head, switching the head torch on as he stared at Patrick.

'Fuck you, arsehole!' he shouted. 'Have her if that's what you're after.' He stepped hurriedly back down the steps as Patrick advanced on him. 'Just fuck off, okay?' he yelled and turned hurriedly towards the drifted tracks, flicking his hand towards Patrick, middle finger extended. Within minutes the light of his torch had been swallowed by the storm.

Patrick turned and stepped into the hut, swinging the door shut with the aid of his shoulder. The woman sat at the table with her head cradled on her arms. He thought that she was weeping. He strode to the stove and slid a metal lever to one side. Immediately the flames caught with a roar as the air rushed in. He unhooked the heavy hot plate and slid it aside to drop a split log into the flames. A shower of sparks burst briefly into life and flame shadows flickered around the hut.

13

Stirring restlessly, Cassie rose to the surface of a fevered sleep. Consciousness returned, followed swiftly by memory as sadness seeped in. It was dark in the fetid warmth. She became aware of the silky skin of the sleeping bag and a musty odour.

When she moved her head she felt the rough wool of a hat slide across the nylon. The hood was drawn over her head. She reached to open it and then paused as she made a hurried mental inventory of her state. She felt warm, although the vestiges of a bone-deep chill clung to her spine and joints with a dull ache. She laid the palm of her hand across her breast and felt the unfamiliar cotton of a man's buttoned shirt, its collar pressed against her throat. She felt the bare skin of her thighs rub against the loose softness of thermal leggings. Thick, ill-fitting socks covered her feet. She remembered the hut and the warm lamplight, and the man angry with Callum and the table top welcoming her sleeping head, but she had no memory of preparing for bed.

Then came a sinister reverberation, almost physical in intensity, as if the foundations of the hut had shifted and she felt the downy hairs on the nape of her neck creep with a frisson of electricity. A bright light gleamed through the slit of the closed hood and she tentatively reached to widen the gap with two fingers and peer cautiously out. Shadows swung round the lamp-lit room. Shapes flickered in distorted, confusing patterns. A hurricane lamp hung on a smoke-blackened hook by the door, its wick trimmed low. A pool of sulphurous yellow light lit a disembodied jacket hanging upon the door. At the table she saw the man seated with his back half-turned to her. A candle protruding from icicles of wax guttered at the neck of a wine bottle. The flame licked with each squall of wind, throwing an uneasy, sallow glow on the book held in his hands. She studied him from the safety of the hood. He seemed

171

preternaturally still. She wondered if he was asleep until he glanced unhurriedly at the long window to his side as ice fragments struck the panes with a glassy rattle. The noise made her flinch.

His movements were slow and deliberate and he stared at the window, watching the storm swirling in the darkness beyond. Then he turned back to the book. She noticed the stumps of his mutilated fingers as he reached to turn the pages and saw the muscles on his forearms flex and the tight tracery of tendons and veins on his wrist.

Slowly, as her eyes adjusted to the muted waver of candle flames, his face came into vision: a stubborn jaw running down from curled greying hair that hung well below his ears and fell, dishevelled, over his forehead. She suddenly remembered his eyes, the arrestingly fierce stare, the controlled undercurrent of anger. He frowned in concentration, leaning closer to the page and biting the corner of his lip.

A man in his late forties, she judged, maybe older, authoritative but with a youthful appearance. He held himself in a taut, athletic way. There was stubble on the tanned skin of his face and she watched deep lines crinkle at the corner of his eyes as he strained to focus on the page in the candlelight. Not handsome, she decided, but there was something about him; something contradictory, intriguingly careworn. His face looked battered, prematurely aged. He had a hard, unsettling presence. He made her wary.

She thought of the anger in his eyes when he had told her of the fight on the porch. It was contained, impressively controlled. His body seemed hard, physically lean, and he moved with an assured muscularity, a lithe, frugal motion. He had the broad shoulders of a climber and moved as climbers do, with easy balance. She liked his intensity and power and purpose and his anger: he seemed coiled between stillness and motion.

His shirt sleeve was rolled up and a heavy stainless-steel watch and wristband glinted against his tanned forearm. The curled hairs caught the light and appeared briefly golden as his arm moved. She remained motionless when he turned towards her and stared directly at the hood of the sleeping bag. She knew he could not see her face back in its recesses, yet he continued to stare. His eyes looked directly into hers. She felt drawn in. He turned back to the book and flicked over a page.

She slowly widened the gap in the hood as he turned away from her and held the pages to the candlelight. Her clothes hung from a climbing rope spanning the breadth of the room. There wasn't much he had not removed, she thought with a wry smile, then she felt the reassuring bite of an elastic waistband cutting into her hip. A faint chiming sound made her peer out once more. The man glanced up and to his right. A grimy clock face hung above the table, its black hands pointing at eleven o'clock. He glanced towards her, then turned his face back to the book. *Where had the time gone?* She tried to recall the events of the day; the late start to the climb, Callum impatient, anger bubbling beneath his curt commands. She had mentioned the deteriorating weather and he had dismissed her fears disdainfully. 'Come on. Less talk, more hurry. We'll be okay.' And she had said nothing. She had always said nothing.

They never argued. Odd that, she thought, as she listened to the muffled sounds of the storm and the noises the hut made in response, as if reluctantly bending to its force. Sudden, woody creaks emanated from above as the ceiling flexed, the stove pipe thrummed to the pulse of the wind and the windows rattled impatiently. She looked at the candlelight playing on her hands, the cracked fingernails, the split cuticles and the bleached, wrinkled appearance of her skin. She clenched her fists and they felt weak and the joints ached. She had always quarrelled with the men that she loved, but rarely with Callum, until this holiday. And each fight ate through the love. Perhaps it was her fault—loving too much, asking too much, until it was gone and she realised they offered nothing but empty companionship. It was strange how you instantly knew it was gone. She looked at him one morning and the love had gone. They carried on anyway.

Callum knew it, too. He became edgy, demanding, querulous and she kept quiet for the peace and because there was no love. It was easier when there was nothing to lose—they accepted the loss. Callum didn't want love: he knew that she didn't love him and that it was easier that way.

Then even the silence became a brawl with no balm of reconciliation, no passion-fuelled forgiveness, only weariness. Odd too, she thought, how I always battled when feeling happiest, feeling most in love. Now, it seemed, she let others do the fighting for her. She remembered the man's eyes when he told her that he had punched Callum and she wished that it had been her.

As she watched the man leaning over his book she felt the warmth of the bag around her and the itch in her scalp from the hat. There were things she ought to be doing. She should be up and explaining herself and preparing. She wondered how she came to be there and why she wanted to be there. It felt strange, unplanned. She had felt weak on the climb, even though the moves were easy and Callum knew it and cajoled her, but she had no energy. The cloud had slumped and lowered over them all day and she had stayed silent until the first snowflakes raced by and Callum became more agitated, glancing angrily towards the summit as she moved slowly up to where he sat on a spiky cockscomb of rocks. The ice field fell bleakly into the northern glacier and the wind cut across the ridge, making her hair blow across her eyes as she stopped beside him and said she was going down. She ignored his silence as he sorted the ropes, clipped the anchors and threw the coils in writhing loops out into the hurrying clouds with furious efficiency. The tiredness had grown, seeping through her until she felt leaden and uncaring as she watched Callum, silent now, because he knew that he had made a mistake and pushed her too hard.

Only near the lower tower, as the storm swirled full force around them, had he shouted above the wind to encourage her with the sight of the guides and the hut nearby. All she really remembered was swaying against him as he set the last abseil and feeling sleep settling through her as she rested her head on his back, feeling dislocated. He had yelled angrily then and she had jerked her head up, trying to wake herself, standing numb as he struggled with the ropes—all the time shouting at her as he tied her in and prepared to lower her. He did not trust her to abseil. She realised now that he was not annoyed. He was scared and the shouting was his fear and to stop the sleep coming—and then they were standing in the wash of light from the hut and the man was there and Callum's frightened frustration boiled over.

Despite the stupefying cold she could see he did not love her and she did not mind. She did not love him either. Cassie understood the fear and respected him for it. He was frightened that he had nearly lost her and that the man had seen his failure. He felt stupid and lashed out and the man punched him. Love was not involved. She pushed the hood wide open and the sudden brightness made her blink. The man was turning towards her.

'Will Callum be safe?' Her voice sounded shrill. The wind seemed suddenly very loud and she glanced anxiously at the snow-streaked window. 'You let him go down alone, in this?'

'So, you're awake, are you?' His voice was calm, amused in a way that made her flush. 'That's his name, is it?'

'Will he get down? Will he reach the village?' She struggled into a sitting position as she pushed her arms through the hood and swung her swaddled legs over the wooden edge of the bed, feeling splinters tearing roughly at the nylon. He was on his feet, moving swiftly towards her.

'Stay there.' He reached forward and pressed her shoulder. 'Don't stand. Lie back. You need to rest.'

'Callum—' He held his hand up, interrupting her, and he stood over her studying her face, staring intently into her eyes.

'He will be safe.' He shrugged as if he did not care. 'He has to be. It was his choice; he cannot escape that.'

'He was cold and tired. It made him angry because he wasn't strong. He wanted to be. You shouldn't have hit him.'

'He shouldn't have hit me,' the man said flatly, keeping his eyes on her face, even as he opened a navy canvas bag that lay at the head of the bed. 'Give me your arm. Roll up the sleeve.' She was quiet as he fixed the blood-pressure sleeve around her bicep and pumped the pressure tight and hard, cocking his head as he took the reading. The Velcro ripped loudly as he pulled the sleeve apart. 'That's better.'

'I'm worried about . . .'

'Quiet now.' The man gave the thermometer several hard flicks, then proffered it to her lips. She opened them and let him place the cool glass rod between them and her teeth and said nothing, feeling child-like again as she closed her eyes. She listened to the battering of the wind and the hut noises until he pulled the thermometer from her mouth, the glass sliding smoothly cold along her teeth as she opened her eyes. He read the gauge carefully then flicked it with a snap of his wrist, before replacing it in the small canvas bag marked with a white cross.

'That is much better,' he said as placed the bag on a shelf above her head and, looking down at her, smiled for the first time. 'Stay there. Don't move. I'll bring you coffee and something to eat. Then we'll talk. We have plenty of time for talk.' He grinned as the hut shuddered under the press of the wind.

'My name is Cassie,' she said as he turned towards the stove.

'I know,' he replied, lifting the coffee pot.

'Short for Cassandra,' she added.

'I know. It was my mother's name.' He poured dark, steaming coffee into a white porcelain bowl. 'The name of a Trojan princess blessed with the gift of prophecy. It means "entangler of men". My name is Patrick,' he said as he handed the bowl to her. 'Patrick McCarthy,' he added as he handed her the coffee.

She held the bowl in both hands, dipping her face into the fragrant steam. It was chipped at the rim, discoloured with age. The coffee was delicious and she felt the heat running down her throat, warming her from deep within. 'Thank you,' she said quietly through the steam but he had turned away and was busying himself at the gas stove, adjusting the ring of flames as he put a pan to the heat.

When she had finished the coffee he took the bowl, wiped it with a cloth and ladled in a rich, thick stew of potatoes and carrots and tough, fatty sausage. He handed it to her without comment. She took the bowl and spoon and embarrassed herself at the speed with which she ate. The meal was spicy and warming and she craved the fatty chunks of sausage, ignoring the pangs of guilt she felt for her abandoned vegetarianism. He watched her quietly as he rolled a cigarette at the table. When she had finished she lay back with the warm bowl on her stomach and closed her eyes.

'They always do that,' he said from the shadows.

'Do what?' she murmured, as she relished the flavours still redolent in her mouth.

178

'Eat as if they are starving.'

'Who do?'

'Victims of hypothermia.' Her eyes sprang open at the words.

'And they do that as well,' he said. He stepped forward and took the bowl from her hands. 'I think you're well enough to get up now, if you want to.' He took the bowl to the stove and splashed hot water into it from the kettle, swirling it gently, then slopping the contents into a plastic bucket and wiping the bowl with a cloth.

'I see you're big on hygiene,' she said tartly as she swung her sleeping bag over the side of the bed. As she suddenly sat up she was feeling nauseous. The loss of blood pressure, a cold, empty sucking, left her faint. The heat and the food and the movement made her dizzy. A strong pulse hammered at her temple and her heart thudded erratically. She swayed unsteadily on the edge of the bed as her face drained of colour and her world went black.

She felt his hands gripping her shoulders and pushing her back gently onto the mattress. She hadn't heard him move. Her vision slid back, her focus sharpening on his face close to hers, the smell of smoke, stubble on his jawline and the intensity of his eyes staring into hers. There was annoyance in the set of his face. He lowered her onto her back, shucking the sleeping bag up and over her head. Reaching inside the bag, he felt for her wrist lying limply on her chest, turned it palm outwards, and she felt the strong pressure of his fingers. His head was turned to the wall, his eyes fixed on the wall clock. She felt a tremor run through her, more fear than shiver. He let her

179

hand drop and then pushed deeper into the bag. She felt his fingers probing for the edge of the shirt and then the dry feel of his palm as it rested with startling warmth against her ribs. She meant to protest, to be affronted. She said nothing.

After a pause he pushed his open hand up beneath her armpit and pressed the ball of his thumb into the pit, fingers spread to reach the muscles on the edge of her shoulder blades. It rested there a minute, then he leaned into her and pushed his arm deep into the bag, lifting her onto her side until his hand slipped round and down to the small of her back, surprising her. There was warmth and coldness, she realised; her coldness, his warmth. He withdrew his arm and tightened the neck of the bag, tucking it beneath her chin, his eyes fixed on hers: the anger had changed to concern.

'What?' she said and he shushed her with a finger to his lips as he straightened and stood over her.

'Stay still. Just lie there. Be quiet.' He moved to reach the shelf above the bed space and she saw him bring down a wide oval of stone, honey-coloured, water-smoothed. He placed it on the bed and reached for a second stone before turning to place both on the hot plate of the pot-bellied stove.

'What are you doing?' she asked, turning her face to follow his movements.

'Warming stones,' he said curtly. 'I said, be quiet.'

She was surprised at the rebuke in his voice, the distant, neutral tone. Candle shadows wavered across the ceiling boards and she felt the hut

180

tremble beneath her back. She listened to the storm and the sounds he made moving around the hut, tin pots clanking, the softened thump of his footfalls, the weight of items being placed beside her and always the wind. It rose and sank with an eerie dissonance, higher notes whistling through bracing wires, a low, symphonic humming across the balcony posts, offset by the abrupt sluicing rattle of ice particles at the window glass. The air was charged, electric, and the wind unnerved her, strangely hypnotic in its discordant, persistent lament.

'Here.' She felt his hand beneath her neck, lifting her head towards the bowl. 'Drink.' She sucked at the warm fluid, feeling it dribble from her chin and onto her neck. The sweetness burst around her tongue as she swallowed and she screwed her eyes shut in revulsion. 'Drink it all,' he insisted and she sucked again at the bowl until she was done and he lowered her head back to the mattress.

He moved away and she heard the clunk of the bowl on wood and then he was by her left side again, thrusting an arm into the bag and placing a heavy, wool-covered stone firmly into her armpit. He pressed her bicep against the rapidly warming wool and told her to squeeze it in place. He placed a second stone on her right side and then he pushed his arm down the length of her stomach. She felt the hot, heavy weight slide across her belly until it lay on her pubic bone as his hand delved further down, pushing her thighs apart.

'Open,' he said sharply. Surprised at his urgency, shocked at her timidity, she acquiesced. The side of his hand slid between her thighs, insistent, levering them apart. The stone slipped between

181

them, set on its edge, high and intimate against her. She was glad of the thermal leggings and thought she was blushing, although her face felt chilled.

'Squeeze. Hold it in place.' She clamped firm around the hot stone and a rush of relief and humiliation ran through her. Then he was gone, his shadow moving huge across the ceiling and the lights moving on the ceiling boards. She listened to the storm, feeling confused and drowsy and sticky from the spilt drink—and she slept.

14

She awoke later, a brief awareness of his hand checking her skin, the stones replaced, opening her arms and thighs without dissent, murmuring her thanks as she felt two fingers firm on her wrist, feeling for the bumping life throbbing against her tendon.

When next she opened her eyes she blinked in the bright glare flooding into the boxed-in space in which she lay. Shelves ran around all three walls above her. Jars, boxes and tins stood in serried, uneven ranks along the walls. She recognised the white cross on the blue canvas bag and saw the tube of the blood-pressure cuff dangling from the shelf. She turned her head and saw the heels of his socks protruding from a blanket at the end of the long bench seat running beneath the window. She could make out the hunch of his shoulders and thought he must be cold. The clock read nine. The wind still hammered relentlessly. It had not woken her.

The stones had fallen on their sides, hard lumps beneath her arms, and she felt the stone at the junction of her thighs and squeezed the hard curve, releasing a luxurious tingling pressure, an effervescent rush up her spine making her feet arch. She struggled to sit up, clawing for the two wool-jacketed stones by her elbows, pushing them from the bag. As she reached down to retrieve the last one she flinched at the heavy, hollow impact of stone on floor.

She turned guiltily to see him looking over his shoulder at her.

'I'm sorry. I didn't mean to wake you.' He grunted and sat up, shrugging the blanket from his shoulders, rubbing his temples with the thumb and fingers of his undamaged hand, squeezing sleep from the bridge of his nose and shaking his head like a dog shedding droplets of water. He checked his watch, glanced at the white-rimed window and then rose to his feet. Metal clanked as he hooked the heavy hot plate from the stove and dropped in two split logs. A flurry of ash spurted into the air from the hob, sunlight flashing on the motes as they rose towards the ceiling. The hot plate clanked loudly back into place and she watched as he reached down and riddled the ash and cinders into the base of the stove. Straightening up, he hung the hook on the stove pipe and placed an old, blue enamelled coffee pot on the stove.

'Feeling better?' He sat by her side, hip to hip, studying her eyes.

'Yes, much.' She looked away. 'Do you always do that? It's rude.'

'Embarrassed, eh?' He reached for her wrist. 'I

183

was checking your pupil dilation. I'll be rude any day rather than lose a patient.'

'A patient?' She turned to stare at him in surprise but he was looking at the clock, two fingers firm on her pulse.

'Nearly lost you last night,' he said in a matter-of-fact tone and turned to push the thermometer between her angrily pursed lips. 'My fault as well. Should have thought of after-drop. Stupid of me. I should never have let anger cloud my judgement.'

She mumbled incoherently and tried to remove the thermometer, but he pushed her reaching hand away and held a finger up at her with a hard, unsmiling gaze. When he had read the temperature he grunted and flicked the thermometer as he stood up.

'You can get up now—slowly, don't rush. Your clothes are dry.' He pointed to where they hung on the climbing rope. 'Put this jacket on afterwards. It has my heat.' He pulled off the yellow down jacket and handed it to her. 'Then come and have some breakfast. You'll be hungry.' It was an order, not a request.

She dressed silently and hurriedly, obeying his brusque instructions to put the shirt back on over her dry thermal top, keep the leggings and hat on, wrap her neck with the red scarf—until she glanced testily at him, but he had his back to her, stirring a pot on the stove. There were bowls and spoons on the table and a hunk of bread on a tin plate, hard cheese and cured smoky dark sausage. He placed the coffee pot and two mugs close by and the bright snow light made the steam dance like smoke. She slipped her feet into large canvas-soled hut slippers, cramming the loose folds of his

184

socks into the sides, then went to sit on the bench beneath the wall clock, zipping the yellow duvet jacket up to her throat. She sat quietly and enjoyed the fragrant coffee vapours. It was cold in the hut, despite the log stove, and she wondered how he had managed to sleep with just the thin blanket for warmth.

He slid himself onto the bench beneath the window and reached out to fill her bowl with coffee, pushing a battered tin of sugar towards her. She held her hand up and shook her head, but he placed the pot on the table and spooned two heaped measures of sugar into her bowl. *Not even teaspoons*, she thought in mute disapproval, but reached for the bowl and stirred the coffee. She seemed to have become accustomed to being told what to do by this strange man. And he was strange, she thought, sipping the coffee and grimacing at its sickly sweetness. She watched him cut the hard cheese and saw through the bread with firm deliberation. He cut enough for both of them, then sliced the sausage, not once asking her if she wanted any. It was as if he was there alone, despite preparing food for two. There was nothing about him that acknowledged her presence.

She thought of the night and all that he had done. It hadn't been concern or compassion, she realised. It was a task, a job to be done as efficiently and effectively as possible. Perhaps that was why she felt comfortable about her near-nudity and the intimacy of the stones. There was no threat from him. The thought was perplexing. For a moment she battled with it in her mind until he pushed a laden plate of cheese towards her without so much as a glance, then stood to lay the slices of bread on the hot plate. Her discomfort began to turn to anger but she pulled the plate towards her without acknowledgement. He weighed down the slices with a plate and the hut filled with the aroma of burning bread. As he turned from the stove she looked up, expecting him to speak, but instead he crossed the floor to scrutinise a small barometer fixed to the wall between the window and the door. She watched as he tapped the glass with his forefinger then carefully turned the bronze dial in the centre of the face until the black and copper arms aligned, indicating the present air pressure. He frowned, a spread of crow's feet crinkling at his temples, his brow creased in concentration, as he tapped the glass again. The pressure had dropped since he had last checked it. He leaned towards her and scraped ice and condensation from the windowpane, peering intently out into the white glare. The wind had not let up its harrying attack.

'It's burning,' she said and nodded at the stove. He rose and crossed to the stove in a lithe, unhurried movement. She watched him flick over the blackened bread and press the slices down, holding them firmly in place with the plate. After a few seconds he lifted the plate and plucked the slices quickly from the smoking metal. He placed the plate beside her and reached for the coffee pot.

'What exactly is "after-drop"?' she asked as he re-filled her bowl. She put her hand over the sugar tin as he reached for the spoon, holding his gaze until he shrugged and filled his own bowl; a small victory.

'You need sugar,' he said as he sat down and

leaned back against the windowsill, partially silhouetted by the stormy white light of morning. He lit a cigarette, the smoke curling blue towards the ceiling, and leaned his head back to exhale.

'You had "after-drop"' he said. 'It can be a killer.'

'What is it? What happened to me?' She was irritated that she couldn't see his eyes and held her hand up to shield hers from the glare, as if saluting him.

'You nearly died,' he replied and picked strands of tobacco from his lips. 'Well, that's my opinion, but I'm no doctor.'

'Have you seen it before?'

'Yes, and I have seen victims die.'

'What, here?'

'Yes, here, right here,' he said nodding at the discarded sleeping bag on the bed. 'It makes you feel pretty helpless. So maybe I am a little cautious when I think I see it again.'

'What is it exactly?' she persisted.

'It's a sort of after-effect. It catches you out, if you're not careful, and I should have been more careful.'

'Hey, I'm still here, full of life,' she said jauntily.

'You didn't see yourself last night.'

'You certainly saw your fair share.' She stared frankly at him, pleased when he glanced away, discomforted.

'I knew you were cold when I saw you outside with your man.' He sat forward, leaning his elbows on the table as he flicked ash into a rusty ashtray. He dragged again at the cigarette, then stubbed it into the tin.

'Doesn't that hurt?' she said as she watched him

press out the ember with the stump of his forefinger. He looked up in surprise.

'Not any more. I could see you were bad. I've seen it before. Clearly your man hasn't,' he added contemptuously.

'He's not my man,' she protested but he looked at her, a sardonic curl to his mouth, and this time she looked away.

'You had all the signs of hypothermia, advanced hypothermia in my judgement—pale skin, blank expression, a degree of incomprehension, slurring your words and confusion when trying to understand your man's argument to go down.'

'His name was . . . is Callum,' she said wearily.

'Yeah, Callum, right.' He finished rolling a cigarette, licked the glue and twirled it into a tube with practised ease. 'Well, Callum nearly killed you.' He studied her with steady eyes. 'There was no shivering. That's the important one. No shivering.'

'I thought you shivered when you were cold? Anyway, I was shivering. I remember shivering. Never bloody stopped,' she said ruefully.

'No, you don't remember. That's the point. And you did stop. At that point you stopped remembering as well. You may have some memory of shivering, maybe not far from the hut, maybe even violently—that's probably why you remember it. When I saw you outside, you had stopped shivering and that's important.'

'Why?'

'You shiver when you are cold . . . up to a point, then you stop and then you're in trouble. Shivering is a stop-gap way of reheating yourself. It works for a while as does physical exercise, but not for long.'

As he talked, her anxiety increased. It had been closer than she had realised. She studied him as he explained the different stages of hypothermia, occasionally gesturing to emphasise a point, oblivious to the mutilation of his hand and always his eyes looking directly at her, holding her attention. He spoke confidently, knowing his subject.

He explained the dorsomedial area of the hypothalamus, the shivering reflex, muscle spasms around the heart and vital organs, core temperatures plummeting, brain functions collapsing, abnormal heart rhythms surging, cardiac arrest, death.

'Simple really, but it gets complicated very, very quickly.'

She liked his voice but looked at his arms as he talked—deep-tanned by the Alpine sun, powerful forearms, the veins prominent, strong fingers, what was left of them. He moved them with surprising grace and she watched them, avoiding his gaze.

He spoke evenly as if it were the best way to block memory. He spoke from experience. Although he was calm there was an increased urgency as he described each step of deterioration and she knew that he had watched them all and been helpless to prevent a collapse. He explained the difference between mild, moderate and severe hypothermia and the way people died—quietly, it seemed, without complaint. They just slept, he said, and stopped remembering.

'So what was I?' she asked, lifting her chin to meet his gaze. He hesitated, doubt crossing his face for the first time.

'Moderate,' he said at last, nodding to confirm it

189

to himself.

'You don't seem so sure,' she said.

'It's not an exact science.' He shrugged. 'Some survive severe hypothermia, some die from mild to moderate effects. Depends on the person. We're all different. They say you should never give up on a victim. They say you're not dead until you're warm and dead. They say a lot of things . . .' he trailed off, his face clouded with some past memory.

'Did you give up on them?' she asked and his eyes narrowed as he looked at her.

'No,' he said a little too harshly. 'They gave up on me.' He looked at her, naively vulnerable. 'The first two . . . well, I didn't know so much then. I've read up a bit since and got a few ideas of my own. The stones—a doctor suggested the stones. I brought them from the river down past the village. It has a long curve with a wide shingle bank: they're good oval stones, water-smoothed granite. They take the heat well,' he added, his expression lightening.

'You're proud of that, aren't you?' she said in a teasing voice and the smile vanished.

'It worked,' he said simply and stood up. The conversation was over. He strode to the door and pulled it open. A rush of icy air and snowflakes span into the hut and he stepped outside and was gone. She watched the door tugged shut against the buffeting wind and leaned across to wipe the window and watch him standing on the porch. He stood, leaning forward, his bare hands on the snow-drifted handrail, and she saw his shirt flapping in the wind. To her it was a maelstrom of wind and snow. He seemed to be reading it, testing

190

the strength of the wind, raising his head to study the teeming sky.

The kettle had begun to steam when the door pushed open again. She poured the water into the coffee pot, watching the grounds swirl and froth. She heard him stamping the snow from his hut slippers.

'Add a dash of cold water,' he said. 'It's a good trick.' As the water hissed she watched the grounds disappear.

'It's going to get worse before it gets better,' he said, from his seat by the window. 'The barometer is dropping fast. Two days, I reckon. Minimum.'

'Two days here?' she asked. 'Can't we get down to the village? Won't the guides come up?'

'What's the point? And, yes, we could force a way down but we're not going to. You're not as strong as you think. It takes time to recover. No point in getting cold again.'

'I'm sorry,' she said, as she placed the coffee pot near him. 'Stupid of me.'

'No need to apologise.' He filled the two bowls with coffee. 'We're even now, anyway. I did a pretty stupid thing last night. Should never underestimate the cold, I know that.'

'So how bad was I?' she sat down and reached for the bowl.

'Worse than I thought,' he said. 'Do you remember anything?'

'Yes—well, I think so.' She frowned. 'I remember Callum being in here. He was shouting. I didn't understand it all. I knew what he was saying, but I couldn't react. It was as if I was outside of it, looking in on us both shouting, but I wasn't saying anything. I remember the door opening and more

191

shouts and you here, looking angry, and then I sat down. At least, I think I sat down.'

'Yes, you sat down. Right here.' He indicated where he was sitting. 'And you put your arms on the table and slept, really fast, no slow going down, just out. I've seen that before so I knew what to do. I took your temperature and it wasn't good—too low—eighty-four, eighty-five, but it's tricky to tell with thermometers. Should have taken a rectal reading but I didn't ... you can guess why?' he shrugged and avoided her gaze. 'Anyway you seemed this side of bad. Pulse slow but not yet irregular, breathing very slow, to be expected. I got you out of your damp clothes, warmed mine and the bag by the stove first, got you changed and into the bag and laid down. I kept checking your pulse and breathing. Your temperature remained steady then rose a bit. Your pulse was stronger so I just waited for you to wake. Should have got in with you, but I didn't.' And he shrugged again.

'Then when you came back, when you awoke, I was thinking of your man, your Callum, thinking angry thoughts, I suppose: stupid, anyway, and that's when the after-drop hit you.'

'Which is?'

'Well, you've re-warmed—or, at least, you appeared to have done so. Trouble is, to preserve your core temperature your body had moved blood away from your extremities, and when you were partially warmed your body started to send the heated blood back out to them again. This blood is now suddenly chilled and comes rushing back, causing a catastrophic drop in core temperature. It doesn't happen that often. I must have had a bad temperature recording from the thermometer, a few degrees out. It doesn't sound much, I know, but it means the difference between moderate and severe hypothermia. And this is no place to start dealing with severe hypothermia, I can tell you.' He stubbed the cigarette out with sharp, jabbing stabs.

'I watched a lad die right there in the same bed two years ago.' He looked across at where she had carelessly left the sleeping bag on the bed. 'His partner was at the base of the lower tower at the time, already dead. I found him on the doorstep. I thought I had him back. I really did and then . . . phut!' He flicked his hand away dismissively. 'He was gone, just gone, nothing I could do. That's after-drop.'

'And you thought that was happening to me?'

'I didn't know, to be honest.' He looked at her. 'I was hoping not,' he added with a half-smile. 'I guess it was the sudden movement of your sitting up that triggered it. All that cold blood rushing back caused chill-down. It looked serious to me. Even with you laid back, stones in place, you had a low eighties reading and that's after three hours asleep in the bag. I checked you every hour during the night. It took a long time and a lot of stones to get your core back where I wanted it.'

'All night?' she asked. 'How much sleep did you get?'

'An hour, maybe two.' He pushed the food towards her. 'Now stop talking and eat. You need it just like you need the sugar. You'll be surprised at how much you need it.'

And she was. The bread was burnt and had a stale, musty flavour. The cheese was hard with an oily, sweated texture and the sausage was spicy gristle. She ate ravenously. He watched her as he pushed his laden plate towards her and she took it without question or thanks. When she had finished and leaned back, washing the last mouthful down with lukewarm coffee, she noticed his wry amusement and averted her eyes, self-conscious, ashamed of her greed, and she heard him laugh for the first time, a strong deep laugh.

'Don't worry. I've seen it before. It's your body overriding your manners. It's a very good sign.'

'You seem to have seen an awful lot,' she replied. 'Or perhaps I should say, a lot of awful things.'

'A few, I guess,' he nodded and the smile was gone from his face. 'But then you tend to remember the bad times more.'

'Really? That's sad. I try to remember the good times.'

'Depends on how bad the bad times are, doesn't it?'

'How bad do they have to be?'

'You ask a lot of questions. The best way to forget bad times is not ask yourself questions.'

He stood and gathered the plates together. As he leaned forward to reach for her coffee bowl, a small gold ornament swung forward from his neck. She reached out and caught it gently. He froze just as his hand touched the bowl and she sensed his body stiffen. Turning the small gold object in her fingers, she noticed that it was not solid gold as she had first thought. It was a tiny, coffee bean-sized sea shell like a miniature conch. There was a blush of pink on the creamy surface of the inner shell and a fringe of orange and yellow where the twist of the outer shell tightened to a point. A fragile rim of gold had been expertly lined along the lips

194

of the shell, ending in a delicate pear-shaped gold loop through which a crude leather thong had been threaded.

'That is so beautiful,' she said as she turned the delicate shell softly between her fingers. It was as if she held him trapped, his body rigid with tension, unwilling to move for fear of breaking such fragile beauty. 'I've never seen anything like it. Where did you get it?' she asked and looked into his eyes, instantly letting the shell fall. For a moment he remained motionless, his eyes fixed furiously on hers. He broke the stare swiftly, lifted the bowl and turned wordlessly, carrying the crockery to the bucket and splashing kettle water over it with abrupt jerks. The kettle banged loudly on the hot plate above the incessant roar of the wind.

'I'm sorry. I meant no harm.' She stared at him in bemusement. He wiped the plates with a ragged towel. 'Have I offended you?' The blood came into her face. She had done something, touched something; she could feel it.

'No. No, you haven't.' He looked across his shoulder at her. 'As I said, too many questions.'

'Oh, I see.' But she saw nothing, understood nothing.

'Best you get back in the sleeping bag and rest some more.' He was ordering her again. His expression serious, the question avoided, dismissed.

'But I've only just got up,' she protested.

'So? What the hell else are you going to do?' He looked meaningfully at the window as a rattle of ice crystals clattered on the glass. Wood creaked in the ceiling and there was an abrupt crack from

195

outside the door as if a steel rod had whipped the wall.

'Jesus!' She flinched and held a defensive hand up as if the windowpane were about to explode. 'What the hell was that?'

'Get into the bag,' he said curtly. 'I'll go and check. Probably one of the stays.'

'Stays? What do they do?'

'Hold the hut up,' he said brusquely and stood up. He reached for a small canvas tool bag from a shelf, checking the pliers, spanners and hack-saw. Moving towards the door, he unhooked a rope, crampons and a sling of pitons and ice screws from their wooden pegs.

'Come on, get into that sleeping bag. We can't burn wood all day just to keep you warm. You can hang the jacket there.' He pointed at a line of rusty nails fixed to the main timber joist running across the width of the hut. 'Put yours on, now that it's dry. If you want something to read, look in the green box under the bed.'

He opened the door and snowy pandemonium filled the hut.

15

It is said that sailors know their seas and mountaineers their mountains—but this is untrue. They know how to exist in these regions, how to explore and travel and survive, but they do not truly know them, for they are ever-changing. Weather changes everything and that is their watchword, not the oceans or the glaciers, nor the

196

waves, nor the rock faces; it is the weather.

They learn how to hoist their sails and set up abseils; they read their charts and maps, understand rip tides and avalanches, read the vagaries of the currents and the snows. They perfect their craft until they are adept at the arcane skills of axe and halyard, crampon and splice, and all the time they look anxiously to the weather. This they can learn about but never be fully certain of. The one truth they have is that, if it so chooses, the weather god can eradicate them in an instant and it makes them respectful and humble—and always a little afraid.

It is the unknown that scares them; the lurking suspicion that a monster may be spawning, the storm of a century, the storm of their lives, a storm about which they know nothing, have no experience by which to understand it and one that will render useless all their carefully acquired technical skills. They learn to read the weather, to predict the possible course they should take, run with the gale or heave to, fight on upwards or prudently retreat.

A storm such as this, a life taker, gathers its power in steady onslaughts, each more ferocious than the last, until the cowering witness begins to suspect that there is some animate purpose to the gale, an uncaring menace in the murderous temperatures, a determined wrath directing the whiplash of the wind, creating the uneasy, claustrophobic sensation of being stalked. Such storms are rare and the witnesses rarely survive. Those who do are forever changed by what they have suffered. The physical scars may heal but the mind never forgets. He never forgot.

The memory of peaceful, tranquil times gave the blinding ferocity of the storm its capacity to numb and overwhelm. It induced a compelling clarity of mind. Madness beckoned in the screaming chaos of wind-driven snow. The witless melancholy, lifeless light and the cruel, seemingly insane gale tortured his mind. He remembered, that day, seeing the mountain in a morning sky of clear air, a light so lucid it appeared as if the landscape was seen through polished crystal. He had clung to that memory; it had been the only way to ignore his whimpering misery.

That perfect light became a mesmerising hope, a remembrance of how the mountain ridges had once been etched exquisitely black by sweeping glacial snow slopes above and below. He remembered the overlapping lines of the ridges marching away in gradated green foliage, emerald greys, dark jade, olive and dry sage—anything but snow white. The colours seemed so rich and clear and the light so pristine that the beauty became physical. It took more than his heart, possessed more than his mind. It included him.

He clung to the memory, to the disturbing ethereal otherness of that remembered landscape. He was left with an awareness of impeccable integrity. His sense of time and place became fluid and then was lost completely. Memory was his saviour, his only assurance that the savage chaos around him would, in time, cease and the clarity and beauty would return.

The storm had become a test of life and sanity, a moment when existence was momentarily held in thrall, beaten into abeyance by something impossible to articulate. A raw, savagely elemental

198

power, simple in its unemotional ferocity. It invaded his mind, bringing with it a feeling that this place of darkness and light, of beauty and power, had supplanted his soul. It had become feral, alive with the sudden, fatal speed of a predator's charge. This was no longer a place for emotion, for appreciation. The storm insisted that he bear witness to its fury; the mountain hidden and shrouded by the maelstrom was an ever-present, invisible dominance. He existed, half-aware, between the two, awaiting the return of the light.

At the storm's end, as it receded grumbling into the horizon of his past, there was a moment of utter calm and the clear light returned and he was reprieved. The mountains were revealed in their fresh storm clothes. They glowed with startling clarity, washed, renewed and cleansed: inexplicably poetic, every colour and form and line and shade intensified, every sharp-drawn peak sacred, suffused by the light as if he were gazing upon a new, unentered world. It was as if the passing storm had been no more than a reverie, a mystical vigil, a vague memory of survival, of obdurate endurance, a time, now forgotten, because the light which he had waited so long for had returned and he would live.

That late morning the storm was still gathering strength, each bellowing roar of wind an octave higher, the cacophony rising by the hour. In the grey light, waves of snow-laden wind surged over the shaking wooden hut. Even as he hauled the door closed behind him he could feel that this was no ordinary storm. He recognised the signs immediately. His back shivered with electricity;

hairs prickled in waves up his spine. His mind blenched at the memory, muscles stiffening and contracting as he forced his body to resist the pulsing tides of wind lashing across the porch, and he was scared again.

By the time he reached the edge of the porch the wind had forced him to his knees, one arm hooked around the balustrade for support. He bowed his neck to the gale, trying to locate the source of the cracking impacts above the shriek of the wind ripping through the notch on the ridge and battering the exposed wooden hut. As he stared fixedly at the gable end, facing the wind, it seemed to be swaying drunkenly.

Then a heavy steel plate came lashing over the edge of the roof to crash against the hut walls, perilously close to the windows. For a moment the support wire lay motionless, almost within reach, draped tantalisingly on the edge of the steps and he dived towards it. The sharp, severed wires ripped across his grasping hand, cutting it to the bone, and his curses were lost in the wind. The wire support stay whipped out of reach and the steel plate, clamped by retaining bolts to its frayed end, disappeared into the driven snow as if it were a paper kite. He heard a sharp crack and saw the hut walls give and the ice-coated timbers suddenly shed their white sheathing. The hut was being wrenched apart. The vortex of wind was beginning to twist it from its foundations.

Patrick knew only too well that the structure was highly vulnerable. He had fitted the system of support stays earlier in the summer. Long steel ringbolts had been driven deep into the surrounding rocks. A double swathe of wire cable shackled around the hut had been connected by two wire support stays from each corner of the gable end, facing the notch. Each doubled wire stay looped through the ringbolts, hard-tightened with a ratchet and clamped in place by the bolted retaining plates, stretched at head height thirty yards out from the corners of the hut. On warm summer afternoons they had made useful washing lines to air the sleeping bags and blankets and dry his few items of laundry. Now one stay was lashing through the air, the heavy retaining plate slamming hammer blows against the roof and walls.

Crouching, Patrick swung the coils of rope behind him and then hurled them up in a powerful, underhand throw. A bunch of pitons and a pair of crampons tied to the rope flew high above the roof, pulled sideways by the wind. Wearily, he retrieved the rope, leaning into the wind as he struggled to coil the loops, and again he hurled it high. The tangle of hardware hit the apex of the roof and the wind bellied the rope out in a crescent, but this time he was in luck. The crampons tangled in the steel cable and he leaned his weight back against the rope, pulling steadily until it came tight against the snag, jamming it on the roof edge. Wrapping the rope around his waist, he jumped backwards and sideways from the porch until, with a harsh, scraping sound and a thump, the plate clattered around his legs and the cable came free. He dived onto the plate, smothering the cable with his knees and arms as the wind begin to pluck at the wire stretched away into the blizzard.

He hurriedly seized the frayed cable end and dragged it into the lamp light spilling from the windows of the porch. Hunching his back to the wind, he worked fast, quickly hack-sawing away the sharp, frayed wires and loosening the u-bolts on the retaining plates. Then he dragged the heavy single wire out of the light and struggled, head down, towards the rocky notch. As he neared the gap in the ridge the wind staggered him onto his knees. He crawled the last few yards with the steel cable biting into his shoulder until he grasped the ringbolt protruding from the rock.

The cable, clear of the ground, swung heavily from side to side as he threaded the trimmed end through the thick metal ring. Fighting against the ponderous swinging weight, he managed to clamp the steel plate, u-bolts and ratchet to the cable. As he tightened the ratchet, the cable straightened between the hut and the ringbolt into a taut bar thrumming in the wind. Hurriedly fixing the plates on either side of the loop, he tightened the bolts until the wire began to flatten. By the time the last of the six bolts had been tightened his fingers were numb, palms slashed deeply by the frayed wire, mouse bites of flesh cut from his knuckles where the spanner had slipped from the bolts, blood seeping from his stumps. The snow around his knees was spattered, the red flecks starkly bright. He slumped back into the shelter of the rock, breathing hard and studying the hut as the snow streamed like a watercourse through the notch a few feet to his side. Occasionally the cable slackened, then snapped back hard and tight and the wind sang on the wire but the hut no longer twisted and flexed.

It took another thirty minutes of effort to crawl along the crest of the ridge and check the second

202

steel ringbolt buried in the snow. The bolted plates were holding, the double cable crushed hard between them. Once back in the limited shelter of the porch he coiled the climbing rope, unclipped the pitons and crampons and then released the latch on the door.

The wind ripped it open, dragging him bodily inside, and he skidded on the floorboards as he swung round to press his shoulder hard against the door to force it closed. He saw the inner latch rise and then drop firmly in place. Still leaning hard against the quivering wood, he grabbed a four-foot length of timber and pushed it down into the retaining arms on each side of the door, leaving a bloody handprint on the timber. Only then did he sink to his knees, rocking back and forth, moaning as the blood returned to his hands and the hot aches bit like blades beneath his nails.

'What's happened? Are you hurt?' She stared in alarm at the snow-spattered moaning figure crouched by the door.

'No, not really.' His voice was muffled as he groaned the words into the cup of his hands, heating them with his breath.

'You're bleeding! What was all that banging?' Cassie swung her legs off the bed and placed the book she had been reading to one side.

'Do you ever stop asking questions?' he said and then began to curse quietly with steadily increasing profanity as the hot blood expanded through his fingertips. She thought to respond, then rolled her eyes, walked over to the stove and pushed the kettle onto the centre of the hot plate, watching his rocking motion with quiet concern. She brewed the coffee and carried the pot to the table and sat and watched as he remained huddled, prayerful by the door. She saw the bloody handprints on the crossbar. He rose to his feet slowly and came to sit by the window, placing his forearms on the table with palms outspread. A pool of dark blood formed in the palm of his right hand. Two deep slits ran diagonally across from the ball of his thumb to the first joint of his little finger. She glimpsed white bone by the finger, and as he tried to curl his hand into a fist, the cut opened obscenely over the muscle of his thumb, exposing meat like scalpel-sliced steak.

'God! What happened?' She reached towards his wounded hand and he drew it away from her.

'It was the wire,' he said, looking at her. 'It was lashing around . . . and did this.' He opened his fingers and blood dripped thickly onto the table.

'What wire?'

'Support wire, the stay,' he answered, reaching for the tobacco pouch by the coffee pot. 'It braces the hut. It snapped.' At that moment the hut shook, the ceiling boards creaked and sooty dust settled on the table. She glanced fearfully at the door as if something was about to burst in.

'It braces the hut? You mean it holds the hut up?'

'It does now,' Patrick replied. 'I fixed it . . . sort of . . .' He pushed the tobacco pouch towards her and then stood up. 'Make me a cigarette, will you?'

'I can't. I don't smoke.'

'Well, I can't either,' he said and squeezed his bloodied fingers into a fist and grimaced. 'And I do smoke, so why not try, eh?' He went over to the bed and reached for the blue medical bag as she doubtfully opened the pouch and pulled out the packet of papers. When he returned he placed the bag and a blue bottle on the table and sat down.

'Before you do that, fill a bowl with some water from the kettle, will you?' She nodded, lifted a plastic bowl from the shelf above her head and stood up. 'Oh, and bring me the salt. It's over there.' He pointed to a shelf laden with tins of processed food and jars of pulses and spices. She found the blue cardboard tube of salt, half-filled the bowl with steaming water and plucked a fork from a cup of crockery near the stove.

She watched him pour a cupful of salt into the bowl and stir it vigorously with the fork. The water swirled in pink tendrils as the blood dripped steadily from his palm. When he was satisfied the salt had dissolved he spread his fingers wide and pressed his hand palm down into the hot water which, in an instant, stained crimson. She watched his face as the pain bit through his hand, his eyes staring hard into the water, a gasp of breath through clenched teeth and then he bowed his head and began to sway his hand back and forth in the bloody water.

'How's the cigarette coming along?' he asked and she looked away hurriedly and reached for the pack of papers.

'I'll do my best,' she said and dug some tobacco from the pouch. 'Was that really necessary?' she asked as she spread the tobacco on the paper. 'The salt, I mean.'

'Good antiseptic,' Patrick replied and she could see it was an effort for him to speak.

'It must hurt.'

'It does.' He winced and flexed his fingers and the water darkened. 'That's the thing about medicine. The things that hurt do you good.'

'Not always,' she replied as she struggled to roll the tobacco into anything resembling a tube. 'It's that old stoic rubbish about having to suffer. Couldn't you just have put some cream on instead?'

'I'm going to. And you're asking bloody questions again. Where's that cigarette?' he snapped and she held up the deformed trumpet of paper with tendrils of tobacco sprouting untidily from each end. He grinned and his face changed, softened from its permanent frown. Chuckling, he reached for the cigarette with the stumps of his left hand. He nibbled the tobacco from the narrowest end, then placed it between his lips. She flicked the flint wheel of his petrol lighter and held the flame to the cigarette. The tip glowed to an ember as he blew smoke across the table, sighed and raised the cigarette to her in half-salute.

'Not bad,' he said, 'for a first go. Not bad at all. Looks daft but it smokes well enough.' He smiled at her and she felt awkward, hesitant. 'Thank you,' he added. 'Now, let's get this sorted.' He held the cigarette between his lips, squinting as the smoke rose past his eyes, and dragged open the zipper on the medical bag. He began to pull out wound dressings and plasters and tubes of ointment and scissors and bandages.

'Bleed them clean and let salt water heal them,' Patrick said as the cigarette bobbed on his lips and he flinched as he clenched and unclenched his hand in the salty water and dark puffs of blood billowed away on each side. When he was done washing the lacerations he reached for the blue bottle by the medicine bag and twisted the top

206

open with his teeth. She wondered how he managed not to drop the cigarette from his lips. He lifted the injured hand from the bowl and quickly dabbed wetness from the palm with cotton wool, then splashed the clear fluid from the blue bottle across his open palm. The pain seared into the meat of his hand. He sucked hard on the cigarette and coughed and grimaced at the sharp burning of the alcohol in the deep cuts. Before the blood welled back to the surface he clamped a wad of cotton to the hand, pressing hard around the ball of the thumb where the cut was long and deep.

'It needs stitching,' Cassie said at last, afraid to break his concentration.

'I know,' he said and looked up from his hand. 'But I'm not much good at doing it with my left hand, so it will have to wait.'

'How long will this storm last?' she asked and, as she spoke, the wind seemed to rise a note higher. She shivered and hunched her shoulders.

'At least another day.' He spoke as he looked across his shoulder at the barometer. 'Probably two, possibly three, the way that glass is falling,' flicking the butt end of his cigarette towards the pot-bellied stove with remarkable accuracy. The damp butt smoked as it hit the hot metal side.

'You've done that before, haven't you?' she said and he nodded with a satisfied smile.

'When I've been bored,' he agreed. 'And these storms do get boring after a while.' The hut bowed to another blast of wind and she noticed that he threw a concerned glance towards the timbers in the far corner.

'This is no ordinary storm, is it, though?' she said and he turned towards her and straightened himself in his seat, careful to keep the pressure on the cotton wool. 'I can feel it. It's not just the wind and the noise and the barometer. I can feel it up my back,' she said and rolled her shoulders again, as if trying to shrug away the feeling of static.

'Ah, that,' he said and pushed his tobacco pouch towards her. 'That will be the *Föhn* wind. *'Sferics* is what the scientists call it; that feeling of electricity, you mean? Bad news is what I would call it.'

'The wind is making me feel like this? This uncomfortable feeling . . . it's not electrical, it's . . . it's weird,' she said, feeling foolish at her words. He looked pointedly at the tobacco and she reached for it and drew the papers out.

'It is and it can get weirder too. Cattle stampeding in terror, men driven insane, mothers miscarrying, children struck dumb, babies born in the storm that follows the wind rendered palsied, forever brain-damaged.' He chuckled when he saw her incredulous expression. 'Well, so legend has it. Old wives' tales, or old mountain villagers' tales, eh?'

'Well, they should know.'

'Yes, true, but there's always a little exaggeration in the stories. Cattle would panic, men might be maddened at the loss of their herds and there is a village idiot born every generation. A storm is a much easier excuse than in-breeding.'

'But you said the scientists have proved that this happens?'

'They backed some of it up. These *'sferics* for instance, some sort of electrical activity. They exist. The wind creates them somehow. The *Föhn* causes them. Comes from the atmosphere, apparently.'

'Do you believe the old stories?'

'No, not really.'

'Why not? People have lived through these things for generations, for hundreds, maybe thousands of years. Why would you not believe them? Maybe in years gone by you could say they had no basis in truth, but if these scientists have proved there is something strange going on, why shouldn't you believe them?' She handed over another cornet-shaped cigarette, lit it and watched as he examined his hand and blew smoke across the table.

'They might have proved that the *Föhn* creates very unusual atmospheric conditions, but they haven't proved or disproved any of that other stuff about madness and miscarriages. Oh and you smoke too much.' He grunted, ignoring her and leaned forward to lift the corner of the cotton wad from his hand. Two dark blood streaks stained the wool but the thumb had ceased to bleed. He was careful to keep the hand very still and gently replaced the wad.

'What they do know is that when one of these storms gets going a number of things happen. The storm is preceded by a warm and extremely powerful *Föhn* wind. This is followed by any number of successive storms, freezing conditions, heavy snowfall, the usual stuff. These *Föhn* winds generate huge amounts of low-frequency electromagnetic waves in the atmosphere, hence the name, *'sferics*. Then weird things happen,' he said firmly and looked directly at her. 'They cause electro-cortical activity in headache sufferers, disturb people's mental ability, screw up attention spans, degrade memory, mess with mental processing . . . but madness and miscarriages, well, they are something else altogether.'

'Can you feel it?' she asked.

'They say it can make you feel all sorts of things. Birds flee, men go mad, something happens.'

'I said, can you feel it?'

'No,' Patrick replied and glanced again at the barometer. 'But maybe I'm used to it.'

'Is this a bad storm . . . worse than normal?' she asked, but he did not answer and kept staring at the ceiling boards above the barometer as if listening for something familiar. The deafening commotion of the wind and the groaning hut timbers began to frighten her. 'Will the hut hold?' she added nervously. He turned slowly from the barometer and regarded her thoughtfully.

'I hope so,' he said at last. 'If the storm comes soon, I think it will.'

'What do you mean "if the storm comes"? What's this?' she said, nodding at the window, which seemed to be in a constant state of humming vibration.

'This is the *Föhn* wind. It's followed by the *Föhnstorm,* sometimes by a succession of them.'

'Oh, I see.' But she didn't really see at all and kept thinking that the storm had been raging for the last eighteen hours and now she was being told that it hadn't even started yet and at this, she felt the fear run through her again. 'Doesn't this noise get to you after a while? I mean, days and days of this?' She waved almost angrily at the surrounding hut. 'Doesn't it affect you?'

'As I said, it can get very boring.' He exhaled a thin stream of smoke at the ceiling. 'But there is some good news.'

'Oh, what's that?'

'The cable is still holding. So long as it holds the hut should stay here.'

'And if it doesn't hold?'

'I'm not sure,' he said and glanced at the barometer as the hut shook. 'But I wouldn't give it long if this keeps up.'

'Then what?'

'Don't worry, we'll cross that bridge when we come to it,' he said. 'We'll hear it start to go, so if we are organised we should be okay. It won't all disappear into the sky, so we should have enough shelter left to stick it out until the weather clears. It just won't be as comfortable as this.'

'How do we get organised?'

'Firstly, we decide what is most likely to be left of the structure if it does go and I already know that. Secondly, we make sure we have a stash of survival equipment that won't disappear into the sky with the hut and which will keep us alive. Thirdly, we anticipate the destruction of the hut and get into the equipment and our chosen shelter.' He noted each point by exhaling smoke and as he leaned forward to stub out the cigarette he gave her a wry look. 'The last bit is the hardest. We have to hope our chosen shelter point will be unaffected by the hut's destruction and that we have enough warning. The other choice is to try and force a route down to the village but I don't rate that as a good option.'

'And that was the good news, was it?'

'Yes. I bet you're glad you stayed now, eh?'

'I don't recall having much say in the matter.'

'True,' he agreed. 'You would have been dead by now if you had carried on down with your man.'

211

'Callum,' she said sharply.

'Oh and the other good news is this.' He ignored her exasperation and held his hand towards her with the cotton-wool wad resting on the thumb. 'It could do with stitching.'

'You want me to stitch that?' she said. 'I've never done such a thing . . . I don't think I can . . .'

'Of course you can,' he replied reprovingly. 'You've made two cigarettes and not so long ago you thought you couldn't do that.'

'It's not quite the same thing, is it? I mean, stitching a wound is serious. I could get it wrong . . .'

'What is there to get wrong? Don't tell me you don't know how to sew? All you can do is cause a little more pain than necessary, and that's my problem.'

'No, really, I can't—'

'Look,' he interrupted her. 'This will not hold together just with a dressing on it, especially if I have to start using it again. It will be too late to stitch it in three days' time. It needs to be done now. I can try using my left hand but it would be hard, for obvious reasons.' He held up what remained of his hand. The stumps had a rounded, calloused appearance. 'Not great for holding needles, you see?' he said, frowning at her.

'Why not strap it tight and try not to use it?'

'Because I may not have that choice. If the hut gives way we're going to have to work hard to stay alive up here or fight our way down to the valley. Either way I would want this stitched and strapped. Go on, give it a try. I'll talk you through it. It won't take long.' With that he delved further into the medical bag until he had found a small

212

metal tube with a screw-top lid. He handed it to Cassie.

'Needles, pre-threaded,' he said. 'You'll only need one, I reckon, if you can tie neat knots, that is. Go on. Get one out and let's get this done. Oh and make me a cigarette, would you? I'm going to need one after this.'

He lifted the cotton wad from the wound. Two cuts, an inch apart, ran across the ball of his thumb. He lowered the back of his hand until it rested on the table and then slowly moved his thumb. The cuts began to open and blood welled from the deepest wound. He pulled his thumb back and the wounds closed. Cassie concentrated on rolling the cigarette, fumbling nervously with the recalcitrant paper and tobacco.

'We'll start on the lower one,' he said, as he dabbed at the blood with the cotton pad. 'It's much the deeper cut and we might not have to stitch the upper one. Five stitches, six at the most and that should do it.'

Cassie said nothing. She set the cigarette carefully to one side and placed the petrol lighter next to it. She had seen the wound open and grimaced. He seemed remarkably composed. She wondered if being stitched without anaesthetic by a complete stranger was an everyday thing for him. Maybe it was just in his nature. She had noticed the contained, lazily efficient way he moved.

She watched him dab the wound, using the pad with deft delicacy despite his truncated fingers. A few stitches, however badly sewn by her, were nothing compared to whatever he had suffered in losing the fingers. She liked the fact that he was unselfconscious about the hand. Indeed, he

213

behaved as if there was nothing unusual about having stumps for fingers. It must have happened a long time ago for him to be so adept with the stumps and so at ease with their appearance. She realised he was watching her as she stared at his hand and hurriedly looked away.

She opened the tube and slid out the foil packages onto the table, then turned to watch the wounds open and close and bleed with grim fascination. She thought about pushing the needle through the skin. Wouldn't it just be like heavy cotton, canvas even? The lips of the wound opened indecently, then closed, leaving behind a bubbled red line of droplets. The edges, she noted, were a perfectly even, clean cut. It would make the job easier.

'Can you do it?' Patrick asked gently.

'Yes,' she replied tersely and tore open one of the foil strips, revealing the curved needle and the coil of thread inside. She looked up from the wound. 'I'll do my best.'

'Here, wash your hands in this first,' Patrick pushed the bottle of alcohol across the table. 'And don't worry. I'm sure your best will be good enough.'

It was easier than she had expected, like stitching warm, wet suede. She winced each time she pushed the needle through the skin and felt her stomach tighten, expecting to hear his pain, but he said nothing and when she looked up anxiously after the first stitch had been knotted down tightly he smiled encouragingly at her. When the sixth stitch was in place she soaked some wool in alcohol and gently cleaned away the blood, dabbing carefully around the dark stubs of the stitches. He flexed the thumb and the second cut opened and blood welled up. She pressed the wool firmly onto the wound, then pinched the edges together to stem the blood and, without asking, quickly laid a stitch across the deepest length of the cut.

'That should do it,' she said as she dabbed freshly-soaked wool across his thumb. 'I quite enjoyed that,' she added cheerfully.

'Well, I'm glad you did,' Patrick replied.

'Oh, I'm sorry,' she said. 'It must have been painful. You were good, no fuss at all. You made it easy for me.'

'It was well done. A neat job.'

He began to pull his hand away but she gripped the wrist firmly and pulled it back towards her.

'It needs a dressing and strapping to protect the stitches.' She turned away, surprised at her sudden authoritativeness, then shuffled through the contents of the medical bag until she found what she wanted. There had been no objection as he had placidly let her take control of his hand. He watched her and she felt his eyes on her hand movements, studying her efficiency, checking she was doing things right, guessing that he always did.

With deliberate precision, she cut a length of Elastoplast into thin strips and pinned them across unstitched sections of the wounds to pull them together and bind them in place. She smeared a generous amount of antiseptic ointment over the stitched wound, then placed a gauze pad over the ball of his thumb, covered it with a dressing pad and strapped it into place with an elasticated bandage. The wire had cut so deep near the root of his little finger that she glimpsed a white flash of bone and the sinewy, silver-grey gristle of tendon. There was no possibility of getting an effective stitch into the wound and she guessed it would be a long time healing, with the movement of the finger.

She pursed her lips, anticipating his pain as she poured alcohol direct from the bottle into the wound. It quickly air-dried and she smeared in a thick glob of antiseptic ointment and wrapped it in protective gauze. Then she strapped firm and hard, feeling his body tense as he winced. She laid broad cross-pieces of tape across the wound, then used the little finger as a brace to strap the bandage around and support the dressing. When she was finished she sat back and admired her handiwork and he flexed his hand gingerly, the fingers moving stiffly in the restraining bandage. She handed him the cigarette and leaned towards him to light it with a flick of the lighter.

'Bad for your health,' she said, as she clicked the lighter shut.

'Most things are,' he muttered, as he stood to reach above her to the shelf running at head height around the hut. With a grunt of concentration, he lifted down a bottle of brandy using his injured hand and holding it by the neck to minimise movement. 'This calls for a celebration.' He splashed generous shots of brandy into the coffee mugs and held one up to her as if to make a toast. She reached for the mug.

'Thank you, Cassandra,' he said, dipping his mug edge to hers. 'A stitch in time,' he added and drank the brandy in one swallow.

Cassie said nothing and sipped the fiery liquor, feeling its heat surging down her throat and expanding into her belly. She watched him refill his mug, the cigarette smoking between his lips. He sipped it this time, giving her a conspiratorial wink and leaning back. She could see that he was relaxing after the pain. They didn't speak. She collected the scattered contents of the medical bag, neatly re-packed them and wiped the blood drops from the table with an alcohol-soaked wad of cotton. She placed the bag carefully on the shelf next to the blood-pressure cuff and tubing. As she walked past him she wondered if he had watched her all the way.

She returned to the table with two small wine glasses and the book she had been looking at before he had burst through the door. She poured the contents of her mug into the glass and did the same with his. She did not ask and he did not object. She poured coffee for them both and sat back on the seat and sipped. It was lukewarm. Cassie was right. He did watch her and he wondered why he kept watching her.

It seemed that a relaxed camaraderie settled between them as they sat around the table. Since regaining consciousness, she had felt disorientated, ordered about, controlled, somehow made useless by cold and the storm and the abruptly alien surroundings. The sense of intimacy felt welcome. It came, somehow, from the act of stitching, from the bleeding and the breath-held concentration. She had regained authority. She had helped him just as he had helped her. There was no longer distance. There was, for the moment, a quiet equality. Perhaps intimacy was the wrong word. It was a loss of strangeness. She felt, somehow, less threatened.

Patrick sensed her ease and glanced at her. She looked across the table at him. Later, it seemed to her in that moment that they had come a long way to be at that table together, but then perhaps it was just time betraying her memory.

Cassie was surprised to feel calm as once again she became aware of the storm noises. Her focus on the needle had been so intense that she had blocked them completely from her mind. Now she listened to the reverberating roar of the wind and the sporadic quivering from the hut.

Sometimes she felt sure it lifted or shifted sideways or moved as a whole, rather than the contraction of individual timbers. Sometimes the sudden movement made her stomach cramp as if the world was slipping sideways for a moment and she would always turn and stare at the same spot in the far corner of the hut where the bed was braced across its width. And always the hut stayed where it was and the wind howled and she would quickly glance at him to check whether he had noticed her sudden spasm of fear. He was outwardly calm, unconcerned, oblivious to her anxiety.

Yet he noticed her fear every time and felt a surge of it himself. The hut was moving and he knew the reason why.

16

Dusk was falling with no diminution of wind strength. There was, Cassie noticed, the same constant chatter at the window and when she wiped a disc of condensation from the glass and peered out into the twilight she saw the snow heaped deep on the porch. She wondered whether the *Föhnstorm* had begun. The hut convulsed on its foundations even as the thought came to her and she grabbed at the table for support.

Patrick had quietly occupied himself in the afternoon hours by building a shelter beneath the bed platform. She had watched as he had dragged out the rows of storage boxes, clearing a space for the mattress which he shoved as far under the rough boards as it would go. It protruded out several feet and he turned the storage boxes upside down and stacked them against the foot of the mattress. He had pulled a length of sun-faded orange nylon from one of the boxes, an old weathered tent flysheet, and, wrapping it around the boxes, he stretched the nylon across to the bed boards. With difficulty, he twisted one of the wooden planks free and rolled it in the loose material until it drew snug and then, with a few sharp kicks, he wedged it tightly back into its original position. The nylon formed a tautly angled roof over the exposed end of the mattress.

When she protested that he would burst the stitches in his hand, he raised the bandages to show that there was no blood on the dressing. She watched him fill two rucksacks with supplies, careful to pack each pan, the gas stove, water bottles and energy bars with his uninjured hand, conscious of her scrutiny. He placed boots, crampons and axe inside her rucksack and did the same with his before tying a pair of aluminium snow shoes to its side panels. When he was satisfied, he laid the rucksacks on top of the boxes, adding their weight to hold the nylon in place. There was a small gap on one side, allowing constricted access into the mattress-insulated shelter beneath the bed, and he shoved the sleeping bag into it and the voluminous folds of a two-man Gore-tex survival bag.

Cassie mentioned that she had a bivi-bag in her rucksack but he pointed out that it was warmer to have two people in one bag, especially as only one of them would have a sleeping bag. He methodically checked his preparations, bringing items that he had forgotten, a hurricane lamp filled with paraffin, the musty blankets from the bunk bed and the two damp mattresses which he laid over the bed boards to give added insulation and further pin down the nylon roof. Then he went through everything again.

Patrick had reason to be quiet. He had watched Cassie stitch his hand and felt things change in some small way and he struggled to see what had happened. He was aware of the way she watched him. She had done so from their first meeting when she had slumped, anaesthetised with cold, staring blankly at his face with wide, unseeing eyes as he had tried to fight off the worst effects of her hypothermia. He had felt in control then. There was a problem to deal with and it was what he did well, but he had let irritation distract him. He was angry with her for her complicity, for letting herself become so cold, and furious with Callum for his mulish, dangerous antipathy. More than anything, he was angry with himself for punching Callum. It was a very long time since he had struck out in fury. He had become accustomed to restraint.

He sat back on his haunches and studied his preparations. They were probably unnecessary but he had felt the hut shift, then shift again. It could mean only one thing—the cable had parted. There had been no sound, no whiplash crack as it flayed the hut walls, which meant that it had sheared where it had been fixed to the hut. When he had struggled to remove the bed boards he immediately knew that the hut had not only moved, but this time it had not been moved back. The frame of the bed was warping with the walls. There was nothing restraining it.

The hut had virtually no foundations that he could recall. Originally a lean-to construction for a maximum of four people, it had never been intended to be any more than an emergency shelter. Over the years he had expanded, enlarged, re-roofed and altered it in a haphazard manner. Now, trussed with wire cables bolted to the surrounding rocks, secure foundations seemed to have been an afterthought. As he watched the walls flex and creak in the clawing wind he wondered how much more strain the structure could withstand. It was weakening by the hour and he could see how it would happen. The whole structure would twist on its axis now that it was held only by the one remaining cable. The roof, gradually sheared loose by the torque of the shifting walls, would catch the wind, unpeel and be torn free. The walls would be steadily stripped away and follow the roof, board by board, into the night.

Since only one of the cables had failed, Patrick reckoned the bed had the best chance of surviving intact. This end had been the original lean-to structure. He watched the corners of the hut where the ceiling boards met the walls. Small gaps sprang open and closed again as the wind struck in a series of buffeting assaults. He stared at the gaps with fierce absorption, as if trying to see what was happening outside in the full force of the storm.

He had never seen such damage happen before and it worried him. He, better than anyone, knew the hut's intrinsic weaknesses. His anxiety was for the building, rather than for himself or his unexpected and perplexing visitor. He realised, with a start, that he was fond of the hut. He had spent too much of his life in the flimsy structure to watch it disappear into the night, too many hours painstakingly adding the small details that had made it home and, most importantly, his. He didn't want to lose it.

Yet now he forced himself to visualise the sequence and speed of events. They would have time. It would not be explosive, not once the roof had peeled away. Constructing a cave around the stout wooden strongbox of the bed was the simplest solution. The support cables were banded around the hut, just above the height of the bed. He nodded to himself as he checked off each point until he was satisfied. There was nothing more to do but wait. He lowered his head and listened to the wind, focusing on its deeper sound, the hidden timbre that might tell him something vital. He felt rather than heard it. He recognised the moment. The storm had changed. It was a memory from a quarter of a century gone, a weather sign that he had logged long ago. The wind was slackening.

He remembered a time of tranquillity when he had emerged from the hammering insanity of the wind to find a landscape of silent, drifting snow clouds shifting and sliding around him and the chaos of the wind-storm finally over. Then came the snow and the intense cold and he looked at the remains of his left hand and clenched them into a gnarled fist. A long time ago. He nodded in acceptance, frowning, until he became aware again of her scrutiny. He busied himself unnecessarily tidying the shelter. Cassie had noticed the moment of rapt concentration as he had appeared to be listening to some message from outside the hut. All she could hear was the relentless moaning of the wind and the hut protesting.

He recovered quickly and looked at her, a stern, fleeting glance, feeling confused. He frowned and tried to look severe, shyness hidden, hating the unfamiliar clumsiness that swamped him when he was in the company of a woman to whom he was even faintly attracted. He felt distracted, off guard. That old feeling, the longing coming back into him again, was unwelcome. He pushed it away and tried to think of the storm, the failure of the cable, the shelter, something else; anything but the way she looked, the way she made him feel, those ancient thoughts returning. He thrust them down, breathed deeply, stared at the bandage around his hand and tried not to think of how she looked. Infuriated, he pushed himself upright and stood up. He thrust his arms into his jacket with impatient abruptness and then reached for the door.

'Just going outside. I need to check something.' He lifted the crossbar.

'The cable?' she asked and saw the answer in his eyes. 'You think it's gone, don't you?'

'Yes, a while back. I felt the hut move.'

'Yes, so did I. Why didn't you say?'

'Didn't seem much point at the time.' He shrugged and looked away.

'I don't need protecting.'

'Really?' he replied sharply.

'Look . . .' Cassie said angrily but her words were lost as he pulled open the door and a flurry of snow rushed into the room. The background thunder of the wind instantly became a fury of noise. Snow blasted against her face as she grabbed at the book and quickly closed its cover. She heard the door banging as he hauled it hard against the jamb and the wind muted instantly. Snow settled, spitting on the hot stove. She brushed the thin layer of powder from the cover of the book and the table top. 'I can look after myself.' She finished the sentence and glared at the door. Then she thought of Callum and the descent of the ridge and the cold eating through her and it didn't seem to her that she had made such a good job of looking after herself. She thought of his long night of caring, the dry clothes and hot stones and barked commands. 'And you would be dead if it wasn't for him,' she added to the empty room.

A sudden gust of wind swept past the hut and again the timbers creaked alarmingly and she flinched. He never seemed to flinch. He appeared not to notice such things, yet missed nothing. His composure irritated and reassured her in equal measure. Even when he spoke it was with a dry, direct efficiency, a caustic thrift, and his gaze was direct, challenging any dissent. Although he moved with unhurried grace there was a bitter frugality to his speech, something hidden about him. It was as if he had built walls around everything he did. The shelter, Cassie realised, had been constructed with the familiar competent deliberation of a man who felt at ease with defence. He was accustomed to shutting the world out and he did it very well.

Cassie had been fascinated and comforted and, at the same time, alarmed at his calm, adept preparations. He knew exactly what to do. There was no fuss or urgency, no sense of unease in his manner. It gave her confidence to watch the shelter take form. Indeed, it even looked inviting and for a moment Cassie was tempted to think that it would be an adventure if the hut blew down.

Yet with that sudden arctic blizzard through the door she remembered the paralysing cold on the ridge with Callum, the night without memory and the tremor of fear that had crept through her as Patrick dispassionately explained hypothermia to her. She thought of the lashing steel cable and the torn flesh on his hand and the force it would take to shift an entire hut. Two days and nights exposed to this storm would not be fun, however inviting the shelter appeared to be. Even as she considered the idea, she was alarmed to observe the expertly organised way in which Patrick went about his task. He had hardly spoken since she had dressed his wound. Clearly, he thought there was a very real threat to the hut and fear at the thought quickly dismissed any ideas of enjoyment from her mind. He was taking it very seriously and it alarmed her. She looked at the closed door and the last feathers of snow melting on the wall and her anger faded.

The door flew open, crashing against the door jamb as Patrick careened into the room, clinging to the handle. His feet skidded on the wet floor as he pressed his shoulder against the door and squeezed it shut. For the briefest moment the door seemed surrounded by a white corona, a fan of pressurised snow spurting around the door jamb as he forced it shut. He hooked the crossbar into its retaining arms and leaned his forehead against the door.

'Has it gone?' she said, as the snow settled like white dust across the room.

'Yes,' he turned towards her. 'It's gone, on this side.' He nodded to the far corner of the bed. 'The other one is holding.'

'Will it be enough? Will it hold?'

'Probably.' He shrugged as if he really didn't care.

'Probably?' Cassie laughed. 'That's okay then, eh?'

'It could unravel fast or it may stay together. Hard to tell. We should have time to use the shelter.'

He shucked his jacket from his shoulders, snow settling around him and she made no reply. She watched as he gingerly pulled his bandaged arm through the cuff.

'How's the hand?'

'Holding up.' He glanced at it, uninterested, then

226

moved to read the barometer, tapping the glass with his finger and resetting the dial before standing beside the window, deep in thought as he watched the snow streak past the glass. Then, as if he had come to a decision, he turned and gathered folded blankets from the side of the bed and began to hang them on the line near the stove.

'It will be warmer if we use the blankets together with the sleeping bag on top,' he said by way of explanation, then moved back to his place by the window.

'So you think the cable will fail?'

'Best to be prepared, eh?' he replied casually. It clearly did not worry him. He was prepared. They would be alright. That was enough for him, she thought, he saw no need to worry.

Cassie gently brushed the new layer of snow from the book she had been looking at, a large-format photograph album. As she swept the table again she studied his expression through sidelong eyes, trying to get some take on how he was thinking. He held his bandaged hand protectively across his chest, leaning forward from the hips as he studied the storm scene sweeping past the glass. His face was surprisingly unlined and youthful for someone who had spent so long in the mountains. The grey at his temples seemed more distinguishing than ageing and she decided he must be close to fifty. His scrutiny was intense, concentrated, as if he were reading words in the window and linking them to the sounds of the storm and so forming an exact picture of what was happening, not just outside the walls of the hut, but high on the surrounding mountains. He was listening to a language she did not comprehend, reading a script that was scrambled hieroglyphs to her. She gave up trying to understand what he was seeing. It was enough that he was calm.

She had noted the sadness that clung to him like wood smoke; an uneasy aura of the tragic, a lived-in desolation. She recognised the sensation. She understood that familiar emptiness cloaking him and she wondered how it came to be. It was something unstated, yet so explicit it was deafening and so simple to observe that it felt intrusive. She found it distressing, a glimpse into his guarded self that he felt sure was concealed, shielded by competence and reserve. It was peculiar to observe. It was as if his veil of invisibility had ceased working and he did not realise it. He wore it like old shoes or a battered hat. He had long since stopped feeling its presence. He no longer gave it thought. She wondered if everyone could see through him as she so easily did.

He turned suddenly, as if aware of her scrutiny, and sat at the table. He had felt her constant gaze, yet her watching was cautious, never invasive. Not for the first time she was surprised at the swiftness of his movements. He moved so effortlessly and with such precision that it startled her every time. He simply appeared in new positions without conscious effort.

'What are you thinking?' She lifted her chin in a defiant stare, challenging him to dismiss her again.

'I'm thinking the change has come,' he said and glanced at the barometer. 'I think the wind may begin to drop soon. It's snowing heavily now. It's colder. The wind will drop and the hut will probably hold. That is what I'm thinking,' he stated with firm assurance. 'I think we'll be alright,' he added and wordlessly pushed the tobacco pouch towards her. Conscious of his attention, she frowned as she pulled a paper free and began to pack it with tobacco, determined to produce a less scrawny cigarette. As she thinned the strands of tobacco in an even line across the fold of the paper she was aware of the silence between them, a companionable stillness like a bubble surrounded by the tumult of the storm. She carefully ran the tip of her tongue along the glued edge of the paper and looked up to see him watching her.

He sat a few feet away, studying her. She caught his eye and looked down as she rolled the paper over with her thumbs, watching the moist glue catch along the paper's edge. The cigarette was evenly rolled and when she had nipped the loose tobacco strands from each end, she twirled it between her thumb and forefinger admiringly. She felt a swell of pleasure at the achievement of the thing. Without thinking, she reached for the lighter, flicked it open, sparked it into flame and inhaled the tip into an ember. She exhaled softly as she handed it to Patrick and he reached for it with a quizzical expression.

'Thought you said you didn't smoke?' he said, putting the cigarette to his lips.

'No, I said I didn't know how to roll them,' she replied as she picked some tobacco from her lower lip. 'And I don't smoke but I used to . . . years ago. It's easier for me to light it than you . . . with your hand,' she stammered through to the end of the sentence.

'Which one?' He held up his bandaged hand and then his left hand and twisted them speculatively in the air.

'I'm sorry,' she said. 'I didn't mean any—'

'Offence?' he said, completing her sentence and she nodded mutely. 'None taken,' he said as he lowered his bandaged hand to the table, the cigarette smouldering between the remains of thumb and finger. He placed it precisely between his lips with his eyes on hers, as if making a point.

'It was a long time ago. I've learned not to take offence. People like to stare. It's curiosity, that's all, but they're ashamed to ask.'

'What happened?' she asked, immediately.

'Frostbite,' he replied and lowered his hand to the table. 'Twenty-five years ago. Lost a glove in winter. Not a good idea,' he added, his lips curled in mock disdain, although his eyes didn't smile. He spoke in a brusque, clipped manner as if the abruptness of his language would avert any further discussion.

Cassie nodded and said no more. Instead, she studied the photographs in front of her and the silence between them became awkward. She brushed distractedly at her hair and stared at the black and white prints. They were precisely mounted on the pages with a date, film speed and f-stop pencilled neatly beneath each one. At first the subject matter seemed eclectic and random— studies of rounded water-washed pebbles, the grain exposed on beach-combed timber, dark-bellied cloud studies, the creaming flow of a petrified waterfall, a moonlit coastline, starlit horizons. And then she realised what she was looking at. It was not the subject but the texture, not the profile but the light which the photographer had captured. She saw it in the curved gold of the wood, the frozen light gleaming in the waterfall, the stream of starlight and the shadow lines of the moon. They were beautiful and as she turned each page the awkwardness was forgotten. She heard the splash of brandy as he re-filled his glass and the scrape of the ashtray as he stubbed out the cigarette, but didn't look up.

Then she came to the first photograph of a mountain scene, a distant range of peaks rising above a series of cloud-forested foothills, as if floating upon them—a full moon hovering incongruously in the daylight sky. From then on there were no more studies of light and texture, no still-life experiments with form. It was as if everything that had gone before had ceased to be, once the photographer had discovered mountains. Yet, as she flicked through the pages, she was again struck by the similarity within each mountain study. The mountains were there, captured in perfect form, close up, far away, in snow and ice and layered, folded rocks; knife-edge ridges slicing to improbable snowy summits, granite pillars stepping majestically up a soaring ridge as exquisite as any cathedral's flying buttress; the chaotic, tumbled beauty of an ice-fall collapsing towards the viewer.

It wasn't the mountains that had been captured, she realised. It was the light—and what light. There was a bewitching luminosity, a radiant clarity, and it seemed to her that with each passing page the intensity of the light study became more acute. Then she turned a page and it was blank and suddenly there were no more photographs. She flicked the page back and examined the last photograph. It was oddly familiar—a view across a mountain face; grim rocks rearing into clouds and beneath them the sweep of an ice field; a falling sheet of grey and white and black striations dropping in a sickening, plunging sweep to the foot of the photograph. The base of the clouds seem to roil as hidden sunlight brightened their surface and where there were small, misty gaps the sun, split into rays, gleamed from the paper with startling brilliance. It was as if the photographer had so completely captured the sense of exposure, the absolute height of the face, that the viewer could not help but be pulled into the scene and have that sudden, uneasy sense of falling. It made Cassie recoil from the page with a start.

She glanced away and then looked at it again. It was a meditation on movement, on the fluidity of light within light. It was the light that pulled her in. She read the date at the foot of the photograph. It had been taken on a winter's day twenty-five years ago.

As she almost reverentially closed the cover of the album she had become accustomed to being observed, she realised. It was his manner. She took no offence.

'These are beautiful; they really are,' she said and saw the momentary surprise on his face before he looked away and immediately she understood. 'They're yours, aren't they? You took these photographs, didn't you?'

'It was a long time ago.' He nodded and leaned forward to pour a shot of brandy into her glass but she placed her hand over the rim to stop him.

'No, thanks,' she smiled. 'Wouldn't be a good idea to fill myself full of spirits just before the hut gets knocked down by the storm of the century.'

He shrugged and filled his glass. 'As I said, I think we'll be alright.' He stood and reached for a row of bottles on the shelf above his head. 'Maybe a glass of red, then?' he said, handing her a plastic bottle. 'I know, I know, it's supermarket plonk but it grows on you after a while . . . and the bottles aren't so heavy to carry up here.' He placed the bottle by her glass and sat down. 'As for the photographs,' he said, nodding towards the album on the table, 'they were a long time ago, back in the days when I used to have to work for a living.'

'Do you have any more? I'd like to see them.'

'Somewhere . . .' He moved quickly over to the bed shelter and began to loosen the flysheet awning. He rummaged underneath it until he had pulled the central storage box free. Jamming a rucksack in its place kept the awning upright, although it no longer looked as taut and neat. He placed the box on the bench seat and began to sift through a chaotic collection of items. Cassie leaned forward to peer into the box. Photographic prints were jumbled untidily amongst seashells, notebooks, rusted pitons with frayed sun-bleached rope attached and a scattering of animal skulls. There were a few bird skulls with long delicate beaks, a marmot, a few fossils—their edges chipped by his axe blows—the fanged upper jaw of a fox and some broken antlers. A tattered copy of a Mountain First Aid manual lay atop a leather roll containing wood-carving chisels. Scraps of used sandpaper were tangled amidst a scattering of warped, wind-polished, half-carved driftwood branches. The contents were overlaid with a fine patina of dust and the base of the box lay thick in sawdust and wood chippings.

233

'No cameras?' Cassie asked.

'No . . .' his voice was a little rough, touched with harshness. 'I stopped using them long ago.'

'That's a shame,' Cassie said. She had noted the defiant look in his eyes, hiding the sadness.

'Well, I'd gone as far as I could with it,' Patrick replied unconvincingly.

'But you never stop with things as beautiful as this,' Cassie protested, as she held up a photograph of sand blowing from dunes. 'They're made out of the love of it . . . aren't they?'

'Well . . .' Patrick shrugged and held out his frost-ravaged hand. 'This made it tricky and maybe I just ran out of love?' And he stared, challenging her to continue the conversation. Cassie bowed her head to the box and gently began to pull the photographs free of the clutter, blowing the dust from each one and laying them carefully on the table.

'Some things never run out,' she said, but Patrick had pushed himself from the table and was feeding logs into the stove.

17

Their quiet intimacy returned with the night. Hurricane lamps hung by the window and the candle flame flickered in the bottle on the table, quivering and dancing to the heave of the wind. They talked softly as the storm fretted at the hut and snow piled against the door. As the hours passed Cassie noticed the flame shiver less and less. Their comfortable amicability or the shift in the storm wrought a noticeable change in Patrick. It was as if he had some affinity with it, some familiar understanding. He no longer checked the barometer or glanced at the far corner of the hut. He appeared to know exactly what was happening and a calm seemed to have settled around the hut and around him, too. He talked of the storm, the fury of nature, of what it is like to die in such weather.

'Can you imagine it?' he asked abruptly.

'Not really, no,' she replied. 'Apart from last night, of course.'

In truth, she still found the surrounding storm overwhelming and claustrophobic. She was startled by the new tone of the wind with its lower, heavier timbre, unnervingly ominous. Her naive anxiety amused him. Yet his efforts to allay her fears by describing what the mountains meant to him was only partially successful. He talked of their beauty, their power and the fear they induced; the way they had become the landscape of his mind, the way his life had been taken hostage by them. He spoke in a quietly distant way and she noticed the tone of regret, as if he were held against his will. She sensed an abiding sadness and an almost bitter enduring without explanation.

What of love? she asked, changing the subject abruptly—and he frowned. Had he ever loved? She persisted and he talked vaguely of a time when he had. He talked more of loss than love. Did she leave him? In a way she did, he replied. He talked of what love is in the unaffected way that a man only does if he has truly loved. Yet not once did he tell her anything about it. Did he want her to leave him? she persisted and he became silently distant and listened to the storm and felt the old uneasiness in the presence of women. She asked too many questions for his liking.

The bottle of brandy gradually emptied as Patrick drank steadily into the night hours with no apparent effect. Cassie occasionally sipped at the sharp red wine but preferred to brew pots of strong coffee and ensure a plentiful supply of logs for the stove. The heady warmth of the stove and the wine soothed the tired stiffness which lingered in her muscles from yesterday's climb but, despite the heat, the marrow of her bones still ached with the chill memory of hypothermia.

'So, is this your work then, your summer work?' she asked and looked at his meagre possessions scattered around the hut. 'Or do you live here full time?' She watched his reaction.

'I tried it once,' he replied with a slow smile. 'The winter was very long . . . too long.'

'And lonely, I imagine. Not many visitors in the winter, eh?'

'Lonely?' He looked surprised. 'No, I was never lonely but it was long and cold and—desolate.'

'Desolate? The winter, or you?' She frowned when she saw his serious face slide back into place.

'Winter is a desolate time, don't you think?'

'So then, is this your summer job? Where do you go in the winter? Home?'

'Hey!' he called out and held up his hands in protest. 'Give me a break from all these questions.'

'Sorry. Sorry. That was rude of me.' She copied his gesture, holding her palms up, fingers outstretched until together they both lowered their hands to the table. 'Looks like we're in for a long wait so what's the harm in chatting?' She ignored

236

his deepening frown lines. 'Come on, Patrick, tell me something. You saved my life. It's only fair I know who you are. Tell me.'

'Who are you?' he retorted and held her gaze.

'No,' she replied firmly. 'I asked the question first. You tell me. Who is Patrick McCarthy? Are you Irish? You sound English to me.'

'I'm English,' he said. 'My mother chose the name.'

'Maybe she loved an Irishman,' Cassie answered.

'Perhaps I'm his son. I never looked like my father's son,' he said a little too hurriedly and they studied the dancing candle flame in silence.

The quiet between them discomfited him, so he talked. The brandy helped and the fact that she listened and nodded and let him talk in a way he had not done for many, many years.

At first the conversation moved on in a desultory fashion, randomly jumping from one unrelated topic to another until, prompted by Cassie, he began to list his life—or so it seemed; a list of things that had happened, nothing more. For the most part he spoke in a strained and oddly detached manner as if somehow disassociated from his own past—as if it were someone else's life. She made no comment but simply listened and observed the strangely callous contradiction in him.

And all the while the storm moved to another phase. She could see the heavy swathes of snow sweeping past the window and when she stood to trim the wick on the hurricane lamp she saw it drifting heavily on the porch. She had riffled through the contents of the box which were strewn across the table. Patrick was turning the skull of

237

some small creature in his hand, examining the profile of the delicate bone structure. There was a collection of bones and skulls on the table, marmots, birds, a fox, scattered carelessly over photographs of long-gone footsteps in snow, on the muddy estuarine banks, in the mica gravel left by a glacial river, of past unremembered lives. A hollow rock, its inner sides jagged with smoky quartz, lay among a scattering of fossils, some whole, some broken through the spiralled backs of long-dead sea creatures. A small geology hammer lay carelessly across the delicate surface of a photograph.

Cassie reached for a small black velvet pouch in the corner of the box. When she released the draw cord two pieces of bone fell into her palm—at least, she supposed they were bone. The larger piece, perhaps four inches long, formed a gentle curve, splintered and jagged at each end. Dark stains lined the smooth inner curve of the bone whilst the top was a dry-bleached, porous ivory. The smaller one looked familiar and she turned it in her hand, wondering what it reminded her of. The bone was tapered, a delicate waist in the middle, almost fluted, each end double-rounded, unbroken. She held it to the light and turned it between her thumb and forefinger, unaware that he had put down the small skull and was staring at her.

'Put it back.' His voice, low and hard, made her flinch and glance quickly at his face. There was a look of fury in his eyes, an implacable, flinty expression, before he masked the anger and looked away. 'Put it back, please,' he said in a more gentle tone and she did, hurriedly averting her own eyes. She replaced the pouch in the box feeling a little ashamed, embarrassed at his sudden, naked anger. She wanted to ask what she had done wrong. She knew it was somehow connected with the bones in the pouch but before she could speak he had gathered the collection of skulls and stones, fossils and photographs and dumped them back into the box. She winced as the geology hammer clattered in last amidst the photographs, cutting a crease across a fine study of sunlight on snow-frosted branches.

As if to baulk further discussion he began to speak as he placed the box beneath the table. He stared past her shoulder and told her about his life in the way a man might describe a series of acquisitions. It was as if the past was compartmentalised like the objects in the box, yet there seemed to be little connection with him any longer. He spoke in a calm monologue and she felt deeply sad. It was someone else's story—not his.

Born to comfortably well-off middle-class parents, his father a dentist, his mother a nurse, he described his life as tolerably unexceptional. He said it with curt disdain, as if ashamed. He came from the north, he said, but did not specify exactly where. He was an only child. A sister had died as an infant, unnamed apparently, and was only once referred to after his mother's death from breast cancer when he was twelve.

His father had given him a camera on the day they buried his mother. Patrick never discovered what had suddenly prompted the uncharacteristic purchase of an expensive camera with lenses and a sturdy canvas shoulder bag. Until that point he had not shown the slightest interest in photography;

239

nor had his father. Maybe it had been his mother's doing; he never did find out. He never asked. Within a month he was back at school, a small family-run preparatory school in the nearby town, which he attended as a boarder because his father said it was good for him. He was allowed home at weekends but preferred the company of friends at school rather than his father's reclusive silence.

As the years passed his father had various affairs. Patrick paid little attention to the awkward meetings with strange women in the formal sitting room. They drifted apart as Patrick edged into adulthood and by the time he attended university and found his own lodgings, their relationship had slid into silence interspersed by uncomfortable Christmas celebrations between strangers and the occasional formal letter accompanying a belated birthday card with a small sum of money tucked in as an afterthought.

He abandoned his medical studies. Academia had never excited him: the formaldehyde scent of cadavers and the desperation of patients repulsed him. Medicine quickly lost out to a burgeoning fascination with mountains and photography. Weekends in the hills with the university climbing club—ostensibly to further his interest in landscape photography—revealed a hidden, natural climbing talent and increasingly the cameras remained in the bottom of his rucksack as his pursuit of vertical excellence became obsessive.

Hoping to forge a career as a photographer, he found a job in London working as an assistant to Peter Fellows, a dissolute, alcoholic wedding snapper. It gave him the basis for a career and enough cynical insights from his teacher to last

240

him a lifetime. The technical details of photography came easily to him and he moved swiftly from darkroom work to shooting a few simple projects himself—most often when his boss was sprawled unconscious across the lightbox, too drunk to load a camera, let alone shoot a wedding party.

Despite his failings, Peter Fellows had once been a fine and famous photographer and revealed to Patrick the subtleties of what he called his 'dark arts'. Patrick devoured his advice and the large collection of art books and photo books at the studio. He was taken to art galleries to study the use of light and to long, liquid lunches in smoky pubs to learn the vicissitudes of life. They were equally fascinating.

Reaching under the table, he selected a sheaf of photographs from the box. He spread them out like over-sized cards and when he found one that caught his eye, he would pick it up and stare intently at it as he talked. Then he would place it before Cassie and point out how the light formed. She noticed the edge of passion that warmed his voice when he spoke of light. He demonstrated how the camera had captured the light and contained it, and how the composition of the objects expressed the light, reflecting it perfectly. He patiently explained the significance of the f-stop, the interaction of film and shutter speeds and what he had written on the back of the photo. Then he discarded it among the skulls in the box below as he continued to talk.

Struggling to earn a living, he had moved on from the shady life of portraits and weddings with Peter Fellows to the world of fashion photography.

'Glamour with frocks,' Fellows had noted contemptuously. Patrick had never really 'got' fashion, either. It seemed ephemeral, vain, solipsistic. Nothing was valued—clothes, models or photographers—for longer than a cover shot was remembered. It was a cut-throat world of artificial light and false promises, ostentatious waste and raging egos. He quickly understood why Fellows had taken to the bottle.

The models were beautiful and intimidating. He had dated a few during location shoots, catching a film, making passable love, filling the emptiness in all their lives. None lasted.

One day a large parcel arrived, his name and address written in an unforgettable, unsteady scrawl on the shabby, bulky, brown paper package knotted sloppily with frayed string. Inside was a classic old camera—a square negative-format 1000F V-system Hasselblad—a priceless treasure. With its renowned 38mm Biogon lens designed by the famous Dr Bertele of Zeiss, it was a collector's dream. Patrick would come to love it for its aesthetics and cherish it because it took everything that he threw at it. At that moment he simply held it wonderingly in reverential hands.

Rooting amongst a jumble of poorly wrapped lenses, he found an M4-series Leica in its original box with the famous 1950s logo *a lifetime investment in perfect photography* on the side. This was the workhorse of an old pro—brilliantly engineered, professional-quality, precise, wonderful to hold and far too expensive for him. He adored the cameras. His love of photography blossomed from then on.

A solicitor's letter explained both the unexpected

death of Peter Fellows and the codicil in his will gifting the cameras to him. He spent less and less time earning a living from the fashion industry. Landscapes had ensnared him and increasingly he made his way to the solitary allure of the hills and the coast. He sold some of his work to photography and outdoor magazines. Despite his disaffection with the fashion world, perhaps because of it, he was in constant demand. His fees rose with every rejected shoot or perhaps because he stopped capturing the clothes or even the models, but continued his experiments with light and landscapes to produce distinctive, surreal shots that appealed to the equally surreal world of fashion. It amused and diminished him by turn.

The camera, he had come to realise, had taught him how to look, how to observe everything that surrounded him. It was not what he saw, but what he was allowed to see that was important. It was, he discovered, all about light. Landscapes, he noticed, were forever changing, always challenging, coolly austere one early morning or vibrantly warm in the settling twilight of the same day. Forms, objects were the mere carriers of light, compositions of light within light. Even now, he instinctively composed shots, using his eyes as viewfinders, as he looked out on the world.

His needs were frugal. He had always tended to be alone, even as a child. His mother had noticed early on that he appeared to live in a world of his own making. Precocious and highly intelligent, he baffled his teachers by being an indifferent, uninterested student. Even as a small child there was something different about him, as if he dwelt somewhere that only others could dream about. It unnerved adults. He lost himself in books, devouring tales of travel and adventure, keeping to himself.

As a child he adored words. They took him to distant realms. They had a physicality about them, a feeling in his mouth when he spoke them aloud. He would relish the way his lips and tongue moved to form his favourite words. He learned that sound, like light, had infinite subtleties.

He spoke of setting out to live an unquenchable life, seeking a longing love, heart-blown, free, and she had smiled at his words because they were not him, but he wasn't watching. 'In the end, all I got is me,' he said, quietly, 'and in a way I am happy with that, even though I always seem to have lost more than I ever found.'

'Sounds like a song lyric.'

'It was,' he replied, 'I liked the words but I could never remember its name. It was one my mother liked.' He looked abashed. 'Words get you like that,' he said, and noticed her unconvinced expression. 'Stories, sagas, lives, they're all captured by words just as cameras capture light. Writing traps words, gives them strength, makes them last, lends meaning to emotion. As a child they gave me dreams and they became reality when I followed them. That's special, don't you see?' he added.

He had always kept himself apart and after the death of his mother he became more reserved still. He had a memory of her lying in bed, pallid-faced, her hair and eyes dark against the pillow. She had held his hand, too weak to speak, and he recalled it as a photograph. He had become so attuned to observing light that his memory seemed entirely constructed of light studies: memory stops, he called them.

He walked away from the fashion world when he buried his father. He had died suddenly—killed one rainy winter morning, crushed between the unyielding steel barriers at a traffic junction and the equally obdurate side of a cement lorry. He was caught in the lorry's blind spot, they said. The driver couldn't hear him scream and the big, heavy mixer kept grinding round as the life was crushed out of him. His father had been in a hurry, they said, late for work, probably.

In an unexpected way it was a life-changing experience. Patrick was quite alone without any surviving relatives, as far as he knew, which was not a situation that unduly bothered him. It was no rite of passage. The fact that he was next in line to die, and childless to boot, meant very little to him. The fact that he was rich did.

He sat in the unsympathetic surroundings of the solicitor's office listening to a dusty little man read out the dry, economical words of his father's will. A low winter sun cut across the space between them, dust motes flickering in the light, and he felt the urge to reach for his camera but resisted and listened in dry-mouthed shock on discovering that he was suddenly a very wealthy man.

This abrupt affluence came as a considerable surprise, greater indeed than the news of his father's death. He need not do a day's work for the rest of his life. He hadn't really considered his father to be a rich man. In fact, since shortly after his mother's death, he hadn't really considered his father at all and had presumed that the feeling was mutual. As an only child and the single surviving relative, his father's estate would naturally have passed to him but, surprisingly, he had been left very little advice on how to dispose of the successful dental practice and the portfolio of shares; how to claim the full value of the life insurance and how best to invest the proceeds. There were even details of the trust fund that his father had set up to manage all his other financial assets, shares, unit trusts and investments.

With the help of his father's solicitor, Patrick swiftly sold the thriving dental practice to one of his father's ambitious and most heartily disliked competitors. The large rambling house and extensive gardens in the Derbyshire Peak District were also sold, along with the old town house that Patrick had been born in. The trust fund swelled impressively. Just as speedily, Patrick abandoned his fashion photography. There was no joy in it for him, no room for artistic expression. He felt lessened, whored by it. 'You are what you create,' he told himself, and he was creating nothing there, so he left to embark on a peripatetic life of travel, climbing and photography.

His mountaineering skills led him to a year spent in Antarctica. The British Antarctic Survey employed him to look after and guide the scientists. It was not a career move, simply an opportunity to photograph the Antarctic landscape bathed in the mesmerising southern light. The dark months of winter were too harsh, too desolate, too long, broken only rarely by the glorious light-show of the Aurora Australis, the Southern Lights. He never forgot the light in that extraordinary continent. There, more than anywhere, he learned what he was capturing.

246

Objects merely reflected light.

His 'snaps'—he pointed at the photographs on the table—appeared in a few minor outdoor magazines and then *National Geographic* called and offered him a professional contract. He was flattered by their interest and deeply satisfied to see the way they published a full spread of his Antarctic photographs in their Christmas edition, but he declined the contract. He had no need to be tied to anyone.

Overland expeditions followed, chasing the light through Turkey and Persia to the Hindu Kush mountains of Afghanistan and the Karakoram of north-west Pakistan. Journeys to India, Nepal and Bhutan followed. Three months in a Burmese jail after being arrested on the mountainous Chinese-Burmese border calmed his wanderlust for a while and he moved to the Alps to recover his health and strength. He bought a small, dilapidated chalet which he gradually converted to a studio-darkroom and which swiftly became filled with the detritus of his itinerant life.

More of his work was published in mainstream magazines and there was some talk of putting together a book of his work, which was, by now, widely admired, but he had little interest in recognition or renown and quietly distanced himself from the idea. He needed neither money nor fame. Happily rootless, they were years of contentment. He was fit, strong and athletic, young enough to be careless of time, rich enough to be independent of others, old enough to be confident in himself. Then he met her and life changed: auburn hair and extraordinary eyes. He loved her at once, he said, with a tinge of asperity, as if love

247

had got in his way.

'Probably the only person you ever loved,' Cassie thought, and listened to his words and felt uneasy. *'He's had an extraordinary life and yet he talks of it in a dulled, disconnected way.'* He described places and mountains, light and photographs in ways she could never have imagined, in words that only someone who has lived such things could use. He had burnt holes in her thoughts, yet she did not know why. He talked of physical things as if they were emotional. He spoke of mountains as if they were sanctuaries of light, as if they could reveal time in colours, textures and shades. To her they were simply huge objects, stone and ice, cold and lofty, nothing more. To him they were a poetic revelation. She understood his words but could not fathom his feelings. It irritated her intensely.

'So, you had it all.' Cassie spoke at last and he looked up in surprise. 'Where did it all go, then?'

'Who said it went?'

'Well, it certainly isn't here, is it?' She gestured at the sparse surroundings. 'And you don't speak like a man who has it all.'

'And how would that man speak?' Patrick said sharply, annoyance creasing his brow.

'Not like you.'

'How do I speak, then?' There was irritation in his voice as he reached for his tobacco pouch.

'You speak as if none of this life of yours has anything to do with you. Everything is boxed: your childhood, your parents, your travels, your love, your entire life. You speak as if you no longer care.'

'Care? What has caring got to do with it?'

'Everything. You've perfected the art of

248

appearing unconcerned, of hiding something.'

'Hardly.'

'You have a separateness about you. It is as if these things were something to you once but you've lost them now. How does that happen?'

'You can't lose memories,' Patrick said sharply and lit the cigarette which he had been rolling intently as Cassie spoke. He tried to appear amused by the line of questioning but his eyes were unsmiling.

'You can lose what made those memories important,' Cassie replied. 'You can lose the passion you had for them. You can fall out of love with your past.'

Patrick shrugged and reached forward to fill his glass, closing her off. Cassie could feel his tension. He didn't like questions. She told him that he was speaking a different language to everyone else, a beautiful, poetic language that meant nothing. He used words that had been true but were now hiding places. She felt she had gone too far and lapsed into a defiant silence. He exhaled and watched her intently and said nothing.

Shaking her head, she reached for the tobacco and rolled herself a cigarette, quietly telling him as she did so that she couldn't understand his world because she didn't see things in his way, had never felt that way about the mountains. She avoided his gaze as she talked, nervous that he would still her flow. She told him that he spoke of the mountains, of light, of art, in words that only someone who truly understood them would use, someone who loved them. They were landscapes of his heart yet he seemed heartless. He remained silent.

Perhaps he made too much of them, invented

them, made them something they were not? Were words his excuse for failing to engage, for being emotionally disconnected?

'Engage with what? Connect with what?' he retorted sharply. And she looked up and caught his eyes, his photographer's eyes missing nothing, framing her. So she asked him about love because there was no love in his mountains. Everyone understood about love, she said quietly and for the first time she noticed him smile, a full, genuine, knowing smile and she knew then that he would speak the truth.

And he did. He spoke slowly and softly and with great deliberation, holding her gaze throughout, insisting that she listen. He told of loss, of failure, of grief and storm and of a long enduring, and she was silent. He quietly told her a story that she wished she had never been told, a story that she doubted he had ever told before and, this time, she believed him.

It seemed, he said, as if he had become locked into the landscape by that one event, as if the mountains were now his jailers. He had stopped imagining what lay beyond them and no longer looked towards a far horizon with expectant eyes. Instead he saw the lines of serried peaks stretching away as a palisade against his dreams rather than the siren hope they had once been. In the past it had been what he had wished to see that had led him on, a desire to find the unknown, the unique, the unforgettable in such adventures. The mountains had filled him with anticipation, a burgeoning hope for what could be discovered, for what he might find in himself. Yet now the longing, the compassion of their beauty had vanished and

250

been replaced by entrapment. He resented them.

The mountains had been a living poetry to him which informed his every thought. There was something sacred within them, fleetingly visible, yet just sufficient to convince him that here there was another reality worth seeking. He had once thought that this poetic, spiritual world existed within the very fabric of the mountains and could only ever be glimpsed when a life was utterly entwined with their icy realms.

He had different eyes now, his senses attuned to a world he no longer recognised. It seemed he now endured the mountains where before he had revelled in them. Once they had revealed something irreducible within him, now they reduced him. He felt lost amongst them.

When he had loved he had convinced himself that it was love in its rawest and purest form and that he had lost it because of the mountains. It was a loss so inexplicably profound he could neither leave them nor rediscover it. He was trapped. There was only the waiting to be endured. When he finished his story she was utterly still.

'I'm so sorry. That is so sad,' she said at last. 'You must have loved her so much.'

'She was my wife,' he nodded and she stiffened slightly at the word.

'There are a lot of unloved wives around, Patrick.'

'She was my life,' he said in a tired manner and she sank in regret. He looked drawn, as if telling the story had been the most exhausting thing he had done in his life. Unwelcome thoughts and cold emotions slid into her mind with a flush of disappointment. There was something about him

251

that held her attention, stayed uppermost in her mind. He had the right to have been married, she told herself. She had noticed that he wore no ring and it pleased her and she felt guilty. He was no longer married. She wondered why she should care at all.

The easy movement, the confidence, the firm authority that had bullied her back from hypothermic insensibility was a beguiling illusion. She noticed that whatever needed to be done was done quickly with a deceptive economy of motion. He wasted no effort. His certainty of purpose was alluring. Yet it was an automatic concern, she thought ruefully, without affection. She thought of the life he had lived and the words he used. They were some parts of the whole that she could put together, stories that fixed him, set him right: the oddly child-like diffidence and the naively vulnerable way he reacted. He gave the impression of being adrift, unfocused, entirely unhurried, yet he had about him a needy innocence, one without self-consciousness. There was, too, the vague sense of an opportunity lost, a moment in time that he had allowed to slip by unheeded. He reacted badly to surprises, discomfited when no longer in control, unable to create the aura of imposed order that he needed always to carry with him. And then there was the distracted, disjointed story of his life, as if he were hiding something, as if his life was a journey that he knew he could not finish; an endless narrative of redemption leading to his pervasive state of unarticulated abandonment. There, she thought, his isolation lay. His grief, lightly worn, was so deeply felt it was visible to strangers, unnerving them into silence as they sensed there was a half-lived man before them.

It was all there. The bitter pill of swallowed-back anger, the deceit of grief, the lost feelings. Grief ennobles but it disables too. Feelings? They had been rejected. He had tried to contain them to discover what he was feeling. Yet he never could quite grasp it. He had let himself become exiled, without identity. She saw how it lent him an extraordinary capacity for emotional silence, blurring the edges of his memory; he was incapable of understanding what had happened, unable to accept it. He held an ineffable memory of his love and clung to it like a drowning man. He would not let it go by moving on. So he stayed. He stayed here, she realised, as if some sort of vigil would hold her memory forever. There lay his flaw, the sense of tragedy dragging him down. That, she thought, was both what attracted her and made her uneasy.

He stared at his hands, one bandaged, one maimed. 'She was mine and I let her fall. I can never forgive myself for that, never forget; could you?'

Something turned around inside her and she averted her gaze in confusion. She felt awkward, felt slowed around him. He did, too. She could see that in the puzzled way he watched the candle flame dancing across his ruined hand. Perhaps he had talked too much and regretted his words. They were more words than he had spoken all day. The confusion and awkwardness left her. He made sense to her now. Surprising herself, she leaned forward and kissed his lips—quickly, before he could flinch away.

'No, perhaps I couldn't,' she answered and felt

253

the confusion coursing through her again. Now that she understood, she could see clearly through his carefully constructed walls and her emotions felt suddenly intrusive.

He listened to the whisper of the storm across the glass and watched her confusion. He felt confessed and guilty. The kiss had ambushed him. It had been a long time without the gift of intimacy; a long time since he had even thought about her death. It was the sudden presence of this woman in his life, he thought. He saw the candlelight reflecting from her cheek: warm light, pretty face, he decided. He wondered at the sudden loss of strangeness between them that had released his words—allowed the kiss.

'You believe that you let her go?' she said at last and looked him in the eye. He nodded and looked accusingly at the stumps of his fingers.

'Is that when you lost these?' She reached forward to hold the fingers.

'Yes,' he said. 'I was lucky to save what I did.'

'You can't be sure, you know.'

'I can,' he replied quietly, slowly releasing his fingers, uncomfortable at the touch.

'You didn't have to choose between the life and death of another. You had no time. Most would say it was a miracle that you even caught her at all. You didn't choose to let her go. It just happened. Things do, you know.'

'I feel . . . it always feels that I could . . . I should have held her.'

'It was too fast, Patrick, impossibly fast.'

'Yes, it was fast but not so fast that I can't remember every detail. I can snap it in my head now,' he said bleakly.

'We can all see, hear and think faster than we can act. You just allow that memory to betray you.'

'Betray me?' He looked genuinely puzzled.

'She may have let you go, Patrick,' Cassie said softly. 'Have you never considered that?'

'No.' He shook his head vigorously.

'Have you never for a moment thought she could have done that for you? Maybe it was her choice to save you? Can't you see that?'

'No. It was not like that.' The words were sharp and hard and final.

She quickly changed the subject. 'When did it happen, Patrick?'

'Twenty-five years ago. A long time ago, Cassie,' he said, holding his hands up in weary resignation.

'Where?' she asked.

'Where?' he looked puzzled at the question. 'Here. On the mountain.' He gestured towards the window. 'On the north face, in winter.'

'In winter?' she said in awe, gazing at the snow-glazed window framing the hidden mountain's distant storm clouds. She looked at Patrick and thought of all that waiting, all that staying in this one place, all that desolation. She had never considered it might have happened on this mountain. It started to make sense. He did not flinch when she leaned forward to kiss him again, nor did he respond. They sat a long time in silence as smoke rose in blue coils above the candle flame and the wind hustled the windowpanes, the touch of the kiss holding on in the quiet. They each knew what the other was thinking but said nothing.

'You never did tell me where you got this,' and this time he didn't pull away when she touched the small gold ornament that swung forward from his neck when he reached for his glass. It turned against her finger to reveal the fragile rim of gold and the blush of the pink and cream inner shell. 'It's very unusual. Beautiful. And rather feminine.' She looked him pointedly in the eye.

'I've had it for years,' he said, a little too guardedly.

'Twenty-five years, perhaps?' she asked. 'No need to answer.' He didn't. When she leaned forward once again, the candle flickering dangerously close to her hair, he reached with a cupped hand to caress her cheek and shield her from the flame. This time he did respond and the surprise registered in her eyes.

18

There was an abrupt, slapping crack as the last support wire lashed against the wall of the hut and the whole building shifted sideways several feet. The hurricane lamp swung in the window, the candle almost guttered and Patrick had gone.

There was a deep, groaning noise of timbers pressed beyond endurance and then the blast of the storm was all around them as the far corner of the ceiling collapsed in a tangle of boards, joists and dust mixed with the snow that swirled around the hut. The candle went out and the hurricane lamp hung drunkenly at the window. Patrick had swung round towards the corner of the hut, even as the floor was still moving, and then in a swift, fluent movement had turned to grab Cassie's shoulder. She was underneath the table with his body across hers as she heard the ceiling collapse and felt a heavy impact shudder around her, heard a grunt of pain as he took the blow, and glimpsed the table part-shattered above her. She wanted to scream, then she just wanted to breathe. His weight was suffocating. As he lay immobile and in the dark beneath the table, she tried to turn her head to see his face but she couldn't move. Struggling to stem her rising panic, she took a few shallow breaths, then held them and listened for his breathing. Was he conscious? Where had he been hit? She felt his chest move against her. He was breathing, at least.

'Patrick?' she whispered and there was no reply. 'Patrick?' she repeated, her voice rising, sharp and strident in the shadows.

'Shush!' came the reply and she felt the panic wash away. 'Quiet. I'm listening.' Chastened by the hard authority in his voice, she listened too. The wind sounds were a constant background clamour. She felt snowflakes melting on her face. In the background there were occasional snapping noises and once there came a long, ripping sound, splitting through the gale.

'That's the roof letting go,' she heard him say. 'Should be okay now.' She felt him move, lifting his protective weight from her. The table shifted and the splintered ends of two wooden joists banged down onto the floor close by. 'Stay here. Don't move,' he commanded although she had no intention of doing so and could not understand his relief at the loss of the roof.

She felt him rise to his knees, grunting with the effort of lifting the table with his back as more ceiling boards slid to the floor. An acrid soot swirled around her and she felt liquid splash against her face and dribble across her lips. She licked at the gritty taste of wine and dust as, with a crash, the table was pushed to one side and Patrick rose tentatively to his feet. She saw the light of the hurricane lamp swinging from its nail in the window frame which had remained intact, and above she could see racing snow and above that empty darkness as she stared, stunned, at the night sky. Raising her head to look down the hut, she saw a crazed jumble of joists and planks laid across the shelter he had built beneath the bed. The room was an oddly twisted rhomboid shape. In the far corner there was no ceiling and she saw snow spurting through a large triangular opening. The roof had been lifted, part-peeled open and then settled precariously back to rest on the twisted walls. The stove still stood, its chimney reaching up through a drunken jumble of twisted ceiling boards. There seemed to be a void above it and she wondered whether the entire roof had ripped off and disappeared into the night.

She saw the harsh white beam of a head torch and heard Patrick moving cautiously through the wreckage. The sound of planks and timbers being moved was audible above the wind and Cassie shivered as she felt its chill bite. If the roof hadn't vanished, the heat certainly had and she began to raise herself slowly from the floor until her head hit the broken table top.

'Stay still!' His voice was sharp and angry.

'I need a jacket. I'm freezing.' More timbers were moved and the light beam flashed from side to side, leaving darkness in its wake. Then she felt the brush of nylon against her hand as he pushed the yellow duvet jacket beneath the table.

'Here. Put this on,' he said abruptly. 'But stay there. I need to sort this out.' With that the torchlight moved away and she struggled into the jacket in the confined space of jumping shadows. From her crouching position she could just reach the base of the hurricane lamp and she lifted it carefully from its nail, lowering it to sit on the floor by her side. Its sodium-yellow light gave the impression of warmth but it also served to blind her from seeing what was happening beyond in the gloomy ruins of the hut.

She watched his torchlight flash in the darkness and listened to the busy sounds of his labour and realised with a start that she felt quite calm. He had known this would happen and he had planned for it.

She wiped dust from her lips and, remembering the kiss, started giggling. When he returned to peer under the table, momentarily blinding her with the head torch, he looked at her with an air of bemused concern.

'It's safe now,' he said at last and reached his hand in to help her out. She saw fresh blood staining the dressing and wondered whether the stitches had ruptured. She passed the hurricane lamp to him and then, ducking forward, crawled out from under the table on her hands and knees. A skim of fresh powder snow coated the floor and as she rose to her feet she saw the white flakes wetting the sides of the stove with tiny spits of steam.

'Yes,' Patrick said following her gaze, 'the hut doesn't look good, does it? Probably be best if it goes altogether. That way at least the walls would 'probably stay put.'

Cassie hurriedly zipped up the duvet jacket and, shivering, pulled the hood over her head.

'Come on,' Patrick said taking her elbow and guiding her past the stove. 'I've made it quite cosy.' He flashed the torch beam in the direction of the bed. The partially collapsed ceiling timbers and joists had been laid across it, protruding out to rest on the storage crates and even as far as the side of the stove. The old tent flysheet was now firmly pinned in place by the weight of wood. He had left a small entrance to one side and pulled back a flap of nylon, indicating that she should crawl inside. Once she had disappeared he threw the glowing torch in after her, blew out the hurricane lamp and then lowered himself feet first into the cramped space beneath the bed.

Cassie watched as his legs appeared in the opening, darkening the interior. She moved over as he twisted himself down into the shelter, pulling the edge of the nylon in behind him. The noise of the wind changed abruptly as Patrick pinned the flysheet securely in place. He rolled onto his side and leaned on an elbow facing her, his head bent to one side beneath the low roof.

'We'll be fine,' he said. 'The stove is full of logs and should last till morning. We have blankets, sleeping bag, hot water in the flasks, food and, of course, cigarettes.' He held up his tobacco pouch with a triumphant grin. 'First thing I looked for.'

'Here,' Cassie said, reaching for his hand. 'Let me look at that.' She pulled the bloodstained bandage towards her and began to slowly unravel the soiled layers.

Patrick threw the blue First Aid bag and a bottle

of alcohol towards her as she delicately lifted the final dressing clear of the wound.

'You think of everything, don't you?' she said, as she unscrewed the bottle.

'I try to,' he replied and gasped as she flooded alcohol across his wounded palm.

'Must be better at this than I thought,' Cassie said, as she wrapped a new bandage tightly around the fresh wound dressing. 'All stitches intact, despite your best efforts. What now?'

'Bedtime,' he replied. 'Get that jacket off and spread it open on top of the sleeping bag. We should be warm enough.'

They were warm, too warm. It wasn't long before they had pushed the sleeping bag and duvet to one side and removed layers of clothing to use as pillows. They lay listening to the thump of another piece of the hut parting company from the rest and watching the candle flame flicker in its tin as gusts swirled around the hollows of the broken building.

Gradually, and without design, they found themselves moving closer. They lay side by side on their stomachs, resting on their elbows, talking quietly. She was conscious of how warm his body felt against hers. She could feel the hard muscle of his thigh against her knee. The warmth moved up and along the length of her thigh, spreading effortlessly, without resistance from her. Years later she would remember that building heat coursing through her and she would stop where she was, staring unfocused, remembering every detail, the feelings inside her as overwhelming as they had been all those years before. When she thought of the hut jerking to one side and the collapsing timbers and the feel of his lips, she would think of what followed, the images clear and vivid and real, and she no longer tried to stop him coming into her from across the years of her memory, the intensity and the heat returning with furious vigour. His curious power would have intimidated her, but she realised as he moved over her that in the time since they had met she had settled into a long anticipation of this moment. She thought she would remain aloof from what they did then. It would be of its time and would stay within that space in her memory and so she could always stand apart from it, but his intensity, his power simply took her control away, all of it, as if he had taken possession of her in all dimensions. There was never any possibility of remaining aloof.

He was on the raw edge of control and she remembered it as clearly as the light in his photographs: the dream-like fumbling of clothes, the heat of the stove washing over her and always his hand moving over her body, feline, held spring-tight by his touch. It was beyond the physical; it was like trapping perfect light.

He used his power carefully for as long as he could, holding himself above her, lips brushing her neck, belly against her belly moving softly, doing it again and again, an ancient dance as he bowed his head to kiss her lips, his tongue tracing the nape of her neck—and always the heat building, their straining bodies slick with moisture.

He made love for a long time, untiring, surprising her, and she wondered at his unremitting control. Sometimes he paused in a soft enlacing, held back waiting, the pressure easing, and she watched the struggle in his eyes as his long, lean body hanging above her regained strength. Sometimes he pulled away to gaze at her, his heaving chest betraying the furiously controlled passion. The sounds of their breathing seemed to swirl around and underneath their urgent quiet motion.

Then he was close by her again, murmuring, and she would feel herself breathless, letting him take her far back within herself, her arm around his waist pulling him to her and her to him. His body pressed fiercely against hers and his eyes gleamed darkly in the candlelight. He reached forward and kissed her and she returned the kiss. She arched into him, small, unintelligible sounds coming from her in a language that he understood completely as his power dissolved and he lay upon her, complete.

She saw then in his trapped expression the way he was: the strength and intensity, the warmth and kindness and the sense of tragedy, clinging like smoke. In his release she watched all the confined emotional power laid bare as, briefly, he no longer had the physicality to contain it.

They lay still and silent and, as their breathing calmed, wondered quite what they had done, why they had allowed it. She knew that from then on he would forever be on the edge of her thoughts, she would feel him somewhere near on the safe, shady periphery of her memory. There were moments when she would think back and believe it ridiculous that she could feel such things about so brief an encounter and she would tell herself it was a claustrophobic reaction to the incessant beating of the storm, that it was nothing more than a few intense days of trapped exposure to each other and a flash of lust. But she knew that she was lying. From then on she never again had the feeling of being alone.

She never spoke of her feelings, and events overtook whatever may have been on his mind and made him silent. It was the atmosphere, she would tell herself, the madness of the *Föhn* storm, not love. It was too short a time for love and she could not bear the thought of being wrong. She thought it might obliterate her.

He became still then, torn-apart silent, and never quite came back to her. He looked up and caught her eye, smiling that hidden smile of his that she had learned to recognise. Neither moved, as if paused in the moment of an unspoken farewell, and they wondered just what had happened there.

It was the silence that woke her: the total absence of sound. No wind noise, no icy slashing at the glass, no sudden cracks of falling timbers, only a deep calm and the soft sound of his breathing, and she remembered it all. They had smoked a while, saying nothing. They had fumbled themselves awkwardly back into half-removed clothes and settled beneath the blankets, sweat cooling between belly and back.

It was dark and, for a moment, she lay confused in the cramped, low-roofed shelter. The candle had guttered in its tin and a draught chilled her back. The blankets had slipped from her and she could feel no heat from the stove. Reaching up, she pushed the ceiling planks to one side, pulling a corner of the flysheet free. Grey light filtered in. She eased herself up through the gap and slowly straightened her legs.

She lifted the plate from the top of the stove and saw a faint amber glow through the white embers. Two split logs and a handful of kindling and wood chips lay in the basket by the stove. She gathered the wood chips and bark in her cupped hands and dropped them through the opening. A puff of ash lifted into the air and the papery bark caught quickly. A lick of flames had burst into life by the time she dropped in the kindling and the logs. She opened the draught vent and flames flared up, sparks hovering around the metal plate as she lowered it in place.

As she zipped the duvet jacket up to her neck she surveyed the battered interior of the hut in the dawn light. Snow coated every surface. Small drifts had formed below the two corners of the hut open to the sky. The table lay broken-legged beside the window. Outside, the snow was high against the glass and a dim glow seeped through a small gap at the top of the pane. The sun was not yet up. The room had a ruined air. She noted the twisted roof, the distorted gaps at each corner, powder snow drifting to settle on the bed, and she listened to the silence. The storm was over.

Cassie picked up the log basket and moved towards the door, surprised that she had not woken him. Then she remembered that he had spent the previous night sleepless, nursing her through the hypothermia. As she eased the door open she blinked and stepped through the deeply banked powder, a wave of snow cresting against her thighs as she waded across the porch. She stopped at the rail and shielded her eyes with her hand as she looked towards the mountain. The frosted rocks of the towers and buttresses were just visible, high on the ridge. As she moved towards the log box at the end of the porch she trailed her hand against the snow-banked window, watching the whiteness cascading to the floor and light flooding into the hut.

She cleared the snow from the box lid, sweeping the basket to and fro until she saw the latch. Releasing the bolt, she pushed the lid up and back in a flurry of disturbed powder, then bent to retrieve the basket from the floor. It took a fraction of a second for her to understand what she was looking at. She had reached in with her free hand, expecting to grasp a log, when she saw the waxen face staring back from beneath its winding sheet of fine snow. The white outlines of shoulders pressed tight against the box sides and hands clasped under a thin frosted veil vaguely registered as a form in her mind as she stared at the face with its raw, gaping eye sockets and the obscene expression of perpetual, horrified surprise.

She didn't register that she was screaming, only that she was moving fast. The lid banged hard down in a burst of snow as she screamed again and stumbled backwards, her boots skidding on the wooden boards as she went down on her knees in the snow. She scrambled towards the hut door, fearful of the horror that lay behind her and, barging into the hut in a welter of snow and sobbing screams, she flung the door closed and crouched on her knees by the stove, swearing repeatedly in fast, panicked gasps, her heart hammering in her chest.

19

The late afternoon sun speared the shattered ribs of the roof, casting fingered shadows across the snow. The hut squatted, twisted and distorted like some forlorn drunk amidst coils of wire, corrugated-iron sheets, ceiling planks and scattered room beams. A thin stream of smoke issued from the black chimney pipe that angled haphazardly up through the stark bones of the roof. From his position on the ridge, Patrick could see down through the gaunt timbers into the hut where familiar objects packed the shelves beneath the open roof. Cooking pans hanging by the stove were half-filled with snow, white-dusted food tins stood in serried ranks above the spot where the table had collapsed beneath the ceiling beams, an almost empty bottle of brandy by its side. The cheerless sight of his shattered home settled gloomily upon him like a passing cloud and he turned away to gaze at the northern glacier.

The glacier weaved its dragon-backed path down into the darkening valley blanched painfully white by the fresh snow, a ribcage of crevasses etched by stony moraines cresting a rise and curling away out of sight. It was a windless, blue-sky day, surprisingly warm. But for the ruined hut and the bandage on his hand, it was difficult to believe the last few days had happened. He stood on the notch in the ridge. The sweep of the north face, streaked with grey, exposed ice where the snow slides had sloughed away, loomed above his left shoulder. He felt its cold chill on the side of his cheek.

On such a day he could feel the mountain, sense its presence around him with its silent purpose, always there, reminding him, awakening the rhythm of his memories. He kept his gaze on the glacier, studying it carefully, searching for the landmarks he knew so well. With the hut gone there was no longer reason to delay. It was time now. She was coming, it was all coming together; he could sense release from that dark place and he had to breathe out long and slowly and let it calm and go.

The sound of shouted voices and laughter came from the hut and he glanced over his shoulder. A cluster of laughing men were bundling a man unceremoniously over the closed lid of the wood locker. For a moment the man held his balance, perched on the edge of the balcony, before the men rushed at him with whoops and shouts and the young guide flew backwards, tripping over the wooden rail and tumbling into the deep snowdrift, disappearing completely in a cloud of powder snow. The group staggered down the steps from the porch, slapping their thighs, bent double with laughter. Patrick smiled at the exuberant energy of the men, even after the hours of hard trail-breaking through deep snow from the village.

They clustered around the twin-wheeled stretcher. Five canvas straps hung from each side of the stretcher rails with steel buckles swinging lightly at their ends. The stiffened corpse lay on the snow at their feet. A dark-coloured canvas tube cocooned the lower torso and legs and a zigzag pattern of white cord stitched up the centre of the canvas from the feet where the lacing opened at the waist. It gave the corpse an insect-like appearance, like some vast larva with its bent elbows and clasped hands like half-budded thoracic wings. Even the blood-blackened eye sockets had the vacant gape of compound insect eyes, immovable, staring blindly at the sun.

Old Peter stood over the corpse, frowning in thought. The crossed arms were still frozen in place, palm against palm, on the chest. Patrick could see the old guide bending to check the lashings for the stretcher, heard his gruff commands and saw the youngest guide floundering in the deep snowdrift beyond the porch as his colleagues hurled snowballs and mocking taunts.

Callum stood awkwardly apart from the group. Even from a distance he had the sulky manner of a spoilt child. There was something wrong with that lad, Patrick thought, as he flexed his bandaged fist, feeling the stitches scratching against the lint and remembering the crunching feel of cartilage as his knuckles had punched hard into Callum's nose. He smiled at the memory of the satisfyingly swift brawl at the hut door only three nights earlier. Watching the surly boy, he wished he could do it again. He disliked the proprietary way he had behaved around Cassie on his return with the guides that afternoon. She had ignored him as if he had simply ceased to exist, been eliminated from her awareness. Patrick had observed their brief interaction, Callum's confusion turning to petulance, and the angry glare he threw at Patrick when he had approached the group. Patrick, for his part, ignored Callum's belligerence as he strode past him to welcome Peter and offer the lads a hot drink, apologising for the lack of wine. He could sense the heated glare aimed at his back and smiled at Peter's quizzical expression and shrug, which quietly let him know that the old guide had as little time for Callum as he did. As they sat on the steps, sipping at bowls of bitter coffee laced with the last of his brandy, Patrick explained how the stay wires had parted and the roof lifted into the night. Peter had earlier walked around the hut with Patrick, stepping over the tangle of wires and broken timber as they examined the concrete base, exposed where the hut had slid and twisted sideways on its foundations. As they drank their coffee, Peter looked reflectively at the man by his side whom he had come to respect and admire over the years.

They quietly discussed the corpse, and Cassie's shocked discovery that morning made Peter chuckle and glance over at the young woman with an amused twinkle in his eye.

'She's a pretty one,' he said as he threw the dregs of his coffee in the snow.

'Yes and difficult too.'

'They are the best,' Peter replied, with a laugh. 'You know they will not repair the hut?' he said and Patrick looked surprised.

'The hut? How so?'

'They are bringing a new one next spring,' Peter replied. 'By helicopter,' he added and grimaced.

'Ah, well,' Patrick said, surveying the ruined building. 'I suppose it had to go one day.'

'It has been a long wait, hasn't it, my friend?' Peter looked directly at Patrick, who nodded his assent.

'Yes, a long time coming,' Patrick murmured.

'What will you do? You can apply to be the warden of the new hut if—'

'No,' Patrick interrupted firmly. 'No, it is time now. I've known it all summer.'

'Do you want my help?' Peter asked and watched with affectionate resignation as his friend shook his head.

'No, this is my work. You know that.'

'Yes, I understand,' the old guide replied and grasped Patrick's shoulder as he levered himself to his feet. 'Come, I must get this lot moving if we are to be down before dark.'

He shouted orders for the stretcher to be retrieved from its hiding place. Cassie had stepped forward protectively as the guides huddled around the open locker, reaching in for the frozen body, but Patrick had put a hand on her elbow and led her to one side. She had angrily pulled her elbow free and strode down off the porch and he had noticed the smirk on Callum's pallid face. He retreated up to the viewing point on the notch, leaving the group to themselves and nodding farewell to Peter as he stalked away.

Patrick watched as Cassie moved to stand solicitously by the corpse. She held herself stiffly, sternly isolated. She turned her face slowly towards Patrick and stared, as if aware of his scrutiny. He tried to read her expression but the distance was too great. Callum, noticing her gaze, stepped towards her to speak and Patrick faintly heard his wheedling tone above the animated banter of the guides. She was silent in response, turning her shoulders away, crouching as if to shield the dead man, keeping her gaze deliberately on Patrick. Callum, more awkward now, lifted both hands at her back, fingers outstretched in frustration, then turned and strode angrily towards

271

where the guides had broken the trail up the drifted path, kicking the snow with evident frustration. The guides pointed and murmured and a ripple of amusement elicited an angry glance.

Peter leaned down towards the corpse, the harsh bark of his gruff voice demanding attention from the instantly silenced guides. Cassie rested a hand on his shoulder and he glanced at her as she spoke softly, then moved aside with a shrug and a nod of approval. She knelt in the snow and laid a hand softly on the man's chest, then reached forward and brushed snow from the ravaged face. Patrick watched as she reached into her jacket, pulled a silk scarf from her neck and lightly covered the hideous, vacant sockets. She reached behind the head, lifting it slightly as she knotted the scarf in place. She rested her hand on the greyed, frozen flesh of his crossed hands for a moment and then pulled the canvas flaps over the head and slowly and precisely laced up the white cords tightly from the waist. He remembered the calm way she had stitched the wound in his hand and he remembered her fury that morning at her discovery of the dead man in the wood locker. Watching her kindness with the scarf made him frown with embarrassment at his own pragmatic approach to the corpse.

The guides, too, had fallen silent. Only Callum, hands in pockets, shoulders hunched angrily, facing the valley, was oblivious to the sudden, attentive hush. Cassie stood and brushed snow from her legs and, with a slight wave of her hand, allowed old Peter to reach for the corpse. As the young guides hurried to lift it with studied care and lower it in place upon the stretcher, Cassie raised her head and looked directly at Patrick. He took a step forward and slowly raised his bandaged hand and she nodded her head and he thought he saw her smile.

The men lashed the blue cocoon tightly to the frame in complete silence as Peter checked each knot with a care not shown during the struggle down the ridge three nights before. Then, with a few abrupt commands, the guides were moving down the track, shepherding the stretcher, Callum striding out ahead of the column, Cassie bringing up the rear.

As the hut dropped out of sight she turned and looked back and Patrick still held his hand up in farewell. It seemed an apologetic gesture, part farewell, part regret. As she stared at the distant figure she saw an avalanche cloud bloom high above him as the summit slopes shook themselves free of the storm fall. It came silently in a boiling white mass, spewing over the headwall of ice-streaked rocks and plunging to the ice fields below. She saw Patrick react as the sound wave eventually reached him and at that moment she stepped away down the path. She turned the first corner and was gone.

He spun around as the avalanche swept across the bergschrund, fanning over the glacier, and slowly let his hand drop to his side. She had gone. He lowered himself into a squatting position and stared ruefully at the distant glacier. A chill wind began to rise from the valley floor, sweeping up the glacier until it washed the cigarette smoke away from his cheek and ruffled his hair. He glanced towards the hut where the chimney smoke now streamed away at forty-five degrees. The skies remained cloudless. Shadows slid across the broken frame of the building. Night was coming on.

He rose, flicked the cigarette into the snow and strode down towards the hut. It was time, at last, to move. Peter had told him what he had already expected. The hut would not be repaired, not this year or next. A new hut would be flown in, slung beneath a helicopter. In the tavern the young guides had been galvanised at the news of a bigger, more prosperous hut. More clients to guide, they reasoned. More bodies to bring down, Peter retorted gruffly, but they ignored him. People always died in the mountains—not guides—they chorused and Peter looked at them pityingly. They would make good money; no more struggle for work in the winter to make ends meet; the tourists would flock to the village—the room hummed with excited chatter as ever more fanciful theories surged around the tavern. The new hut would be the making of them, they predicted confidently, and Peter shrugged his shoulders and muttered darkly. 'More girls,' the youngest cried and his ears were cuffed to the ribald taunts of his drinking companions and the amusement of the barmaid. His face flushed crimson and her smile silenced him instantly.

The youngster had moved to sit beside Peter and suggested that there would be more use for his new stretcher, with all the extra bodies to recover, and he would be rich and Peter had grunted and stumped away to another table and shouted for beer. He had sat morosely, both hands around the foaming glass, a bearish, scowling presence that even the brash youngster knew not to disturb.

Peter knew the real worth of the wheeled stretcher. Like its inventor it was an old, unfashionable idea. Helicopters would render them both useless. The beer-fuddled youngster was being kind or stupid—likely both.

The old hut would be cleared at the end of the season, he had told Patrick as they finished their coffee. By helicopter, he added a little bitterly, and both of them sat quietly in the sun and thought of all the loads they had carried so painfully up to the remote security of the hut.

As Patrick stepped up onto the porch and pushed the door ajar he knew with a sinking heart that this would be the last night he would spend in the hut that had taken up twenty-five years of his life. The rucksack that he had packed earlier that morning was propped against the steps. Stepping into the hut and sweeping ceiling joists from his path, he pushed the table top onto its side and reached down for the box of photographs, fossils and bones and carried it outside. When he stepped back inside he stood amidst the jumble of possessions and broken wooden timbers and looked slowly around the remnants of his home. He studied the shelves lined with tins and pots, the cooking utensils stored close to the stove and the temporary shelter he had built beneath the bed. He selected a hunk of hard cheese, its waxy rind dusted with snow, and placed it in his rucksack. He also packed the slim bottle of brandy that Peter had surreptitiously handed him when his men hadn't been looking.

The weather settled and the sky cleared, heralding a cold night to come, but there was no need for the shelter any more. He reached beneath the tent awning, pulled out his sleeping bag and flung it into the doorway. One of the mattresses was soon dragged from beneath the bed and he cleared space for it on the floor, brushing the table and ceiling boards to one side with his leg. He dropped splintered shelves and broken joists into the stove until no more would fit and then replaced the lid with a metallic clang. He found the hurricane lamp still hanging from its nail by the window and, hefting its weight in his hand, he guessed that she had filled it that morning. A search of the shelves turned up an assortment of candles, two cigarette lighters and his store of tobacco and papers. As he sat on the mattress rolling a cigarette he glanced around at the ruins of the hut; a forlorn, abandoned mess of broken memories.

Only then did he remember the wooden storage chests he had used to pin down the tent flysheet. Roughly flinging the flysheet and the ceiling planks to one side, he pulled free the nearest of the wooden boxes and lifted the hinged lid. Crouching on his knees, he quickly sifted through the contents until he found what he wanted—a small wooden case, the name and crest of some long-finished wine stencilled into the lid and sides, lay part-hidden by tattered paperback books. He placed the old wine case on the mattress with reverent care and slowly eased the wooden lid free. Reaching in, he carefully lifted out a soft canvas bag and pulled the draw cord open. Inside, two cameras nestled in tissue paper within their lidless cardboard boxes and four lenses in their padded leather cases lay alongside. He held one camera in his hand, turning it in the softening evening light, the memories flooding back to him. The M4-series Leica, classic black body and stainless steel showing the years of use: scuffed corners, knurled dials worn by his thumbs and fingers over time, the V-shaped dent on the back cover where his ice axe had been carelessly dropped.

'A lifetime investment in perfect photography,' he quoted aloud, remembering the old advertising slogan. Then he carefully settled it back into its cushion of tissue paper. He tightened the draw cord and carried the bag outside, placing it in the box which contained the photographs and fossils. The lid closed snugly on the cameras and he slid the wooden peg through the hasp to lock it in place.

The shadows lengthened steadily across the snow. Occasional flurries of powder drifted down to dust his hair and shoulders as a breeze ghosted through the skeletal roof. He would set off in the early morning, four o'clock at the latest, he decided, and lit the cigarette. There was little more than an hour of light left in the day. He rose and leaned against the door jamb, looking at the tracks churned in the deep snow. With luck they should be in the village before nightfall.

20

Cassie walked behind the stretcher, watching as it bounced and juddered over the deeply posted path that the guides had laboriously broken through the storm drifts. Only as they approached the village nestled against the side of the valley did the going improve and she no longer felt the urge to reach out towards the cocooned body to steady it. Occasionally, Peter had thrown her a reassuring look and ordered a decorous silence from the guides as the sight of the twinkling lights in the houses had revived their boisterous spirits. She had smiled her thanks for the old man's thoughtfulness. Beyond him, she saw Callum striding forcefully ahead, a good two hundred yards beyond the stretcher party, and the smile died on her lips.

She thought of the name. Karl. His name was Karl. It was important to know his name, she thought, as her gaze lingered on the mummified shape on the stretcher. She thought of the moment of shock when she had opened the locker and gazed numbly at the eyeless glare of the corpse, the crashing noise of the door as she had blundered into the hut on her knees, Patrick's perplexed expression as she had screamed and cursed and gasped for breath by the stove, her arm pointing helplessly out to the porch. As she had regained some control she had watched as Patrick had wordlessly pulled himself from the shelter and padded out to the porch. The lid of the locker had shut with a sharp, woody thud, making her flinch, and he had returned and sat on the storage chests. The argument had been short and furious and pointless. *It was the best place for him,* was all that he would say and his dry pragmatism only drove her to a greater fury. *He didn't care, he didn't care,* she had yelled again and again. *He was dead, there was no more to care about,* he replied and she swore again and shook her head.

A taut silence had followed. Patrick had shrugged and rolled a cigarette and peered around the shattered interior with studied detachment. She had brushed the snow from her legs, calmed herself with deep breaths, then slowly walked out onto the porch and faced the wood locker. When she tentatively lifted the lid she kept her gaze firmly averted from the face. She reached to touch one of the pallid, icy hands, pausing the moment before contact, half-expecting to be abruptly grabbed in a deathly grip, echoes of childhood nightmares haunting her mind. It was hard, wooden, a lifeless, grey solidity.

She could feel her cheeks tightening, lips pinched in a constantly twitching wince, as she pulled at the ice-stiffened zippers on the jacket pockets. They were empty. Pressing the torso gently, she felt delicately in the inner pockets. It was a curiously intimate search and gradually her revulsion subsided. At last, a sharply outlined edge pressed against her fingertips. As she eased the chest zipper down, lifting a stiffened elbow, ice crackled through the nylon teeth, spitting a fine spray of shards onto the bright red wool of his sweater. With the nervous apprehension of someone undressing a sleeping stranger, she meticulously brushed the wool clear, resisting the urge to murmur an apology. At last she could peel aside the hem of the jacket and reach into a deep chest pocket, feeling the hard, rectangular edge of a booklet and, lower still, the bulge of a leather pouch.

She opened the passport with exaggerated care, as if it might snap and crumble to dust in her hands. The colour photograph showed a smiling face, unusually for a passport, framed by tousled blond hair, a strong jawline, prominent cheekbones and a dominant nose. Handsome, she thought, and glanced nervously at the face she had so studiously avoided. The shock of the obscene gaping sockets made her inhale sharply and step back, almost dropping the passport. She forced herself to study the waxy, ashen face and glance at the passport photograph.

'Karl Brandler. German, eh?' She spoke quietly, addressing the corpse. 'Well, then,' she said looking at the body, 'now we know who you are, Karl.'

She opened the pouch. There were a few credit cards in leather sleeves, a sheaf of notes held in the middle by a brass Spanish clip which she folded to one side, and behind a small plastic window a creased and faded colour photograph. Karl stood head and shoulders above the dark-haired woman, bending slightly as if to kiss her, and she looked back across her shoulder at him. Cassie looked at Karl staring blindly at the porch ceiling, a gauzy drift of snow settling on his face, and placed her hand on his.

'We'll take you home, Karl. We'll take you home,' she whispered.

As she lowered the lid of the locker she made a last check that all the zips and pockets were closed, the hands back in position on the chest, the shadows of the closing lid throwing his ravaged face into darkness. By the time she walked slowly back into the hut the pouch and passport were safe in her pocket. She said nothing to Patrick. He knew that she had returned to the locker and, apart from a quizzical glance, he asked nothing.

She sat outside in the sun, sipping coffee, thinking about Karl, thinking about Patrick; an oddly pensive grief. She knew little about Karl Brandler except that he was German and had a lady in his life. There had been something sad about the happiness frozen into that small colour print. Patrick? She knew a lot now about Patrick. And, she thought ruefully, she knew nothing.

It was the eyes. In Karl it was the absence of them; a sight she would never erase from her memory. In Patrick it was their unforgettable electric quality. His eyes were uncommon, forcefully individual. He was quite unaware of their hypnotic effect. He had that unnerving habit of staring into your face as if you were the only soul that he had ever encountered. Most people looked away, unable to hold his gaze. It must be strange, she thought, for so many people to look away from you. She found at first that she could not look long into his eyes and, when she averted her gaze, she noticed not a sense of triumph in him but a barely masked loss, a vague air of bereavement. It was the loss felt by those who have spent too much of their lives by themselves and when she recognised this she forced herself to hold his gaze. When he spoke it was with that same intently uncivil directness. His enforced isolation seemed to have stripped him of the sense of conversation as most people understood it and that, too, was why they looked away.

Yet when he looked at her she felt unsettled. Of course it was his eyes: the eyes, then his voice, measured and curt at the same time, then the easy way his body moved: the poise and the air of loneliness. All of it added up to her being changed forever. He drew her in and rearranged her and felled her barriers in old, subliminal, whispered ways. That is where it began. It began with his eyes upon hers.

After only a few seconds he had drawn her in and he didn't even know it. And she would always see him clearly down through the passing years, down through the flow of her memory, when she remembered his eyes: blue-grey eyes, always looking for the light, that took her aback and drew her in, and that flooding sensation of bubbles rising through her that made her smile. She would remember his eyes all down the years long, long after he had died.

She was jolted from her thoughts by a cheerful shout in the distance and, looking up, she saw several figures coming towards the little party. Already the lights in the village were brighter and when she glanced back only the summits were bathed in the last soft rosy light of the setting sun. She saw Callum march rudely past the figures with a curtly dismissive gesture of his arm in their direction. The figures paused and stared at his retreating back, their dislike apparent, before responding to the halloos and yells of the guides and striding towards them.

Later that evening Cassie found Peter in the tavern, nursing a beer by the fire. She placed the passport and the pouch on the table by his glass.

'His name is Karl Brandler,' she said, as the guide reached for the passport. 'I meant to give these to you at the hut.'

'Thank you. We were having problems with identifying him. He was alone, didn't stay here, just went straight up to the mountain, so there was no record of him.'

'Well, you have him now,' Cassie smiled. 'And thank you for today, for understanding . . .'

'No, no. I should thank you,' Peter held up his glass in a mock toast. 'We see too much of these things,' he said, pausing, searching for the right words. 'Sometimes we lose our respect. You showed us how to regain it.'

'What will happen now?' Cassie asked and Peter shrugged eloquently.

'Paperwork for us, family informed, if he has any, of course—and then it is in the hands of the authorities, the police, that sort of thing.' Cassie listened and nodded.

'What about Patrick? Why did he not come down with us? What will happen to him?'

Peter told her about the helicopter in the spring and the plans for the hut.

'He is leaving,' he added. 'In a few days, I expect.'

'Leaving? Then why didn't he come down with us?'

'He has some things to do first, then he will be coming down.'

'Do? What is there to do up there now?'

'He has been there a long time.'

'Twenty-five years,' Cassie interjected and Peter looked at her thoughtfully.

'Yes, twenty-five years. A long time, eh?' He took a deep draught of his beer and wiped the foam from his lips. 'He will come down in his own time, I think.'

The bunkroom in the basement of the tavern was stiflingly hot and noisy, the boiler intermittently roaring into life, pipe-work clanging and the ancient timbers of the tavern creaking and groaning. Sleep was impossible and Cassie swung her legs off the bunk and switched on the light. The room was austere, bare and functional and the bright, whitewashed walls made her blink in the sudden light. There were no others to disturb. Callum had gone soon after arriving at the village, still angry. He would always be angry, Cassie thought, as she watched him pack his rucksack with abrupt, almost violent force. She watched as he marched through the picturesque old village towards where the jarringly modern bus had stopped. There was no backward glance, no wave of the hand and she was glad of it.

It took only a few moments to pack her rucksack with a few essentials and the bottle of brandy that she had purchased from the barmaid after Peter had left the tavern. She turned, flicked the light switch and the room plunged into darkness as she groped for the door handle. As she stepped outside in the early morning dark her eyes slowly adjusted after the brightness of the room. She pulled the door shut, pressed her thumb and forefinger to each eye, then blinked and looked around, testing her vision. There was the same flickering sensation around her, an unfocused, washed-out colour. She took a few cautious steps out from beneath the arched basement doorway and began to climb up the stone steps leading to the road. Stepping onto the street, her eyes were drawn to the sky and she stopped mid-stride and gasped.

The night sky was moving. Cassie swayed forward onto her partially raised foot, tripped and almost fell. As she regained her balance, her eyes

284

still fixed on the sky, she was overcome with a feeling of dizziness. A feeling of emptiness swept over her, a sort of breathless unsteadiness as if she would fall at any moment. The colours waving across the heavens induced a giddy vertigo and for a moment she continued to stumble into the road and she was forced to look away.

She was staring up the valley northwards towards where they had descended from the hut. The ghostly outline of the peak, shimmering in the air, seemed to float above its anchoring ridge lines, back-lit as it was by a mesmeric light-show drifting across the sky. Beneath it, a wash of moonlight made the mountain appear to be rising from a sea of silvered waves.

'Pretty, eh?' Peter's voice made her jump and she glanced round to see the old guide standing by the front door of the tavern.

'What is this? What's happening to the sky? What does it mean?' Cassie said, hearing a tremor in her voice.

'Mean?' He smiled and stepped towards her. 'It doesn't mean anything, unless of course you believe in old wives' tales, in which case those are lost spirits making their way to heaven.'

'Spirits?' Cassie whispered as she gazed at the effervescent sky. Brilliant pinpricks of starlight flickered behind the streaming curtains of lights.

'Murdered souls, they say,' Peter added quietly and Cassie realised he, too, was bewitched by the sight. 'They say that the lights are their torches leading them away from the world. If you listen, it is said that you can hear their laments.'

Cassie could hear nothing. Instead she felt herself enveloped by a gentle soundless tranquillity, a profound stillness and a feeling of helpless, surrendered vulnerability. She watched the colours pulsing like deep inhalations.

'Gorgeous,' she whispered. 'So beautiful . . .'

'Yes—and rare,' Peter replied softly. 'I've only seen it once before, many years ago . . .' He paused and watched the sky thoughtfully. 'And again, it was after a great storm,' he added.

'What's happening?' Cassie asked, unable to drag her eyes away from the heavenly vision.

'The Northern Lights, Aurora Borealis. I think that is their real name,' Peter said and lit a cheroot, the flare of the match momentarily switching off the light display. Cassie blinked and watched as the pastel light slowly bled back into vision.

'But we are not in the north.' She glanced at the bright orange ember of Peter's cheroot and saw him nodding agreement. 'I thought you needed to be in the Arctic to see them.'

'Well, we're seeing them now and I've seen them before. Don't ask me why. Just enjoy them while they last. Here.' He offered her a silver hip flask and she took a swig, coughing as the peach schnapps burnt her throat. 'It is not often you see them twice in a lifetime, I can tell you.' He smiled as she handed back the flask. 'Maybe it's a good omen, eh? Maybe the lads are right after all and good things will happen to us now.'

As he said it there came a distant low whistle and then a shout and one by one doors and windows swung open and heads leaned out to stare at the sky. Soon figures were crowding into the street, their chattering voices dying to silence as they gazed awestruck at the heavens. Within a short

286

time a delighted crowd had spilt out onto the street as people whispered and pointed and offered drinks to each other, rarely turning their heads from the flamboyant sky.

'Going somewhere?' Peter nodded at her rucksack and raised his eyebrows. 'A bit early, isn't it?' he challenged and his cheroot glowed bright as he inhaled, keeping an amused and speculative gaze on her upturned face.

Cassie tore her eyes reluctantly from the sky and turned to stare at the grizzled old guide, feeling her face flush hot and red, glad of the cover of the night.

'Oh, this,' she shrugged the rucksack nonchalantly. 'Couldn't sleep. Thought I'd go for a walk.'

'A walk?' Peter chuckled. 'At three in the morning? Where would you go at this time?'

'As I said, I couldn't sleep ... and it's a full moon, so I thought I would walk and came outside and then I saw this ...' she paused. 'You know, it's odd but I got the feeling that I knew this was happening ... it drew me outside ...' She tailed off and fidgeted with the hip-belt on her rucksack.

'Calling you?'

'Yes. Sounds silly, doesn't it?'

'There are lots of things we cannot explain.' Peter replied quietly. 'Lots of things we don't need to explain. You see all these people?' he said, indicating the milling crowd. 'They will talk of it for weeks. Everyone will have their own theory. But it's the old ideas that people will believe, the ones they have heard since childhood, the stories of the spirits, the stories that they want to hear because they are comforted by them, because they want them to be true.'

'I don't think they are spirits. I wasn't being called. It was just a feeling . . .'

'And what is wrong with feelings, eh?' He took a swig from the flask and glanced sideways at her. 'These people know it is not true, but in the end—well, they are villagers and the stories are very old, so they say they believe them. Village life is like that. Things are held up to be eternal and true only because people want them to be so. You can't resent the inevitable. It is just the way they are. Anyway, you haven't answered my question. Where were you planning to walk?'

'Oh, anywhere . . .' Cassie replied, feeling flustered under his gaze. 'Up there maybe.' She nodded towards the distant, floating peak. 'The moon is bright, the track will be firm, it would be nice to—'

'—Meet Patrick again?' Peter interrupted and Cassie blushed. 'I see your man has left the village,' he said before she could answer.

'My man?'

'Callum. That is his name, isn't it?'

'Oh, yes, Callum. Yes, he has gone . . . and no, he isn't my man,' she said firmly, with a hint of anger that only made Peter's smile widen.

'Well, we could all see that.'

'And what else could you all see, Peter?' she said with asperity, her face reddening.

'That you liked Patrick and that he liked you,' he said with infuriating equanimity. 'He liked you a lot,' he added.

'You said you have seen these lights before, a long time ago? How long?' She abruptly changed the subject.

'The lights? Oh, a long time ago, more than twenty years. It was in the winter—'

'After a big storm, like the one we just had?' Cassie cut in.

'Yes, after a storm.'

'Twenty-five years ago?' she said, challenging him to contradict her.

His smile faded as he studied her gravely. 'Yes, it was twenty-five years ago. What of it?'

'He told me about the storm. He told me what happened.' Cassie bowed her head and then raised it to look at the distant peak. 'He's up there alone and it's happening again. He's alone,' she said and, to her chagrin, her eyes began to fill. She brushed angrily at them and pursed her lips. 'I was going. I am going . . .' she corrected herself, '. . . to thank him. I have a present for him.' She looked at Peter, who nodded and flicked his glowing stub into the snow.

'Well now, he has been talking, hasn't he?' Peter shrugged his jacket tightly around his shoulders and pulled the zipper to his neck. 'Come to think of it, it is a nice night for a walk. Shall we go?' He offered his elbow and Cassie hesitated. 'It's alright. I'll just see you out of the village, make sure you're on the right track. Can be tricky on nights like this, you know, all these spirits around.'

Cassie linked her arm through his and they walked through the jostling crowd. Soon the village lay twinkling below them and they crunched slowly up the track, snow crystals squeaking beneath their boots. They didn't speak and Cassie felt saddened when at last Peter stopped. He had walked much further than he had promised— almost three-quarters of the distance to the hut.

They stood quietly, as they watched the weakening light display in the northern sky. Layered banners of pale sea green and watered blue pigments still quivered across the sky, but with each hour they had steadily faded to a faint colour wash as if the pulse of the earth was slowing, the exhalations drawing to a close, the light weakly shifting between bone-hard moonlight and the dying auroral colours. It was like a bereavement.

The dazzling pinpricks of the stars glinted with diamond ferocity, a shower of sparks swirling up into the dark night sky far above a blazing fire. The full moon gave the mountains a spectral appearance. Ice crunched beneath their boots as they swayed silently, heads back, watching the sky. Away to the east a faint sky-blue line of dawn showed beneath the inky edge of night.

'I'll leave you now,' Peter said. 'I have work to do.'

'Thank you, Peter.' Cassie gave him a hesitant hug and he patted her back, then pushed her away and held her at arm's length.

'Be careful with your heart,' he said. 'Be careful with his. Perhaps it is too damaged. Perhaps we all are, eh?' he said and, despite the levity, she sensed the sadness in his tone. Even as she lifted a hand in farewell he had already turned and was striding quickly down into the darkened valley.

21

Darkness seeped around the hut like a flooding night tide. Patrick craned his neck to peer out of the door at the snowy peak rearing far above him. The last wash of alpenglow tinged the underbellies of the high, streaming clouds as inky shadows clawed the summit rocks. In a moment he had made up his mind and, rising to his feet, he grabbed the rucksack and swung it onto his shoulders. Gripping the edge of the mattress in one hand and draping the sleeping bag across his shoulders with the other, he trudged up to the notch on the ridge. Once there, he flung the mattress onto the snow, propping one end up against the rocks so that he could lie facing the mountain.

By the time the blue flame of the gas stove was flaring noisily under the pan he was settled into his sleeping bag and the final vestiges of sunlight had left the summit. He lay back watching as darkness swallowed the mountain. He smoked the last of his cigarette and thought of the coming day with a chill of apprehension. He realised that he would miss the blue skies and endless horizons and the long light of these mountains though the years since her passing had been almost too much to bear. The thought struck him that he had always lived with her absence; she clung to him still, a solitary fading scent in his memory. Perhaps tomorrow she would leave him. As he pulled the hood of his sleeping bag over his head and turned his back against the sapping wind slipping silently up from the glacier, he knew it to be a forlorn hope. His mind numbing with the stupefaction of sleep, he thought of her again as he drifted into lightlessness.

He dreamt he was floating on air, a gliding bird sailing above the face of the world. On either side stretched vast numbers of birds, wings fixed in soaring flight, ghosting across the trackless heights. It was an exquisite thing to be part of, he thought, beautifully inexplicable, seeking the edge of the world. He was in a hallowed place.

Then the dream darkened and, try as he might, he could not pull himself back to the heady lightness of flight. The dark shadow of a raven swept across his memory and he flinched at the carrion odour and its baleful shrieking cry, talons extended, reaching for his eyes. Gaping, bloodied eye sockets jumped into his sight, then he felt the raking talons and its weight settling upon his shoulder. He struggled and twisted, moaning as he saw again the deathly pallor of her stricken face. She mouthed inaudible words, dislocated, accusatory sounds and her sorrow flowed around him. The harbinger still squatted on his shoulder, fixing him with its depthless stare from lidless eyes before sweeping away across a winter's sky.

Shuddering and crying out, he thrashed in the silken cocoon of his bag, trying to escape the feeling of being stalked. He had fallen into a dream so enfolding that he could no longer resist it. On the edge of fragile sleep he jerked awake to the sound of the lights in the sky. He snatched at the drawcord of the bag in panicked haste, desperate to escape the nightmare. As his head emerged into the chill air he drew in hurried breaths, trying to calm his racing heart. The dreams had plagued him for so many years, yet he was still shocked that they had caught him out again. He had thought that he knew the symptoms, knew when they were coming and he would prepare and somehow he could lessen their impact, cut them off before they started, but this one had slipped under his guard and caught him fully exposed.

He felt his chest heaving as if he had run a hundred yards, a chilling sweat running down his spine. When he pulled his fingers away from his eyes he saw them trembling like a drunk's and forced them into painfully clenched fists. As he stared at his hands he noticed the soft play of the light and slowly raised his eyes to the night sky. He was silent for a moment as the light-show swept across the stars. It was happening again, he thought; he must still be in the dream, but the pain of fingernails biting into a fisted palm told him otherwise. The colours wafting across the sky sent him lurching back twenty-five years as if everything had happened only a moment ago.

He gazed at the sky, trying to marshal his thoughts and suppress the hysteria rising like sour bile in his throat. *How could he dream of such things and then wake to see them happening again?* He glanced around, bewildered. The hut still squatted amidst the dancing shadows as moon and starlight lit the ribcage of its roof. Everything was as it had been and yet he had this unanchored feeling, this awful lightness, the tugging sensation as if he were a party balloon pulling at the hand of a child. He had the terrible suspicion that the child would let go; that he would be released, blown

293

away, tumbling, swept on an unceasing current.

The blown-away feeling always surprised him. Over the years he had come to recognise the signs and could prepare in small ways; hold on to something, secure himself. It started with a quiet sense of desperation, a tendency to panic which, even if swiftly repressed, left him with a feeling of giddy unsteadiness as if at any moment he might be loosened and set adrift, floundering and rolling. At times the raw, windswept sensation eased, at times it kept coming on. When the skies were vast and the horizons limitless he knew he would be overwhelmed.

Now the feeling had come again, the haunting emptiness, and his mind drifted back down the long river of his memories to the beginning and he was alone again on the mountain. This time it was so strong it was as if he were being swept along on the flood and staring at the colour-washed sky just made the torrent carry him on faster and faster, without hope of holding on.

He knew he was in the grip of something incomprehensible. He glanced at the veils of light and memories surged up through him, filling his mind with images—her falling noiselessly away, the shattered thigh bone and her grey, frozen skin and then the faces came to him, all the dead people rolling like river-borne leaves through his mind. He had seen too many corpses down the years and he told himself it was of no import yet the sight of them made so much sadness engulf him that he feared he couldn't contain it. He quailed at the thought that the world could see his fear, despite his effort to show nothing at all, to show cold control.

As the warden, he had seen too many shattered corpses carried past the hut, some he even failed to save from dying, and as they went past the blowing-away feeling would sweep through him and he would have to hold on hard.

In death, he noticed, people shrank. They looked small—withered, diminished: the adults like sad, broken children, the children like shattered dolls. They had the same unnerving, empty-eyed stare. The violence of their deaths reduced them as they died and shrank away from life. They diminished him too.

He remembered that morning with Cassie screaming and the fury in her eyes because she had seen the dead man. She hadn't held on to anything, had not anchored herself inside, and she had rounded on him, furious and scared. She had not understood that he had locked himself away and let her fury wash over him.

He shook away the train of thoughts and stared angrily at the pulsing sky, wondering how he had let himself be caught out so easily. He had always had an affinity for danger. Few landscapes were more threatening than steep mountainsides. Yet he had always felt that he could smell danger before he saw it. At the first hint he would inhale slow and deep, tasting the adrenaline odour, the slight acidity in his mouth. A subtle scent, easily ignored, but he had learned to recognise it.

It all added up: the nervous air, the suddenly stilled birdsong, the uncanny quiet, normality suddenly and inexplicably strange, and he would know, grow tense and go still: a fragile anxiety energised by a flush of fear; then he knew something was about to happen. If he sensed things were about to go wrong they usually did. He had learned to respect his senses. He was proud of that acquired skill and yet now he seemed to have lost it.

Sometimes he could feel bitterness swirl within him at the memory of the mountain and what it had taken. He had played the game, relished the fear and anticipation, stepped out on the great faces and airy ridgelines and he had loved it all for the strength it gave him. Like capturing light and trapping words, there was an elusiveness about the mountains that drew him in, drew him back again despite knowing at some point he might face that killing storm. Yet he had never anticipated such a cost.

After she had fallen he had stayed strong, fought well and hard, but he had always known there would come a time the fight was over and he would let go and let death accept him. The euphoria of that moment of release, that long resignation, still lived with him.

He had wanted to break the habit of fighting and die in calmness. His breath came despite himself. Sleep would quickly, painlessly destroy his will, cease all striving, make him accept the time when his breath should stop. Death would ease inaudibly into his torpid coma.

But he had seen the glory of that auroral night and it had driven all ideas of death and surrender from his mind as he stared in mute wonder at the heavens. He had heard the pulsating lights, listened to them float down the night sky. He was certain of this—a weak beat, the faintest murmur sensed on the edge of his dying consciousness. It had flicked his frozen eyelids open and he had gazed at the slow ebb and throb of pastel colour through the snow shroud entombing him on the ledge. Then he had breathed again.

He remembered watching the leaching sky, crouched motionless on the ledge, awed by the avalanche's reprieve. It was an animal state, a form of courage all of its own, a wild nakedness as he stared hopefully upwards to see the sun slowly bleach the darkness from the edge of the horizon, a soft, pale blue line lifting steadily above the retreating black thread of night. And he knew then that he would live.

And now he sat again beneath the glowing heavens, amazed that twenty-five years had swept so swiftly by. He seemed now to be returning haunted from a long night of passing lives, left half-consoled, alone again—and always aware of the sensation that there was a face in the crowd looking out at him; a face that no one noticed, but which was always there, watching him, always waiting. Perhaps it was her, waiting for him down all these years. He watched back, peering at the sky, calling silently to her. He found that he was crying.

He took a deep breath, crushing it deep into a place where he still mourned her and all that had been lost. He knew that it had to be locked away where it could not destroy him—somewhere he always wept. With the passing of time there would come a day when he would no longer mourn—or not as relentlessly—when the details of her face would fade, when he could no longer suddenly be cut adrift at the recollection of her name.

At these times when he struggled to recover from the cold flood of sorrow, he told himself, that in time it would pass. But how much time? Nothing erodes grief like time. There is no reasoning with it. It wears away slowly like the face on a coin. Yet even then he knew that as time softened the features and the image faded, melting back into the worn metal, there would always be her ghostly face just visible, from far back in time. Grief hanging like a shroud outlasts us all.

He had let the years drift by, welcomed the balm of time's distance, numbed, silent, trying to forget, heart blown, locked in an empty space—a place he had made where he could live a life of sorts, the future only bounded by the day that would come, that had now come. He had given no thought to what would happen afterwards. He was losing his place, his sorted life.

Sometimes, in feeble defiance, a craven self-protection, he came to think of love as a terrible mistake, the worst disillusionment. It was pity, he knew that, but some days he needed that quiet condolence. He needed to be able to crush it out of existence.

How many hours he lay staring at the fading light-show he did not know. It seemed he was trapped within an endless film of memories as the colours faded slowly and the heavens returned to a placid scatter of diamonds against the black ink of space.

In the first grey light of morning he found himself numbly staring at the pale edge of the sky that heralded sunrise and warmth and the promise of another day. He struggled stiffly to his knees and swung the rucksack onto his shoulders. He discarded the sleeping bag on the snow, kicking a few rocks over it to weight it down.

He paused a moment, trying to force the memory of the night from his mind but the sadness was deep and no thoughts came to drive it away. He turned and walked away, wordless, without direction. His path took him down from the notch to the glacier's edge. The pallid dawn cast a dead, flat light across the glacier as he jumped lightly from the rocky bank to land knee-deep on the snow-covered ice. Distance was difficult to judge and the telltale creases in the snow revealing hidden crevasses were impossible to detect. He carelessly forged a path to the centre of the glacier, ploughing a knee-deep wave through the layers of storm snow, then turned and headed along the crest of the glacier as it curled towards the distant valley.

As the sun rose, lifting serenely above the surrounding peaks, the grey light evaporated and suddenly he saw the first of the cairns built early that spring come into sharp relief. A faint snow-rounded hummock that only moments before had been invisible threw a weak shadow across the snow. He could just make out the silhouette of the next cairn three hundred feet further down the crest of the glacier. As he passed each marker he counted off the years, as he had always done. Twenty-five times they had been re-built and repaired when the winter snows had melted.

As he lost height the snow cover thinned and patches of bare, gritty ice began to show through. Rocks and boulders carried along by the flow formed distinct banded lines across the humped spine of the ice, and with the abundance of building material the cairns became more elaborate constructions, taller and more distinct. The mounds of rocks were stacked shoulder-high with splintered canes poking from their tops. Sun-faded strips of nylon fluttered with incongruous gaiety in the early morning breeze. They reminded him of prayer flags.

Rivulets of water coursed, vein-like, across the surface of the glacier, cutting clean, blue-green ice channels through the granular surface ice. His boots crunched loudly as he followed the tributaries until they melded together and a single channel, deep and fast-flowing, surged alongside and the gurgling sluice of the water drowned the sound of his boots. He followed the stream as it contoured across the glacier, swept around the base of a huge boulder and gathered speed as the ice steepened in its fall towards the valley.

A short distance beyond the boulder the sound of the water became a steady, thudding roar and he slowed his pace until he came to the *moulins,* a circular sink hole of water-smoothed blue ice dropping vertiginously into the depths of the glacier. Several tributaries spewed into the hole from converging channels to thunder in a solid, heavy plume of white water. Above the boom of the waterfall he could hear the occasional heavy thump deep below his feet and the steady rock-gouging grind of the glacier.

Leaning forwards, he peered into the deep, glistening shaft cutting down into darkness, watching the light blue ice darken in colour until, leaning as far out as he dared, it became a sinister, inky well. He thought of all the years he had crouched besides this *moulins,* his thoughts as dark as the well below, savouring the hypnotic draw of the falling water tugging insistently at his eyes, urging him to take a step forward. Every year it had been harder to resist its call and he had normally broken away from the path of the channel to avoid it.

Now he stood on its rim, staring intently into the depths. He thought of the water deep beneath his feet, a frigid Styx, a black river surging relentlessly towards the snout of the glacier. At intervals he could see the edges of stones and larger boulders protruding from the sleek ice walls. Carried down from where they had fallen from the mountain decades earlier, they now clung precariously to the ice on their slow journey to the valley. As he watched, a man-sized rock crackled free from the ice and tumbled into the shaft, ricocheting from the walls with dull, thudding echoes.

Patrick stepped back from the edge and raised his eyes to the mountain. The skirts of the peak lifted from the pristine snow of the glacier in a sweep of grey, corrugated, rock-pitted ice. He narrowed his eyes as he followed the fall-line up the ice field to where it licked against the rocks of the headwall until he spotted the distinct angular shape jutting out over the sweep of the wall. He

301

turned to peer down the receding bulge of the glacier until he found what he was looking for. At the narrowest point of the distant snout of the glacier a great, flat-topped rock broke the skyline, perched on a fragile column of dirty ice. A small cairn of stones had been piled on the centre of the rock, a faded strip of red nylon lifting gently in the early morning breeze.

He shrugged his rucksack into a more comfortable position on his shoulders and stepped away from the roaring presence of the *moulins*. His stride was hesitant at first and his gaze unfocused. Then he remembered the night of pulsing colours in the sky and the blown-away feeling and the unsettling sensation that he was being called for and he let go his hold, his stride quickening, jumping meltwater channels, leaping narrow, mud-soiled crevasses until he found himself breaking stride into a loping run, heedless of the dangers around him.

Ahead lay a chaotic maze of water channels, fissures and open crevasses where the crest of the glacier heaved itself up and over some deep hidden bulwark of rock, the surface cracking open like splintered toffee. A quarter of a mile beyond the hump the ice smoothed itself into a gentle flow. The short, treacherous ice-fall needed cautious navigation, yet he ran straight through in a maddened breathless rush, swept down the glacier in a flood of panic, the childish fear of an ominous shadow at his back, his boots pounding the ice, stones skittering into crevasses as he flew from one edge to land in a scrambled rush on their furthest side, only to leap again before his momentum plunged him into the depths.

The panic began to ebb, replaced by a crazed, reckless charge as he ran faster and faster, leaping each crevasse as it appeared, not caring about what lay beyond, adrenaline surging through his veins as the heady excitement of dying urged him on. He reached such a speed that he knew that there was no chance of stopping without slithering helplessly into a waiting crevasse. He found himself grunting with each heavy impact, then springing immediately clear, a strange, incoherent roar breaking the thudding noise of his boots, and he realised with surprise that he was screaming and he grinned manically and leaped again, vaguely conscious of the giddy drop beneath his flying body.

At last he skidded to a halt close by a cairn, ignoring the shower of loosened stones skittering into the maw of an adjacent crevasse as he slid on his hip, grabbing at the heavy rocks at the base of the cairn to halt the slide. Slowly he rose to his feet, brushed the grit from his legs and stood shakily examining the way ahead. He was startled to see how far his maddened charge had taken him. The great flat-topped boulder perched on its pedestal of ice stood out against a backdrop of trees no more than half a mile ahead of him. He was far down the glacier, which had narrowed to a dirty moraine-strewn ramp of ice. The crevasses revealed the rocky bed of the glacier barely a hundred feet below.

As he approached the boulder he felt the exhilaration ebb away, to be replaced by a leaden apprehension. Pressing his hands against the base of the tabular rock, he paused a moment to steady his breathing as his heart thumped hard against his chest. Dropping to his knees, he was relieved to see the shape of the wooden chest resting far back in the cool shadows of the eroded ice plinth. He edged beneath the roof of stone in a low crouch, sensing the immense weight poised above him, held up only by melting dirty ice. At full stretch his hand closed over the leather strap of the chest and he heaved it back hard and scrambled out from the claustrophobic menace of the boulder.

The lid of the chest was still firmly closed as Patrick grabbed both handles and swung it out into the bright sunshine. He checked that the wooden wedge was still jammed tight in the hasp, before shifting the chest under his left arm and pulling it hard against his armpit. He heard woody knocks and froze at the sounds of the contents sliding from side to side. He felt his breath stop for a moment. The world spun around him and he held on hard and tight to the reassuring solidity of the boulder.

A shelf of dirty ice led down past the boulder, forming an easy ramp bounded on one side by the shadows of a crevasse. At the foot of the ramp he paused to watch the torrent of water exploding from the base of the glacier. A great tunnel of ice, twenty feet across, had been gouged from the melting snout of the glacier and the sound of the water seemed to be amplified as it erupted out into the sunshine. From deep in the dark recesses of the tunnel he could hear strange, hollow echoes as the water pummelled towards him. A small brown lake dotted with spumes of foam and broken chunks of ice had formed at the mouth of the tunnel. He watched as the lake spilled past his boots to tumble through a cascade of jumbled rocks, forming a steep tree-lined ravine. The trees were close by. He could smell the moist tang of pine needles on the breeze and the rich aroma of earth lifting on the valley wind. He stared fixedly at the rushing mica-grey water, trying to force himself to turn away.

The glacier was now an ugly sprawl of blackened ice, curving whale-backed towards a broken boulder field. Fresh-cut blue blocks and the scatterings of shards of ice showed recent collapses. Dry-bedded crevasses cut dark V-shaped fissures deep into the foot of the glacier. Behind him, one of the largest crevasses cut sideways into the ice away from the foaming melt water. The walls angled steeply on either side, throwing the interior into shadow. A thin stream trickled from the bed of the crevasse which was dotted here and there with fallen rocks. Fifty yards deeper, where the walls narrowed to barely an arm's width apart, a great boulder lay jammed in its base.

Patrick shucked the rucksack from his shoulders and left it on a prominent rock beside the lake before he reluctantly turned and began to walk slowly into the open jaws of the crevasse, feeling the chill air surround him. The walls blinked out the sun. He paused a moment to let his eyes adjust to the gloom, then hefted the chest tightly under his arm and continued his progress, shoulders slumped, head bowed, oppressed by the enclosing walls. When he reached the boulder he stopped, leaned his forehead against the ice-smoothed rock and breathed deeply, willing himself to go on. His chest felt tight and the air around him, although cold, was oppressive and menacing. It felt decayed and old and the shadows were unwelcoming.

He felt the light-headed sensation begin to flow through his mind, the weightless panic rising, the blown-away, unanchored feeling swamping him. Pushing himself from the rock, he stared up at the sliver of blue sky framed a hundred feet above him by the glistening icy walls. The sound of the torrent had faded, replaced by the spatter of constantly dripping water. Occasional echoes of ominous shifting movements rumbling far back in the depths of the crevasse made him flinch and pause, head cocked, listening for the sudden collapse of the walls.

The ice around him seemed to exhale a drawn-out, breathy groan which ended with a rifle-shot report. He sprang back, turning on his heel, ready to flee, heart hammering. From behind and above him came the heavy rumble of some great mass settling and he heard the crescendo of collapsing ice walls peeling from the melting and disintegrating glacier. The sounds softened and he watched droplets spinning down from the walls above to spatter the grit-strewn ice at his feet.

Once past the boulder, he proceeded with exaggerated caution up the narrowing defile of the crevasse floor. Ahead, he just could see through the gloom to where the walls pinched closed. The metallic scent of ice and crushed stone was replaced by a fetid odour. He wrinkled his nostrils, recognising the nauseating smell, getting the sour taste of it as it slid down the back of his throat. It was the sweet, infectious scent of corruption and he swallowed convulsively. When at last he stopped, the walls were brushing his shoulders. He kept his eyes fixed ahead to where the ice walls pinched shut, trying to let them adjust to the half-light. He could not at first force himself to look down. The sickly odour, sharp now, caught in his throat.

He glanced back at the boulder, studying the stone-strewn bed running with a thin stream of water. He was glad to see that, just as had been the case in the spring, nothing could be washed past the boulder. He saw a few telltale white fragments and bowed his head and swallowed again, feeling the nausea and sadness swelling around him. Turning, he pulled the wooden wedge free from the hasp and slowly opened the lid. The faded remains of the harness, torn, frayed nylon and the glint of the locking buckle came into view. It was laid upon a bed of white shards like beach-combed wood. Torn fragments of colour-bleached cloth were crumpled to one side, partially concealing the skeletal hand. A foul stench wafted up into his face as he pushed the lid fully open and he threw his head back, teeth bared in a grimace and gagged, swallowed and retched again, his eyes flooding with tears. When at last he had controlled himself and turned to face the open chest, the glint of gold caught his eye. The wedding band still circled the startling white bone that lay alone in one corner. He reached forward tentatively and plucked the bone from the chest, a mixture of revulsion and love confusing his mind, and he found himself murmuring softly in the gloom as he eased the gold ring from the bleached finger. He gently replaced the bone and turned to face the end of the crevasse.

Cold water seeped around his knee caps and he was oblivious to the needle-sharp pain of the stones. His eyes had adjusted to the gloom and he sat back on his haunches to study the changes wrought by four months of thaw. There were fewer than he had expected and he combed the ice walls with his fingers searching for evidence, shadows in the ice, suggesting more was hidden within. He was both relieved and saddened to find no signs. The jumble of debris that had fallen' to the floor lay in a ragged, crushed scattering of dark shapes. He reached for the nearest piece, brushing away layers of grit and stones until he could prise an edge free from the ice. It released with a sucking noise and particles of ice skittered onto his thighs.

It was indistinguishable from the layers of dirt that he had just brushed from it and he turned it slowly in his hand, at a loss to understand what it was.

When he shook it gently more grit fell away, exposing a smooth surface. He registered the stitch-like marks running across the bone and realised that he was holding a segment of skull. The partially crushed upper half of a jawbone swung loose below his fingers from a thin, gristly tendon. He spoke quietly, soft reassurances in the gloom. He placed it carefully in the chest. As with all his hard-won finds, it looked pitiably small.

In truth, he had always known through all the long waiting years that the probability of finding anything was virtually non-existent and always he had pushed it to the back of his mind, until the early spring morning four months earlier. It had been another exhausting and fruitless day searching the chaos of the ablation zone, peering into innumerable constricted fissures, creeping beneath precariously balanced boulders, sifting through the grey mica sand leaking from the melting ice to beach the shores of the pool, losing hope with every passing hour, every year ticked by, as he completed yet another cairn.

He had counted the yards, marked the cairns as he trudged back down the glacier, calculated to within a few years when she might be likely to appear. Then, as he had turned wearily to leave, he had spotted in the gloom of the far recess of this crevasse a white shard lying on the dark stream bed. Stumbling into the open, clutching the bone tightly in his fist, he had hardly dared believe what he had found. Each day he returned and unearthed another clue: a strip of discoloured cloth, discarded domino tiles, chips of shattered ribs strewn on the ice and the metal buckle of the harness glimpsed behind its glassy wall. He had knelt on the mess of stones and bones, hacking with his ice axe, his arms cramped in the constricted space. Eventually, his heaving and wrenching freed the nylon belt and part of a leg loop in a splintering of ice. The shredded belay loop had taken another hour of excavation until it lay at his knees with the screw-gate karabiner still clipped in place. The gate, he noted, was open.

He knew then how lucky he had been as he had stared wildly around the enclosing walls, looking vainly for telltale shadows in the ice. In another year this place would be gone, melted away and its contents swept down the grey, rushing torrent to the river valley below. Perhaps the rest of her was already there, swept along in scattered fragments, completing her journey to the sea. These wretched scraps were enough.

He ran his hand through the stones and soft

309

bundles, sifting through the debris, picking the rags and bone chips from the slush and grit. They rattled like poker chips as he dropped them into the chest, the noises clicking in echoes from the walls. Just as he had decided there was no more to be found he saw a strange, dark, elongated shape lying far back in the crevasse. At first he thought it was the edge of a buried stone protruding from the ice but then his fingers touched the yielding surface. It was the shape and colour of a bark-covered stick, yet felt soft, mushy to the touch. Apprehensively, he dug his fingers under its edge, pulling it free and turning it over.

The seven vertebrae seemed to shine with obscene paleness in the murky light and, as he stared, something rolled inside him, an uncoiling of sadness. Fragments of grit and cloth fell away as he lifted it in his hands. Gristle and fronds of gelatinous brown softness attached to the underside of the spinal column swung wetly against his hands. He felt slickness slime his fingers and a putrid stench soured the air. Blindly, eyes shut, tears leaking from the lids, he placed her gently in the chest, talking quietly as if to a child, talking to himself. He could not be there any longer. The urge to flee, to be blown away, overwhelmed him and he crouched forwards, resting his hands on the ice, head lowered, as the world swayed around him. He had nothing to hang onto any more.

His vision had gradually adapted to the murky light and he had become accustomed to the smell. He glimpsed the bundled, formless shapes in the chest and felt the sudden clench in his stomach. Here and there a pale bone gleamed. He could look upon them impassively. They were dry, inanimate parts of a puzzle that he could fit together and understand. It was the ragged cloth and the decayed flesh that unnerved him. He was glad of the shadows.

He forced himself to stare at the pathetic, rotted remains. He wanted to honour her but revulsion tightened his throat. He closed his eyes and let himself be swept to those suspended hours in the crevasse when he had held her in his arms, lain beside her, talked to her and promised to return. And for an endless moment it seemed he was hovering above his own body, looking down, absently observing, caught between the past and the present, as he watched himself kneeling, monk-like, penitent amidst the screes and the mud and the leaching glacial ice. Her voice called his name and seemed to echo around the chamber. He heard, as from a distance, low, heaving sobs reverberating from the surrounding walls and he sensed her presence close by his side. He could hear from a far distance, all those years gone, the time when he had wept softly.

He had found her lying peacefully on her side, ghosted with powder snow. Asleep, it had seemed to him, until he had seen her ice-shredded nails and the ravaged, amputated fingers and the mutilated leg bent back on itself. He had hurriedly swept them beneath the snow so that the sight of the exposed bone could not hurt him. Then he had lain by her side and convinced himself she slept safely. She had been waiting for him to come and wake her. He whispered hushed sentences, reassuring her, reassuring himself, looking for affirmation in the cool, porcelain features that he

311

cradled in his hands.

He blew softly on her face so the fine, silken folds of her snow shroud disappeared and the utterly stilled sleeping face rested in calm repose. He had seen the trace of a tear and touched the cold, ice-raised weal, seeking the softness beneath—a moment of tender, unconscious grooming that he had never been able to forget.

That was the moment when he had let go of his hold on life. Gazing helplessly at her fading beauty, he had felt his consciousness and control floating away into the shadows and the unanchored feeling had surged around him and he had never quite found his life again. He should have stayed with her. He knew that now, held the ravaged hand that he had let go of and slept on by her side. It would have been easy then to have stopped his breath. *We would be here now,* he thought, looking around the gleaming walls of the crevasse, *together.*

'I'm sorry,' he said and the words echoed from the walls and echoed through his memory. 'I am so sorry.' He had vowed to come the next morning and take her home but, exhausted, he had failed her, again. He had tried to convince the guides to mount a search and even then he had failed.

Time had swept past unnoticed until the midday sun slid across the slitted roof of the crevasse far above where he crouched. Light streamed into the chill, sepulchral gloom, the ice gleaming wetly as sunshine refracted from melting, mirrored walls of green and blue. Patrick glanced up and winced, closing his eyes against the fierce glinting reflections. Sunlight flooded the chest and his vision of her sleeping face instantly evaporated.

The bones and filthy rags and glistening, decomposed flesh lay tangled in a bright wash of light. He reached towards the skeletal hand and laid his palm across it and bowed his head.

'Oh, Patrick.' The words came from above him in a hushed whisper. He slowly lifted his head, scarcely knowing what he was hearing. Through the brimmed prisms of his tears it seemed as if a crowd of faces was staring at him, staring endlessly, and he recoiled as he heard his name whispered again. 'Patrick. It's me, Patrick. Cassie.'

He blinked his eyes clear and saw her leaning over the boulder jammed in the bed of the crevasse. A look passed between them, a fleeting, wordless exchange, a raw, unguarded moment.

'It's okay, Patrick. It's all okay.' And she held out her hand.

He hesitated, then reached tentatively to grasp her outstretched hand and winced as he pulled his knees free from the sharp bite of the stones. He swayed drunkenly and felt her grip tighten and pull him back into balance.

'I didn't know that you were waiting for her,' Cassie said, but his eyes were blank, disengaged, devoid of emotion. He was not with her.

As the sun rose she had come upon the abandoned hut, the sleeping bag at the notch and the cairned trail down the spine of the glacier. Looking down from the flat-topped boulder, she had spotted the rucksack lying by the edge of the pool. Gingerly descending the ramp, she had called Patrick's name and searched the chaos of the melting glacier for some sign of his passing until she glimpsed the set of prints heading directly for the largest of the crevasses at the end of the glacier. As she hesitated to enter the intimidating shadows of the crevasse, the ice she was standing on trembled with a deep, shuddering groan.

There was an immense, thudding impact and she glanced up to see that the flat-topped rock had crashed to the ice, pulverising the ice pedestal. It was slowly toppling over the ice wall rearing above the base of the ramp where she stood. Fear gone in an instant, she was running towards the open mouth of the crevasse before she had even torn her eyes from the colossal, tumbling boulder. She heard the thunder of the rock smashing into the ramp and bounded in one huge leap to land in the centre of the pool. She was still running, barging off the narrowing ice, when the wave of mud and grit and freezing water washed her from her feet and surged past her, dragging her in a grating, tumbling rush along the walls of the crevasse. As the water ran out of force it flooded back past her and she found herself drenched and shivering in the hushed chamber, adjusting her eyes to the gloom and trying to calm her beating heart.

She approached the boulder jammed across the walls and decided there was no point going any further. Even in the murky dimness she could see that not much further ahead the walls had crimped shut. It was a dead end. When she turned to retrace her steps her eye caught an unnatural white gleam near the foot of the boulder. She crouched to look more closely and a momentary golden flash seemed to glint from the dark, stony stream bed. When she looked again it was gone.

She reached for the white chip nestling against the base of the boulder. It came away from the frozen grip of the ice with a light clicking sound

314

and she held it to her eyes, noting the odd, musty odour surrounding her. She turned the object between her fingers. It seemed familiar and alien at the same time, light and smooth on its sides, fractured at each end. Her first thought was that it might be a piece of wood, water-worn, bleached by the ice. She searched around the area by her feet but there were no other fragments of wood and then she saw it glint again, the tiniest flash of gold and then again and she marked the spot. She dropped the piece of wood and reached to where she had seen the glint. As her finger touched the spot a shaft of sunlight spilled into the crevasse and the walls gleamed and sparkled around her but she stared fixedly at what her finger had swept clear. Gold.

She dug with her fingernail, flicking grit and ice to the side until the nail snapped. By then the thin band of gold appeared to be attached to a pebble, or a bone perhaps, and with that thought she turned to stare at the white wood chip lying where she had dropped it and she knew then exactly what it was. She remembered his angry words when she had opened the velvet pouch in the hut and found the bones. She had been surprised at the icy fury in his manner and how, with unblinking eyes, he had settled such a stern gaze upon her that she had hurriedly dropped the pouch and looked away. A deeply unsettling sensation seemed to surround her and she shivered.

When at last she had prised the gold object from the ice she rose unsteadily to her feet and held out her palm to a shaft of sunlight. The delicate sea shell, flushed pink and cream, gleaming in the sunlight, lay becalmed in a watery slush of mica

315

grit and ice fragments. The lips of the tiny shell were rimmed with a fine band of gold and the pin of the earring had been bent back, but she recognised it at once. She had asked Patrick several times about the shell that hung on its leather cord around his neck and each time he had said nothing. As she stared at the earring she became aware of a low murmuring sound. It was a mixture of words and sobs and so low in register that she could only just hear it. It seemed to come from beyond the boulder.

At the right-hand end of the boulder there was a low gap and she stepped forward and leaned over to look at what was beyond. Below her, Patrick knelt in a crouch, a strange, low, keening moan keeping time as he rocked back and forth. Sunlight washed across a wooden chest at his knees. Horror and pity swamped her, tore away her words as she stared at the grisly contents, the skeletal hand and segmented spine and the stench and the broken, swaying figure.

'Oh, Patrick,' she whispered involuntarily again as she dropped down by his side. 'Patrick?' There was no answer.

He had ceased his rocking and pulled his hand clear of the chest. She watched the battle for control ripple across his features but he had no control, had long since lost his anchors.

'That's enough now, Patrick.' She tried to hide the tremor in her voice. She closed the lid of the chest and, wedging the hasp, turned to him, taking his face in her hands, forcing him to look into her eyes. 'It's done, Patrick. You have her.' She rose unsteadily and held out her hand.

He took her hand, eyes unfocused, all fight gone,

and struggled to his feet, swaying as if against a powerful wind, reproachfully hesitant.

'You have her,' Cassie reassured him as she bent to lift up the chest and hand it to him. 'We can take her home now.' And, holding his hand, she helped him over the boulder and led him out towards the light.

Acknowledgements

I am indebted to the following people whose advice and opinion has been so valuable to me during the long time it has taken to finish this novel; Mary Weston, Nadine Towers, Marek and Karen Kriwald of Parliament Communications and my brother David Simpson for their patience and honest opinions. The love and support of my partner Corrinne helped me weather my crises of confidence and banish the doubts. Milly's tireless hours attempting to sit on the keyboard were a useful comfort break. Thanks also to Phil Kelly for saving my digitally disappeared chapters. My literary agent Vivienne Schuster for her wisdom and help. Dan Franklin of Jonathan Cape for his judicious advice in the final stages as the book came to print.

This was the last book I worked on with Tony Colwell who as an editor, friend and mentor had taught me so much over the years. At the time I didn't think that eight years would pass before it came to print nor did I realise I would have to do it all without him. I found the novel as hard to write as Tony had promised me it would be and without Val Randall's unstinting encouragement and support I am not sure I would have completed it. She has been an enormous help to me during the many drafts, re-writes, edits and more edits—as keen eyed, judicious, and uncompromising as Tony Colwell.